P9-CAZ-302

Praise for
Barbara Michaels

the best

"Simply the *best* living writer of ghost
stories and thrillers in this century."
MARION ZIMMER BRADLEY

great story

"With Barbara Michaels,
you always get a great story."
OCALA STAR-BANNER (Florida)

ingenious

"This author is ingenious."
KIRKUS REVIEWS

supernatural

"Michaels has a fine downright way
with the supernatural."
SAN FRANCISCO CHRONICLE

popular

"A writer so popular that the public library
has to keep [her] books under lock and key."
WASHINGTON POST

entertain

"This author never fails to entertain."
CLEVELAND PLAIN DEALER

Books by Barbara Michaels

Sons of the Wolf

ELIZABETH PETERS
WRITING AS
BARBARA
MICHAELS

HARPER

An Imprint of HarperCollinsPublishers

HARPER

An Imprint of HarperCollins*Publishers*
10 East 53rd Street
New York, New York 10022-5299

Copyright © 1967 by Barbara Michaels
ISBN 978-0-06-124783-5

First Harper paperback printing: July 2008

Visit Harper paperbacks on the World Wide Web at
www.harpercollins.com

10 9 8 7 6 5 4 3 2 1

*To Kay and Carol
with love*

Chapter

1

March 29, 1859

THIS MORNING I STOOD BEFORE THE GLASS AND LOOKED AT my face.

It has been a long time since I indulged in that vanity—if vanity it could be called. Black hair, straight and coarse as a horse's mane, brows black and threatening, a skin so swarthy that I fear Grandmother's unpleasant comments about my Italian mother are correct—there may be Moorish blood somewhere in that family tree. My coloring will win no crown of beauty in this land of pink complexions and flaxen curls, and the shape of my features is no more encouraging. I know what a physiognomist would say about them: the brow too high, too wide for a woman's, the nose too strong, the chin a square, uncompromising block. The mouth is wide and generous. But generosity, of that sort, is not a virtue prized by gentlemen—at least not in their wives and daughters.

The high-collared, long-sleeved black dress deadened my skin; I scowled at it, and my ominous eyebrows dipped like little black crows. I hated both the black color and the hypocrisy it represented. My grandmother was dead. But she had hated me since the very moment of my birth. And ever since I had been old enough to understand that hate and the reason for it, I had returned the sentiment with a vigor that did my character and my Christian upbringing little credit. If I had dressed to suit my feelings, I would have blazed forth in crimson and gold.

As I stood scowling at myself the unsightly vision in the glass was obscured. Ten small fingers clasped themselves over my eyes and a sweet voice caroled in my ear, "Guess who it is!"

"Who else could it be?" I answered rudely and pulled the little hands away. The wrists were as delicate as those of a child; my own long fingers more than circled them. Over my shoulder, reflected in the glass, was Ada's face.

She must have been standing on tiptoe to reach so tall, for normally the top of her shining yellow head just reaches the bridge of my nose. She had tried to confine her curls, but they would break loose, a cascade of ringlets and waves and curls that resisted the sober black ribbon. The color of death, which is so hideous on me, only purified the delicate pallor of Ada's face; she looked even younger than her seventeen years. Now her blue eyes were wide with hurt affection, and her mouth was puckered into a pink rosebud of distress. She looked as sweet and winsome, and about as intelligent, as a Persian kitten. And, as always, guilt at my unkindness overwhelmed me. I turned and put my arms around her.

"I'm sorry, darling," I said.

She gave me a hearty hug in return; for all her delicate looks, there is nothing frail about Ada's constitution.

"It doesn't matter, dearest Harriet. I came on you too suddenly. You were thinking of—of dear Grandmother."

She is a creature of volatile moods: first hurt, then affection; then the blue eyes swam with sudden easy tears and the little chin quivered.

"Nothing of the sort," I replied—too sharply, for one tear slipped loose and flowed down the curve of Ada's nose. I made my voice more gentle as I went on. "If I was thinking of Grandmother, I assure you those thoughts don't deserve your tender consideration."

"She was always kind," Ada murmured, dabbing at her eyes with a lacy handkerchief.

"To you, perhaps—in her way. But you are her favorite daughter's favorite child and you look just like the well-bred young man of fortune she picked to be her daughter's husband. Whereas I—"

Ada's eyes sparkled. She glanced guiltily over her shoulder. The room was empty; it was my own bedchamber and, now that Grandmother was dead, no one would enter it without knocking first. But Ada has a childish love of mystery. She spoke in a thrilling whisper.

"Harriet. . . . Now that Grandmother is—is gone. . . . Oh, I have always wanted to know! What did your father do that made her so bitter toward him?"

"If you wanted to know, why didn't you ever ask me? I would have told you; there was nothing of which I am ashamed."

"But—but—Grandmother said it must never be spoken of."

"Yes, although she spoke of it herself, in hints and sly allusions, which made it worse than it was. And you never dared violate her commands, did you? No . . . come, Ada, don't cry. Darling, I am sorry! I will tell you all. It was nothing, really—nothing except an imprudent marriage against a dictatorial old woman's wishes. But that was the ultimate crime, for her."

"How can you speak so, when she is still . . ." Ada's hand

made a fluttering gesture and I was reminded, with a sudden shock, that the mortal part of my grandmother was still in the house. Downstairs in the darkened library, surrounded by flowers . . . how she would have hated those sweet waxy lilies, she who had never allowed a fresh flower in the house! I laughed, to Ada's shocked surprise, and leaned forward in my chair to pat her hand.

"Our parents, as you know, were brother and sister," I said, trying to make the story simple enough for easy understanding. "Children of our grandmother. So we are cousins."

"Sisters," said Ada softly, and bounced from her chair to give me a quick kiss.

"Now sit down and be still," I said, pretending to frown at her, "or you will not follow my lecture. We are cousins by blood, if something dearer by affection. My father was the elder, as well as the only son. He was a gay, handsome fellow and Grandmother's pride; but, alas, he had inherited her arrogance and pride as well as—they say—her handsome looks. She had arranged a suitable marriage for him; but while he was on his Grand Tour, in Rome he met a young Italian peasant girl and married her. He didn't tell his mother until after the deed was done; he knew, I suppose, that she would have done anything, moral or immoral, to prevent the match."

"Your mother must have been very beautiful!"

I laughed and touched my cheek.

"According to Grandmother I am very like her. So you see it must have been her charm and wit, rather than her beauty, that won my father."

Ada bounced at me with hugs and kisses and protestations; I had to scold her again before I could go on.

"When Grandmother heard of the marriage, she was furious. She told my father that not a penny of the inheritance he had anticipated would be his. His father—our grandfather—had left him a small amount of money, to be given to him on his twentieth birthday. On this, and on what he could earn by the work of his own hands, he and his bride had to live. If he ever showed his face again at the door of his home—so his affectionate mother informed him—she would have the servants whip him away."

"How terrible!" Ada leaned forward, cheeks pink with excitement. "How could she do such a wicked thing?"

"She would fight anything that threatened her authority and her pride of lineage," I answered bitterly. "Her mother's name, as she never tired of reminding us, was Neville; she always believed that her ancestors were of that noble northern house. 'A Neville was once Queen of England, my dears.'" My voice was savage as I mimicked the voice that would never again taunt me.

"Yes, yes, I know. But to disinherit her own son—"

"They say," I remembered, "that it hurt her grievously. It was after that that she became so biting and withdrawn. And he did not suffer. He had no time for that. The climate of Rome, so healthful in summer, is deadly in winter. He died not long after I was born."

"Then you do not remember him?"

"No."

"Poor Harriet! And your poor mama!"

"How can I mourn him when I never knew him?" I asked reasonably. "I do remember my mother—just a little—as a soft warm voice singing sentimental Italian songs. And as a pair of flashing black eyes and a hard brown hand—I was a very bad child!"

Ada shook her head reproachfully.

"You pretend to have no sentiment, Harriet. But I know you better than that."

"How can I feel sentiment for a pair of ghosts? They are no more than that to me. They did nothing for me except bring me into the worpld. Before he died, my father, like any well-bred fool, had spent every penny of his little inheritance. My mother was no more inclined than he to save. She was a true child of Italy—gay, improvident, and selfish. Heaven knows I heard that often enough from dear Grandmother—that, and how she rescued me from the depths of iniquity into which my mother had fallen."

"Iniquity?" breathed Ada.

I hesitated, but only for a moment.

"In Rome, the girls from the provinces dress in their native costumes and stand on the stairs near the Spanish Embassy to be hired out by artists. She was an artists' model when my father met her. After he died, she went back to her old life. Well, she had to have money, Ada. What else could she do?"

Ada was shocked into silence; her blue eyes were as wide as saucers. I was wicked to tell her, but not wicked enough to add that other bitter conjecture which my grandmother had hurled at me once, in the heat of anger—that I was not her son's child at all. A well-bred young English miss is not supposed to know about such things. But my grandmother had not spared me the knowledge. I thought of the stiffening form which lay below in the library, hands folded on its breast in unaccustomed humility. She was no colder, no less remote, than she had been in life. My voice was just as cold as I said:

"When Grandmother heard of this through her Rome agents, she sent them to my mother. My mother sold me to them—for fifty pounds sterling. She was living with a French officer at the time and she was delighted to have the money. Our grandmother told me of that tender maternal gesture quite often. She also reminded me frequently how, but for her generosity, I would now be a starving urchin in a dirty alley in Italy. Generosity! I would rather be left to the charity of strangers than endure such generosity. As," I added darkly, "I may yet be left."

Ada, poor child, is accustomed to my wild moods. She had been patting and soothing me as I stormed, but at that last remark she sat up and stared at me.

"Harriet, what do you mean?"

"Ada, has it never occurred to you to wonder what is to become of us? Does the future hold no apprehension for you?"

"Why, no. There is Grandmother's money. We will have that now."

"I suppose so," I said, without voicing my own suspicions on that point. "But how and where and with whom will we live?"

"I don't care," Ada said simply. "So long as I am with you. Oh, Harriet, promise me—we will never be separated, will we? You will always take care of me, just as you do now?"

I do have some shreds of conscience. I could not look at that candid child's face and infect her with my own pessimism or even vex her with the unaccustomed effort of thinking.

"Of course I will," I said gaily. "But the time will soon come, Ada, when you will prefer another sort of protector. Someone young and handsome, with moustaches like those of the young gentleman who turned to stare at you in the park last week!"

I sent her away laughing and blushing and protesting, but even her affection could not lighten my dark mood. Of course she will marry, and soon; she is so sweet—and will be so wealthy! Suitors will overwhelm her and she will take the first one to propose, simply to keep him from feeling unhappy.

I began to pace up and down the room, as is my habit when I am worried. The sunlight of early spring lay in a narrow strip across the matting beside my bed. The window shades were drawn, naturally, in deference to the rigid form that lay at rest in the library. Her death had been sudden. One moment she had been sitting upright in her chair scolding Hattie, the housemaid, for some fancied neglect of duty; the next moment her face turned a strange dusky red, her speech died into harsh gurgles, and she fell forward onto the floor.

There has been so little time. I cannot accustom myself to this new freedom; sitting in my room, I still expect the door to burst open, without the courtesy of a knock. I expect to hear a harsh voice demand why I am moping, with idle hands, in darkness. I need not hide my diary any longer! I am sure she found it, no matter where I hid it; very little escaped her prying fingers. Once or twice, after I had written an account of a particularly bad day, I fancied her little bright black eyes regarded me with more than their usual irony. Oddly enough, she never said anything. Perhaps, after all, I imagined those looks. . . .

Still, I feel more free now that those bright black eyes are closed forever. Although I said what I pleased about her in these pages, defying my own uneasy suspicions, I never dared voice my wilder fancies; I could not expose them to her mockery, her harsh chuckle. My diary has been a great blessing; it was the only outlet for my rages against Grandmother, for of course I never dared shout at her directly. She did not break my spirit, but she bent it rather badly.

Now, though, my diary can be an even greater solace. I can tell it my innermost thoughts—as I would speak to some unseen friend, and know that that friend will never criticize or answer back! I love Ada and would cheerfully die for her if a suitable occasion ever presented itself, but some of my thoughts are not fit for her ears.

Of course my freedom is only temporary. The Magna Charta, the root of England's liberties, was written *by* and *for*

English*men*. In our great modern England women and children have no liberty. As soon as possible, "they"—that ambiguous, vaguely threatening "they"—will enslave me and Ada again. Grandmother's money will be managed for us, by some man or other; some man or other will choose our home and our servants, possibly even our bonnets. Then "they" will marry Ada to one of themselves. I told her I would take care of her. I could do it, too; I could guard her against swindlers, help her choose a good kind man from among the many fools who will propose to her—I could even manage her money. But "they" will not let me. "They"—the smug, pompous, selfish gentlemen of England. I wish Providence would wipe them all off the face of the earth!

April 2

That horrible old woman! That witch, that crone, that hateful, malicious hag! I have been too well brought up. I have exhausted my store of expletives.

We had the "Reading of the Will" this afternoon. The capitals are those of Mr. Partridge Junior—a nasty, smirking young man who is so thin he looks like a lamppost in his long black trousers, not at all like his dear old father, who was one of Grandmother's best friends, as well as her family lawyer. But Mr. Partridge Senior is confined to his bed by a stroke, brought on, they say, by Grandmother's death; so we, perforce, had to make do with his beanpole of a son.

I could tell by Junior's manner when he greeted us precisely what he was going to say. He gave me the coolest of nods and almost knocked his forehead against his knees being obsequious to Ada. So it came as no surprise to me to learn that Grandmother had left the "Family Fortune" (again, the capitals are those of Partridge Junior) solely to Ada. No surprise, and no anger. What did infuriate me—my fingers are still shaking!—was the one clause in the will which referred to me. I can still remember every word. I doubt that I will ever forget them.

"To my granddaughter Harriet I leave my ebony workbox, with the hope that she will apply herself assiduously to its contents if she is ever to attain that station in life which she deserves. I also commend her to the care of my dear granddaughter Ada, knowing that the said Ada will never allow her cousin to be in financial need."

At that Ada squeezed my hand fiercely and tried to smile at me through eyes brimming with tears. She had been overflowing, like a flower filled with rain, since the funeral. I am writing only for the eyes of my "Unknown Reader," so I will admit that the last clause did not please me; of course Ada will never let me want for money, but it is maddening to be dependent on anyone, even a dear one. However, Ada is too unmalicious to catch the sting in that first, worst, sentence. I shan't point it out to her; it would be rubbing salt in the wound. That station in life which I deserve! A milliner, perhaps? Or could she have meant I might aspire to being a lady's maid? How dare she—and in front of that smirking young whippersnapper! I am tempted to take the ebony workbox and smash it against the wall. I won't, of course. I have had too many years of Grandmother.

Next day

I was so enraged yesterday that I forgot to record, or even to ask, the most essential question of all concerning Grandmother's will. However, my omission was rectified today when Mr. Partridge Junior paid us another call. I would have refused to see him, but Ada asked me to go down with her. Ordinarily she is not at all alarmed by young men—and why should she be, when one smile reduces them to red-faced adoration?—but she is alarmed by lawyers, and, both as young man and as lawyer, Junior is a particularly weedy specimen.

Junior (I like to think of him by that name) had news for us. I knew, naturally, that some member of the great male sex would be the arbiter of our poor little lives from now on, but I couldn't imagine who the fortunate gentleman would be. If I had my way I would have selected Mr. Partridge Junior's father, who is a dear old man. But that seemed too great a stroke of luck.

I was correct on both counts. Mr. Partridge Senior had been declared our trustee and guardian. However, Providence had intervened to cancel my grandmother's wishes. (I can almost hear her hoarse indignation at His daring to overrule her.) With Mr. Partridge ill, there was no one, seemingly, to take on the alarming responsibility of Ada and Harriet, and our lawyers had been in a quandary until the day before the funeral.

"That day," Mr. Partridge Junior explained weightily, "we received a letter from your grandmother's half brother's son."

"Aves-vous la plume de la grand' mère de ma tante?" I murmured and stifled a giggle as Mr. Partridge stared at me indignantly.

"This gentleman, Mr. John Wolfson by name, has kindly offered to take charge of you young ladies. We have naturally made inquiries about him, and all our sources report him to be a gentleman of means and of position. He is also the sole remaining man of the family, so it is with great relief that we have accepted his offer."

"But"—Ada put her lace-trimmed handkerchief to her lips—"I do not know this gentleman. Harriet, have you ever heard of him?"

"Certainly, dearest, and so have you. Don't you remember Grandmother's famous, boring genealogical chart? Mr. Wolfson must be the son of Grandmother's young brother. Her father, you recall, married twice. But we have had no contact with that branch of the family for years—"

"An unfortunate circumstance," Junior interrupted. "Mr. Wolfson explained that his father and your grandmother had not spoken for years—the result of some foolish childhood squabble. But his position is irreproachable."

"Is he a—a kind man?"

If I had asked that question, Junior would have pronounced it the irrelevant absurdity which it undoubtedly was. Kind? What concern was that of ours, who would only be dependent on this man for paternal affection and care? But since Ada had asked it, and looked appealingly at Junior with her wet blue eyes, he tried to smile. He was not very good at it.

"My dear Miss Ada, who would not be kind to one so charming and . . . ?" The impertinent puppy caught my eye and had the grace to blush and cough. He finished his business in a great hurry after that. We are to leave for Yorkshire within the week. It seems like a short time, but, as Junior pointed out, what have we to wait for? It also seems very far away. But since Mr. Wolfson lives in Yorkshire, and Mr. Wolfson is henceforth our lord and master . . .

Grandmother would say that is irreverent. I daresay she would be right.

My boldness does not deceive even me. I will write it very small: I am afraid. Afraid of the future, afraid of this Mr. Wolfson. Perhaps my forebodings are bred of the twilight that darkens this gloomy, starkly furnished room. I am a superstitious Italian peasant at heart. Grandmother always said so. And she was always right.

April 14

I have been shockingly remiss with my poor diary, but I have not had a moment for more than a week. Even this moment will not last long; behind me in the big bed Ada still sleeps, her tumbled curls spilling out from under her nightcap, but when she awakes, she will want all my attention. She is torn between excitement at travel and strange new sights, and childish terror as she remembers the unknown future, now pressing close upon us.

It is so early that the housemaid has not rekindled the dying fire, and the room is bitter cold; my breath forms a pale cloud and my fingers are so stiff that I must stop and rub them before dipping the pen to take more ink.

The view from the window also slows my pen. We are high over the rooftops here, in this respectable inn; but above the gables and chimneys I can see the twin spires of the noble minster—the heart of York, which is in turn the heart and capital of the North. It is an English church and an English city, but it looks so strange to me; when I reflect on our surroundings and their distance from London, I can scarcely believe my senses. Four hundred miles north and two months back into winter; it was spring when we left, but here a blanket of snow carpets streets, rooftops, and spires. To the north lie the heaped stones of a structure older by centuries even than the walls of hoary York Minster—the stones of Hadrian's Wall, built by an emperor of Rome to guard young Britain against the wild barbarians. To the east, not far distant, lies the sea; to the west, mile on mile of rolling moorland, broken only by rude hamlets and isolated farmhouses, and the crumbling ruins of abbey and castle. Only the south seems warm and familiar.

Ada stirs. I must hasten, recording events rather than "foolish Italian fancies."

We left London on Thursday in a flurry of haste, rain, and tearful farewells from the cook and housemaids. The first day of our journey Ada wept—no, that word is too strong; she seeps at the eyes like dew. When she is in these moods, she is, uncharacteristically, silent and subdued, so I spent the time reflecting on Mr. John Wolfson.

I had told Ada that I knew of him, but the mere fact of his existence was all I knew. Rack my brain as I might, I could not remember Grandmother's ever mentioning him; but I did have a vague impression that there had been some disagreement between the two branches of her father's family. That in itself would have been nothing against Mr. Wolfson; anyone who disagreed with Grandmother was automatically an ally of mine.

Even in the confusion of those last days in London I found time for some quiet inquiries concerning Mr. Wolfson, and my efforts were rewarded by—of all things—a guidebook to Yorkshire. Apparently Mr. Wolfson is, as Junior claimed, a man of property in those parts and his home, Abbey Manor, is one of the most elegant mansions in the North Riding. According to the book, the mansion is built near the ruins of one of the abbeys destroyed by Henry VIII; in fact, it is built *of* the abbey, the stones having been looted to supply building material. There was an engraving of the abbey ruins in the guidebook, and they looked very picturesque, with sprays of ivy twining over the tumbled stones. In some places the walls still stand, and the stone traceries of the empty windows made a lovely shape against the sky.

But I see my fancy is leading me astray again. What is most important, to Ada and me, is the hint of our new guardian's character given by one chance sentence in that helpful book. We will be more fortunate than most touring parties; we will be allowed to view the old abbey. Mr. Wolfson, it seems, does not allow visitors on his property, which includes the ruins! Even the engraving was taken from a distance.

The author of the book was quite bitter about Mr. John Wolfson; but, contrary as I am, I am inclined to sympathize with his unkindness to amateur antiquarians. If I owned such ruins, I would be inclined to keep them to myself, so that I could wander the roofless cloisters and stone-floored cells in peace—meditating perhaps on the vanity of fine architecture and the transitory nature of even monkish aspirations. Or merely enjoying my ownership of something other people covet!

It seems certain, though, that Mr. Wolfson is not a man of yielding character. I have a picture of him in my mind: a vinegary, peppery old gentleman with white whiskers and hair, who rushes at invading parties of travelers brandishing his cane. Yet I know this can't be right; if Mr. Wolfson is the son of grandmother's younger brother, he must be younger than my own father would be. Well, I shall soon know the truth. We leave for Abbey Manor this morning. Mr. Wolfson's carriage is already here; the landlord informed us, when we arrived last night, that we should be prepared for an early departure. The manor is a long day's journey from York, far to the northwest. Only sixteen more hours before we know . . .

I may as well be frank. My efforts to sympathize with Mr. Wolfson are feeble subterfuge. I dislike him already, without ever having seen him; I will dislike him, whether he is white-haired and peppery or handsome and bland. He is our guardian—our guard. That is enough to turn me against him, or any other man.

Later

The date should really be April 15—it is long past midnight—but I cannot sleep without recording the impressions of this most eventful day. Let me say it at once: My apprehensions were groundless.

I sit now in a tastefully furnished chamber, equipped with all modern comforts. Heavy velvet portieres are drawn against the chill of the northern wind, and a fire burns on the hearth under a handsome marble mantelpiece. The bed which awaits me is new, and it is piled with quilts; the table on which I write has pen and ink and even a folder of writing paper. Bed, chamber, fire, all are my own. Ada's room, which is as comfortably and elegantly equipped, adjoins this one. The door which connects them was just cut last week, and it is open now, for fear Ada should be nervous in a strange house. She sleeps so peacefully that no such apprehension concerns me; but how thoughtful was this idea of Mr. Wolfson's!

Yet no more thoughtful than all the other arrangements he has made for our pleasure and comfort.

We left York early this morning, by the Aldersgate; I craned my neck out of the coach window, braving the biting air, to get a last view of the ancient city walls, with the great spires of the minster towering above them. The sky was a pale clear blue, foretelling sunny weather; but it was so cold that I shiver now at the memory of it. We kept our heads well inside the coach for the rest of the journey. Not that there was much to see; it is a pleasant, rolling country which may look pastorally beautiful in springtime—not at all the bleak moorland of my fancy. But now a heavy coating of snow reflects the sun and makes the eyes water; the bare trees and shrubs look dismal and deserted. The area is certainly remote. We passed through several villages, but all of them were small. The houses, of gray stone, seemed to have shut their window-eyes and huddled themselves inside their thick walls against the cold.

As evening drew on, the sky was obscured by clouds. Now all was gray—earth, sky, houses, and fields—except for a lurid reddish glow in the west. Ada, who had been chattering brightly, fell silent. I sensed her mood; it was like my own. Some nervousness was understandable, in our situation, but I was aware of an odd despondency, almost fear. Nothing justified such a feeling. The coach was a splendid vehicle, upholstered in blue plush and supplied with cushions, wraps, and foot warmers; the horses were a pair of matched grays; the coachman wore a dignified but expensive livery. Certainly our new guardian was a man of means and taste. Yet it seemed to me that the crimson of the sunset clouds gradually took on the vague but menacing shape of a great animal and that we were racing toward its outstretched claws at breakneck speed.

I write this only to show how foolish such flights of fancy can be. No doubt Grandmother was right about my peasant Italian imagination! Darkness had fallen long before we reached the house—a darkness the likes of which my town-bred eyes had never seen. When I looked out the windows, it was as if I had been struck blind. Not a light, not a shape was to be seen, except for the glow of the carriage lamps. How the coachman kept the road is a mystery, but I suppose he knows the route by heart.

The first lights we saw proved to be those of the gatehouse, and very pleasant those yellow-red squares of windows did appear. We were expected; as soon as the carriage rolled up to the iron gates, a man darted out of the house and flung them wide. We did not pause but drove on through the gates onto a graveled drive which seemed to stretch on forever into the darkness. It was several minutes more before the lights of the manor came into view; it is some distance from the gates and completely screened from sight by a large plantation of firs.

The vehicle crossed a wide carriage sweep and drew up before a flight of steps. The coachman opened the door and extended his arm; Ada took it and stepped out. As I followed her, the door of the manor opened, emitting a flood of yellow light, and the figure of a man could be seen outlined against the glow. Ada clutched my arm; I could feel her shivering.

But the great encounter was yet to come. The figure in the doorway emerged, holding a lamp, and I realized it was that of a servant. We followed him up the stairs into a brightly lighted hall. Its warmth was a pleasant shock after the chill wind outside; I had only a dim impression of velvet hangings and great mirrors before the manservant was asking for our wraps.

His voice, as well as his manner, had told me that he was London-bred. A tall man of middle age, he had the stiff dignity of the well-trained servant. His impassive features did not alter when he looked at us, but I thought I noted a subtle change in his attitude as he received first my plain black cloak and then Grandmother's magnificent sable cloak which Ada was wearing. Neither of us had thought twice about her right to wear it; she loves furs, and she and Grandmother were almost of a height. Now I realized, with more amusement than chagrin, that the cloak was a symbol—and a very accurate one.

"My name is William, miss," said the servant, addressing Ada. "Mr. Wolfson is waiting for you in the library. Will you follow me, please?"

As we started off along the corridor, Ada's hand crept into mine, and I was glad to take it. I am not easily humbled, but as I followed that dignified specimen of manhood to a meeting with another male, who would henceforth dictate my comings and goings, I felt as small as Ada—a new sensation and not a particularly pleasant one. My heart was beating more quickly than usual as William opened a door and bowed us into the room.

I had wondered why our guardian had not met us at the door and hoped it was not a demonstration of his feelings for his new wards. But then I realized that he might be old or ill, and in my mind I placed the white-whiskered gentleman of my earlier fancy on a couch by the fire, with a shawl covering his limbs.

There was a great oak desk piled with papers and a man sitting behind it.

His hair was not white; it was a silver gilt that blazed like a helmet where the light struck it. A long moustache drooped over his lips, but he was beardless. Eyelashes and brows were of the same fair shade but thick; instead of looking hairless, as so many blond men do, his eyes seemed to be framed in gold. And the eyes themselves were so extraordinary that one hardly noticed their frames—a deep, brilliant blue, clear but oddly cold, like water that has frozen and yet retained its ability to mirror the sky. He might, at first glance, have claimed almost any age. The shoulders and arms were those of a man of vigorous youth, and there seemed to be no lines in his face.

Then he smiled, and the extraordinary ice-blue eyes lost their chill. They fascinated me so that I hardly noticed the shape of his lips, except to sense that there was something unusual about his mouth.

"Ada and Harriet," he said, stretching out his hands. We advanced shyly to take them, one in each of ours. "Forgive me for not rising," he went on, "but, as you see, it is my misfortune rather than my lack of courtesy which forbids me the pleasure."

Still holding our hands, he emerged—there is no other word for it—from behind the desk; it was a weird sight to see the unmoving head and torso glide sideways, without rising. But when he was away from the shelter of the desk, I understood. Part of my imaginary picture had been accurate. Mr. Wolfson was seated in a wheelchair, and—yes!—a lap robe covered him from the waist down.

Yet it was impossible to connect the frail invalid of my fancy with this broad-shouldered, vigorous man, even when, as I saw him closer, I realized that the gold of his hair was faded to gray and that his face was seamed with the fine lines of physical suffering.

"Sit down," he said, relinquishing our hands and waving us toward a velvet settee. "I know you must be cold and weary. A light supper and then bed, eh? Perhaps you will sit with me while you sup; I am anxious to know you and to make you feel at home."

The words were kind in themselves, but the tone, the extraordinary charm and warmth of his voice, made tears come to my eyes. We did as he directed, and soon the heat of the roaring fire, fatigue, and sheer relief made me sink into a dreamy haze. I remember only one other thing about this evening, but it woke me like a dash of cold water. We were sipping a glass of wine—against the chill, Mr. Wolfson said—when out of the corner of my eye I saw something move in the shadows behind the desk. I paused, with my glass at my lips. Somehow the shifting shadows were all wrong. The movement could not have been made by a man; it was located at waist level, as if something crept on hands and knees behind the desk.

Mr. Wolfson saw my look of apprehension.

"I have forgotten to introduce you to two important members of the household," he said with a smile. Extending one hand, he snapped the fingers. From the shadows emerged the creature he had summoned.

The glass fell from my fingers and shattered on the hearth. The creature was a dog—but such a dog! Its head was on a level with Mr. Wolfson's breast when it came, obediently, to stand beside his chair. Its coat was grayish and short; the long bushy tail and elongated nose were those of a wolf, and as it lapped at his fingers, in a horrid parody of doggish affection, I saw the long white fangs gleam wetly in the firelight.

"My dear child!" Mr. Wolfson turned a look of concern upon me. "I am sorry. Are you so afraid of dogs?"

I could only shake my head dumbly and shrink back into my chair. A second dog had followed the first. It was somewhat darker in color, but the same immense size. With its mate it flanked the man in the invalid chair like animals on a coat of arms.

Ada leaned forward, holding out one clenched fist to the nearer dog's muzzle.

"Harriet has been terrified of dogs since she was bitten as a child. I protect her from dogs; she protects me from all else."

"Indeed?" Mr. Wolfson considered us in turn. "And a pair of charming protectors you are. I am afraid, my dear Ada, that Fenris will not respond to your overtures. She and Loki are perfectly harmless, but they have not been trained to be pets."

The dog had turned its head to sniff at Ada's hand, but once it had made this gesture it turned back again without giving any demonstration of interest or normal canine affection.

"They are certainly formidable," I said, regaining my wits

with an effort. "How still they sit! They look like statues of dogs. What are they, if not pets?"

"Guards." For a moment Mr. Wolfson's face lost its good humor. His lips drew back. Suddenly I could see a resemblance between the animals and their owner. He had a set of excellent teeth, large and white as— But that *is* folly, and I will not write it. He went on calmly, "We live in a remote district, my dears, and I am a poor helpless invalid. Loki and Fenris are my protection, and very effective protection they are."

"You—a helpless invalid?" I exclaimed. It was involuntary, and I blushed as soon as I had said it. But Mr. Wolfson seemed pleased. He laughed and dismissed the dogs with a small movement of his hand. They trotted back behind the desk and subsided. We did not see them again. But I did not forget them.

I do have a mild fear of dogs, but I thought I had learned to control it; half my public fear was for Ada's benefit, since she so loves to protect me from something. Evidently it is not all pretense! It is fortunate the animals are so well trained; beasts of their size and strength could do much damage. And what extraordinary names! Loki, I know, was an ancient Norse god. And not, if I recall, a very pleasant fellow. Fenris—that name is unfamiliar, but it must be Norse as well. I must look it up.

April 21

We have been exploring our new home and its surroundings.

Ada, with her love of animals, found her way to the stables the very first morning after our arrival. I am shamefully lazy in the mornings, so I did not follow until later, and when I came upon her, she had already acquired a mount and a cavalier.

We had little time in London for shopping and dressmaking. Our supply of mourning is limited. So Ada was wearing a sky-blue cloak and hood, lined with white fur, which framed her rosy face. She looked enchanting. The horse was a dainty brown mare which stood, already bridled and saddled, in the stableyard. The cavalier was obviously one of the grooms, from his rough clothing—a tall, dark boy with the slender bones of a horseman. His manner was perfectly correct as he helped Ada to mount, but as she turned her head to smile down at him in innocent (I think!) thanks, the wind blew one long golden curl across her cheek, and his whole frame stiffened in response. I could hardly blame him; but of course I advanced at once, feeling like an elderly duenna.

"Harriet, how late you are! Do hurry!"

"Slowly, slowly, Ada. I know your passion for animals, but have you Mr. Wolfson's permission to ride his horses?"

"Begging your pardon, miss, but Mr. Wolfson gave instructions that you ladies should ride whenever you like. Pamela here is gentled, and there'll be another mare for you."

I looked at the speaker. He was even younger than I had thought, not much older than Ada. His high cheekbones and dark skin seemed alien to Yorkshire, and this suggestion of foreign blood gave me an uneasy sense of kinship.

"What is your name?" I asked.

"David, miss."

"He is the second groom," Ada explained, "but he hopes to be first when old Adam retires."

"How nice," I said blankly. "David, is it safe for us to ride hereabouts?"

"Mr. Wolfson did say, miss, that I or one of the other boys was to go with you. But the horses are safe and gentle. Not that Miss Ada needs a gentle mount."

"She rides like a centaur," I said, smiling. "I am the one who needs the gentle mount."

I got her—a docile old mare named Fanny—and the three of us set out for an exploratory ride.

The abbey ruins are certainly the dominant feature of the landscape. They lie, I suppose, only a mile or two from the courtyard of the manor, and as we approached them I saw that they were much more extensive and better preserved than I had imagined. The walls of the church still stand, although the building is roofless, and one side of the cloisters is relatively intact. At the far end of this side there is a great block of rooms which looks almost habitable. At least the roof is still there, and the windows are solid. I wonder what this portion could have been. Dormitories for the monks, one would suppose, yet the tall tower at one end is more like part of a castle than a monastery.

I was fascinated by the ruins and wanted to ride over at once to explore. But David refused to go.

"They an't—aren't—safe in winter, miss. There's pits there and broken stone underfoot, all covered with snow and thin ice. When the ground's bare and you can see where you're stepping, then I'll take you."

He has an unexpectedly firm jaw, this young man. I might have persisted in spite of the jaw, but I saw the sense of what he said. The ruins will have to wait till summer.

April 27

The weather still continues clear and cold. I wish Ada were not so set on daily exercise; those long chilly rides freeze my bones and bore me to distraction. There is nothing to see but snow and barren trees. We have not even ventured as far as the nearest village, a small place called Middleham. It is three hours' ride, and David does not recommend going so far.

David's recommendations would fill a volume. Not that he is at any time disrespectful; indeed, I rather like him. But there is a quality about him, despite his youth and station, that makes one listen to his remarks and respect his judgment. We have seen a great deal of him, since Ada insists on spending most of her time in the stables, and I—I have complete confidence in Ada, but—

It is so nebulous I feel foolish recording it. But I cannot forget that one look, the first morning they met. After all, he is a young man. And Ada is not only beautiful, but charming and friendly. I feel sure David is too intelligent to forget himself; he is ambitious and has asked us to correct his English, which is far better than the speech of his fellow servants. He—well, I may as well be honest in these pages. It is not David who worries me, but Ada. I do *not* have full confidence in her. Her very virtues—simplicity, candor, kindness— make her untrustworthy. She has an open, loving heart, and David is an extremely personable boy. They share an interest in animals—his is profound and intelligent—and always seem to find something to talk about; they chatter and chat during the whole ride, while I huddle on my saddle, trying to keep warm.

The whole thing is ridiculous, of course. Now that I have written out my suspicions, I can see that. I will martyr myself to frozen fingers and noses, and keep a proper chaperone's eye upon them. That is all I can do and I probably don't need to do that. If I hadn't formed a habit of worrying about Ada, I would never have thought of this.

To turn to pleasanter topics: our guardian, Mr. Wolfson. I call him guardian, since it is hard to think of a familial term that describes him without sounding like a French exercise book. The son of my grandmother's half brother! Does that make him my half great-uncle? "Cousin" is certainly simpler; I will ask if I may call him that. In law, probably, there is no relationship at all.

We have not seen much of our cousin-guardian; despite his handicap he is a very busy man. I suppose the management of this vast estate and of his fortune takes a good deal of time. Occasionally he has visitors from London and York on business matters. Once or twice, though, we have dined with him.

It is a curious performance, dining with Mr. Wolfson. On the first occasion William showed us to the room; we found a handsome apartment, brightly lighted; the table shone with the finest of crystal and silver and china. But no one else was there. William seated us, in his usual frigid silence. I would have thought that we were to dine alone, except that there was another place laid at the head of the long table. Our own seats were to the right and left hand of the master's place—except that the master was not present, nor was there even a chair at that place.

I had only time to exchange an inquiring glance with Ada before William marched to the folding doors at the other end of the room and threw them open. In came Mr. Wolfson, chair and all. Stalking behind him, like a pair of peculiar footmen, walked the dogs. I was torn between laughter, fear, and—pity.

Yet once our cousin had taken his place the strangeness disappeared. His invalid's chair is of just the proper height; he might have been seated in an ordinary dining chair. The dogs subsided, out of sight. One hardly remembered that they were there, especially after Mr. Wolfson began to speak.

He is a brilliant conversationalist. Although he confesses to having little taste for music or drawing, he is widely read.

At first that struck me as incongruous. As he sat there, very handsome in evening dress, his hand seemed too large and muscular to play with anything so fragile as a wineglass. He looked the perfect country gentleman, and that breed is not notorious for serious pursuits. The breadth of his shoulders and chest is that of a man of action rather than thought. It was with a shock of real surprise that I remembered the invalid chair and realized why an active, restless mind must, perforce, have turned to books.

I fear the conversation became a dialogue. Ada reads very little, and she does enjoy her food; she is happy as a listener, so I never try to bring her into a general discussion. But gradually Mr. Wolfson seemed to become aware of her silence. More and more often his eye turned away from me, and I could see by his look that he was much amused by the contrast between Ada's dainty form and features and her well-bred but determined intake of nourishment. He deftly made the talk more general, and then asked Ada point-blank how she had been amusing herself. She at once thanked him for his courtesy in providing us with the means to ride.

"I admire your hardiness," he said with a smile. "Have you really been riding in such cold?"

Ada nodded; then her attention was distracted by an apple tart which the footman placed before her, so I answered.

"Ada will ride anything on four legs and in a hurricane. Her bravado is justified only by the results—she has never been thrown or run away with."

Mr. Wolfson's face sobered.

"Very well, but I do beg you to be careful, Cousin Ada. Overconfidence can be dangerous; you are, after all, only a slight young girl. When I spoke to Adam about your riding, it was only as part of the general arrangements I made for your coming. I had no notion that you would venture out so soon."

"You are very kind to be so concerned," Ada said placidly. "But you needn't worry, Cousin, truly. David goes with us everywhere."

"David? Ah, yes, the gypsy boy. He accompanies you?"

"By your orders, Cousin," I said. And then, seeing his expression, I added anxiously, "Is it not by your orders?"

"No." The word was softly, almost pensively, pronounced.

"But then—"

"David is an excellent servant," Mr. Wolfson said carelessly; there was, however, a slight emphasis on the last word. "He was following the spirit, if not the letter, of my instructions."

"Is he really a gypsy?" Ada asked.

"His mother was a member of the band which comes every summer to camp in the east meadow. They have their regular paths, you know, like animals—which they greatly resemble in their filth and freedom from moral and legal restraints."

"And his father?"

"The son of a prosperous tenant of mine. You wrinkle your pretty nose, Ada; do you find the thought of such a match distasteful? So you should. But some of these gypsy wenches have a kind of charm. . . ."

He caught my eye and at once he stopped speaking, while the half-smile on his lips smoothed out into an expression of proper gravity. But I am sure there was a slight droop to his left lid, the slightest suggestion of a wink, as he addressed Ada.

"The less you know of such matters the better, little Cousin. Let us only say that the lad's mother was a pretty girl. David was brought up by his father's people, however; he is a proper dull Yorkshireman and has rejected his wilder heritage. He will eventually marry a pink-cheeked village maiden, and after a few generations the dark gypsy strain will disappear. A pity, in a way, for he is a handsome young animal. At least I imagine a woman would think so."

He lifted his glass, as if dismissing the subject, but I knew he was watching Ada closely over the edge of it. To my relief she failed to respond to the cue. She chattered on, praising David and the horses equally, and at last Mr. Wolfson's attention relaxed.

So Ada's heart is untouched. It was careless of Mr. Wolfson to tell that romantic story, though. Some girls might be moved by it.

May 4

Life is full of surprises—trite, but true. We have inherited not only a new guardian but a whole family. And to think that I never suspected it until today!

It has been pouring rain since last night—not just rain, a solid gray mass of water, which discouraged even Ada from her daily ride. She was napping this afternoon, but I am too restless to sleep in the daytime, so I decided to explore. Though new, this house is large and rambling. Today, with the clouds pressing on the very window panes, it was quite dark. I wandered up some back stairs near the library and found myself in the south wing. It is luxuriously carpeted; my feet made hardly any sound. Turning a corner suddenly, I came upon a man, a complete stranger, curled up on a window seat, reading a book and looking quite as if he belonged there.

I would have taken him for a ghost if I had not known that ghosts do not wear cravats, the latest in trousers, and pearl stickpins. But his presence startled me so that I stood stock-still gaping at him, until he looked up from his book. He was not surprised to see me; he rose, smiling, and extended his hand.

"You must be Cousin Harriet. A belated welcome to Abbey Manor, Cousin. I am Julian."

I shook his hand, no wiser than before, and let him lead me to the window seat.

"I do beg your pardon—I should know who you are—"

Again he smiled, and then I knew him. Mr. Wolfson's smile is brilliant, while Julian's is so melancholy in its charm that it makes me want to pat his head. But the resemblance was plain.

"I see. My father has not yet seen fit to acknowledge my existence. My apologies, Cousin. Did you take me for the ghost of Abbey Manor or merely for an impertinent stranger?"

"Why should you apologize? It seems to me rather—"

I had no business criticizing his father and my guardian. I stopped speaking, in some confusion. Happening then to see the title of the book he was holding, his finger still between the pages, I found a safe topic of conversation. It was a new work by Mr. Thackeray. Grandmother would never let us read Mr. Thackeray; she reveled in him herself, but she said his irony was not fit for young ladies. Of course I found her hidden volumes and read them all, so I was delighted to discover that Julian was also a reader. As we discussed *Vanity Fair* I had a chance to study him more closely. The resemblance to his father was not really so great. The coloring was the same—the silver-gilt hair and lashes, the long pale face, the blue eyes. But Julian's eyes are a lighter blue and his hair is almost flaxen. In all things he is a faint copy of his vigorous father. But his softer manner is appealing. We talked for hours; it was not until the failing light obscured book title and faces alike that I realized I must go back to

Ada. Once again he made his needless apologies, and by this time we had become such friends that I let my unruly tongue run away with me.

"I can't understand why your father never mentioned you. He has been very busy, but still—"

"I assure you, my dear Cousin, it is not surprising. My father has been disappointed in both his sons, but my dreamy ways vex him most. He prefers to pretend I don't exist." My face must have expressed my feelings; Julian's attractive but melancholy smile curled his lips and he took my hand. "My dear Harriet, don't distress yourself. My father's jeers leave me unscathed. He allows me my books and my pianoforte and a few pencils for sketching; what more could I ask? And now that you are here, I foresee many hours of shared enjoyment in these simple pleasures."

"Yes. . . . Both his sons, you said?"

Julian laughed. It was a musical sound, but almost as sad as his smile.

"Poor Harriet! To have two such cousins thrust upon you! Yes, my brother Francis is a ruder edition of my father, just as I am a faded copy. He has the vigor I lack, but no refinement whatever."

"Where is he now?"

"In Edinburgh. Studying medicine, of all the ugly, distasteful subjects! How he can bear to touch, let alone dissect— On this one subject my father and I agree. He wanted his eldest son and heir to be a gentleman, but something in Francis' nature seems to attract him to all that is coarse and vulgar. And when Francis makes up his mind, he is, I assure you, impossible to reason with."

"I have always admired physicians," I said. "It seems to me the noblest of all callings—to heal broken bodies, soothe pain. . . ."

"How beautifully you express yourself! If I thought that

was Francis' reason— But there, perhaps it is. Who am I to judge my neighbor's motives, let alone those of my brother?"

He smiled again and it was all I could do to keep from putting my arms around him—in a purely maternal fashion—and telling him that everything would be all right. I do feel that physicians follow a noble profession; if I were a man, I might pursue it myself. But, on thinking over what Julian said, and—more important—what he omitted to say, I am glad it is he and not his brother who is living at the manor. Francis sounds a most unattractive person. We are to meet Julian again at dinner and will, I hope, see a great deal of him in future. He really is a charming young man.

May 7

Today Mr. Wolfson paid me a great compliment. At least—no, I am sure he meant it as such and that is how I will take it.

He summoned me to the library this afternoon, the first time I have been invited into his sanctum since the evening of our arrival. He was working busily at some papers when I entered. Once again I was struck by how normal he looks seated behind his desk. Normal only in the physical sense; he is actually far more attractive and alert than the average gentleman.

He motioned me to take a chair and then came immediately to the point.

"Do you find life dull, Cousin Harriet?"

"Why . . . no . . ."

"Of course you do. A young woman of your intelligence—no, Cousin, don't bridle and look displeased. From some men that might be a left-handed compliment, but I see no reason why the ladies should not use the brains God gave them. Intelligence, properly applied, only adds to a woman's charm."

The brilliance of his smile, the look in his blue eyes were so compelling that I would have agreed that I had two heads, if he had made that assertion. Under the circumstances I admitted the truth. He nodded, as if satisfied.

"You as much as told me, the other evening, that you were not a horsewoman. I know you well enough, I believe, to sense that the silly nothings of a woman's day do not amuse you. You prefer activities that have some meaning, some use."

"I could embroider you a pair of slippers," I said daringly, "with pansies or a sprig of mignonette."

He threw back his head and laughed resoundingly.

"That's precisely what I mean. Embroidery, sketching, music—activities for empty-minded dolls of young ladies." His eye became dull and abstracted; I could almost read his mind. He was thinking of his son, my cousin Julian. Of course I said nothing, and after a moment Mr. Wolfson shook himself, like a thoughtful lion, and resumed.

"There is something you could do for me, Harriet, if you will. I suggest it partly to give you some employment, partly because I need your help."

"Of course," I said eagerly. "You have been so kind to us—"

"No more than you deserve." He dropped his eyes, and his long fingers played absently with a pen holder. "In fact, less than you deserve. Harriet, I am an unfit guardian—a sinner, in sober fact. I lied to your grandmother's lawyers about one thing. There is no lady of the house here, no chaperone. I'm sure you noticed this at once. Why haven't you come to complain to me?"

At first I couldn't think what to say. Then he looked at me

from under his lashes, and I saw that, although his mouth was curved downward in a parody of repentance, his eyes were alight with laughter.

"I did notice it," I said severely, "and I have already written to the Lord Chief Justice of England about the matter. Dear Cousin John, after all your kindness—"

"I detest the name 'John,'" he interrupted. "My friends—when I had friends—used to call me Wolf."

"Oh, dear! I don't like that at all."

"Well, call me whatever you like, so long as it is friendly and informal. You make me feel young again, Harriet. If my feelings for you were not those of a father, we would really have to do something about that chaperone."

"As for that," I said quickly, in an effort to hide my silly confusion, "I think such antique customs quite outmoded in this day and age. Really, I think of myself as Ada's chaperone."

"You make the very point I was about to press," he said, looking pleased. "You see, after my dear wife died, I couldn't endure another woman about the house. William manages the place well enough, and we are overrun with housemaids and cooks and the like. Still, I sometimes feel that we lack the finer domestic touches. Would you care, my dear, to take on the duties that my daughter, if I were fortunate enough to have one, would assume? To carry the keys?"

"I would be honored," I stammered. "But I have had no experience—"

"I can't imagine that it requires much experience. Any well-brought-up young lady knows what is to be expected; she has only to demand it. William will be your intermediary; you need not even put that elegantly chiseled nose into the kitchens. But if he might report to you instead of to me for instructions, it would relieve me of a minor but tedious task."

There was no way of rejecting such a request without

sounding churlish. Yet I had reservations. As I sat nervously twisting my handkerchief in my lap, Mr. Wolfson seemed to read my thoughts.

"You may wonder why I don't make this request of Ada. She is a dear child, and I am fond of her. But she is like a butterfly; she has not the maturity for such a task."

"You are right. But someday she must learn—"

"Not necessarily." His eyes met mine; they were grave and kind. "My dear girl, I know of your grandmother's will. It was typical of her—from what I have heard of her—and I found it disgraceful. But we must face facts. Ada will marry well—so well that she may never have to manage a household. She will, we hope, have you to do that for her, until you find someone who values beauty of mind and body above a dowry."

No man had ever spoken to me in that way. (Admittedly, my standards of comparison are narrow; Grandmother regarded eligible men as noxious weeds, to be frozen out if they dared to raise a head.) I know my cheeks were scarlet, for I could feel the heat of them. My eyes fell before his penetrating stare and I lost the use of my voice. I did manage to shake my head, although I'm not sure precisely what I was trying to deny. Mr. Wolfson interpreted it as doubt.

"There are such men; the world is not made up altogether of fools. But since the connoisseurs are far rarer than the fools, you may be living with Ada for some time after she marries. Then you will want to manage her house well, to keep her from being cheated or bullied by her servants."

I laughed, forgetting my embarrassment. It was easy to visualize Ada being bullied by some burly cook or grim housekeeper.

"You're right, Cousin. I am happy to be able to learn my lessons now."

He called William in at once and explained his plan. The butler accepted it with his usual frozen calm, but I think he was pleased. A housekeeper might resent being supplanted, but William probably has more than enough to do being butler and valet. I will begin tomorrow by going over the domestic offices with William. Later I will introduce Ada to a few wifely duties, just for the fun of it; she can hardly go riding without me, in any case.

That was a strange word he used—connoisseur. Of what, pray tell? I am such a fool. I looked in the mirror—and saw the same swarthy, black-browed face. He was only trying to be kind.

May 9

I am weary tonight, but filled with a pleasant sense of duty done. I have been a model housekeeper today.

William and I went over the entire house. The walk alone would have been wearisome; it is an enormous establishment. And full of people—I felt like a child in a fairy tale, who wakes at midnight to find her room populated by busy elves. How selfish human beings are; we simply accept our comforts and pleasures without ever asking whose hands produced them.

There are a dozen housemaids, round, red-cheeked girls whose Yorkshire accent is so thick they might be speaking another language. There are a cook, laundry maids, a dairy maid, footmen, grooms, two coachmen, herdsmen, shepherds. . . .

Luckily I have nothing to do with the outdoor servants; the inside group is big enough to daunt me. I recognized three of the maids, having seen them in the corridors, and one of the footmen looked vaguely familiar. It will take me weeks just to learn their names!

The cook interests me, perhaps because I can understand about half of what she says, in contrast to the others, who are completely unintelligible. She looks like a cook; they ought to proclaim the worth of their wares in their persons. Mrs. Bennett is heavy rather than fat, and her brown eyes have a certain shrewd intelligence. She was quite affable, especially after I rejected her suggestion that I make out the bill of fare. Her selections please me well enough, and I told her so. If I have a special dish I wish served, I will notify her; otherwise she may manage her kitchens as she pleases. The duties certainly will not be onerous. William has the place running like a well-oiled clock, and the equipment is superb—all the most modern conveniences.

Candidly, I think I shall find the whole business rather dull. But I am determined to do well at it; I would hate to have Mr. Wolfson look at me as he looks at Julian. . . .

May 10

The last entry was interrupted by an enormous yawn which threatened to spill the entire contents of my pen onto the page in one big black blot. I took the hint and went to bed, for the subject of Julian and his father is difficult enough to require my full waking concentration.

I saw them together for the first time at the dinner table. Julian had kept to his room for nearly a week, with a slight cold, according to the message he sent me through William. His father rarely dines with us, preferring a tray in the library. I suspect he dislikes having his infirmity emphasized, as it is at the conclusion of every meal. He cannot rise when Ada and I leave the room.

That evening we were greeted by sweet strains of music

when we came down to the drawing room. Ada, who is fond of Chopin, darted ahead of me with an eager exclamation. We found Julian seated at the pianoforte. He smiled at us but continued playing until he had finished the ballade.

Evening dress becomes him. Above the severe black and white, his fair skin and pale hair resemble a delicate watercolor. He is tall and rather slight; as he bowed over Ada's hand, I could not help noticing how well they looked together. But I suspect that his languid looks are a fair indication of his health, whereas Ada, who appears fragile as a flower, is only too healthy.

At Ada's request, Julian played several other pieces for us. His performance is excellent but a trifle pallid. Eventually I tired of the pensive airs he prefers and asked for Beethoven, which he played well but without fire. When William announced dinner, Julian showed his mettle; faced with two ladies, he offered an arm to each, and in we went.

Mr. Wolfson was already seated. He greeted Ada and me with his usual charm, Julian with more reserve, but with perfect courtesy. Yet the meal had hardly begun before he made his first attack.

"Your playing has improved," he said to his son. "But that last was beyond your powers. You should not attempt Beethoven."

That was all he said and he said it in the mildest of voices. Julian, however, flushed up to the lock of fair hair which had fallen over his forehead. He did not reply. Ada went on devouring soup, placidly unaware of undercurrents.

Mr. Wolfson continued in the same vein throughout the meal. He seldom addressed Julian, but when he did it was always in the same manner: calmly, gently, the words themselves unexceptional; but there was always a sting, a veiled contempt in the speech, which never failed to hit its mark. The climax came with the dessert. The conversation had turned to horses—it usually does when Ada is present—and Mr. Wolfson mentioned that he had a new acquisition.

"He is a beautiful creature; by some freak of nature the various intermediary strains have canceled out and he is a throwback to the pure Arab stock—but wild and fierce as the desert itself. You must promise, Ada, not to try to ride him until he has been completely broken to the saddle. Harriet and Julian, I know, need no such caution."

There it was again—the implication of cowardice and effeminacy. By this time Julian's fingers were shaking as he wielded knife and fork. It really was uncomfortable and I was trying desperately to think of some innocuous remark to break the silence which followed Mr. Wolfson's sneer, when Ada innocently saved the day.

"Oh, I have seen him," she exclaimed eagerly. "He is a love, black as coal, with such lines! But he is not dangerous, Cousin. Yesterday he took a lump of sugar from my hand, and—"

"And you still have all your fingers?" Mr. Wolfson shook his head. "Cousin Ada, Cousin Ada—I have done you a disservice by employing your guardian angel in household tasks. Surely Harriet told you you must not visit the stables alone?"

His voice was light, but even Ada sensed the steel beneath the silky tone. She hesitated, unwilling to incriminate me. Julian watched us with a faint smile. I thought, perhaps unjustly, that he rather enjoyed seeing someone else withered by his father's disapproval for a change.

"No," I said, to save Ada from the lie she was considering. "I didn't tell her, Cousin. I fear I simply didn't think."

"And why should she?" Ada cried. "She assumed I would know better!"

She looked quite lovely and unafraid, with her cheeks flaming and her usually mild eyes alight. Mr. Wolfson stared—I almost wrote "glared"—at her for a moment, and then, unexpectedly, he began to laugh.

"That is the most ingenuous excuse I've ever heard," be said between chuckles. "You did know better, Ada, didn't you? Precisely what is the attraction of those dirty outbuildings?"

"Why, the horses," Ada said at once, meeting his eyes without evasion. "And now the black. He is so-o-o-o beautiful. . . . You will let me ride him, Cousin, when he is tamed?"

"Certainly, my dear." The crisis was past; Mr. Wolfson regarded her with amused approval. "But in the meantime, Ada, you must promise not to ride without a companion—and I don't refer to the grooms. Wait until Harriet can accompany you. Or—now, here's an idea—Julian can ride. Not well, of course; he does few manly things well—"

I was hardly surprised when Julian thrust back his chair and leaped to his feet. The glare he bestowed upon his blandly smiling father was not especially filial.

"Sit down," said Mr. Wolfson coldly. "You have not been excused. You will ride with your cousin whenever she condescends to put up with your company, is that understood?"

Julian stood still, half-crouching, with his eyes fixed unblinkingly on his father's face. Then his tall body wilted. He slumped into his chair.

"Yes. Sir."

We should have lingered, I suppose, and tried to restore peace with our gentle female presence, but I suspect that not even a saint can restrain Mr. Wolfson when he is out to make mischief. I caught Ada's eye and we rose to retire. Julian was on his feet at once, opening the door to the drawing room. He would not look at me and I saw that he was still pale—with fear or fury, I wonder? We left them to their port, and Heaven knows what went on after we had gone. Julian was not being overly sensitive. His father does despise him and makes no effort to hide it.

May 15

I have been so occupied these last few days with household matters that I have scarcely seen Ada alone. (The linen presses are in a shocking state; William makes a fine brave outward show, but, like all men, he does not worry about what goes on behind closed cupboard doors.) Today when I went to the drawing room for tea I found Ada by herself, so I told the parlormaid that I would pour. As soon as she left, I asked Ada what she had been doing.

"Riding."

"And how do you like our cousin?" I asked, knowing that she must have been riding with Julian.

"Not at all," said Ada promptly.

It took me a moment to interpret that insult properly.

"As a horseman, you mean."

"Yes. It is a pity. He is a well-set-up young man—I would have expected him to ride beautifully. But he is fidgety; he makes the horses nervous too, and then of course they misbehave."

She investigated the biscuit plate and took a particularly rich one, filled with jam.

"Well," I said, smiling, "if he does not ride well, nothing else matters. I suppose it would be useless to ask how you like him otherwise?"

Ada considered the question, her mouth open to receive the next bite from the sweet poised in her hand. With a

sprinkle of crumbs on her upper lip, she looked like a con-
templative cherub who has been raiding the biscuit box on
the sly.

"He seems pleasant enough," she said, and bit into the
sweet.

I abandoned the subject of Julian. I don't know what I
had expected; he is the first "suitable" young man Ada has
met here, and I suppose I thought . . . but I ought to have
known better. No man can charm Ada unless he is part
equine.

What a spinsterish old matchmaker I am getting to be!

May 19

It is spring! I never noticed it until today.

This morning just after breakfast I was changing into my
riding clothes. I have those linen presses in order now; be-
sides, I remember Mr. Wolfson's concern about Ada's visits
to the stable, a concern which I share. So I was preparing to
go with her. But before I left my room a summons arrived
from the master. I went at once to the library and found not
Mr. Wolfson but William awaiting me.

"Mr. Wolfson, miss, asks you to go for a drive with him.
He will meet you in front of the house."

Talking with William, I have discovered, is like conversing with an automaton. He says "yes" or "no" or "thank you,
miss," and that is all. So I did not express surprise—which I
certainly felt—or pleasure. I nodded and went on my way.

Uppermost in my mind was the question of how Mr.
Wolfson proposed to go driving. In the few minutes' walk
from the library to the front steps I considered several possibilities: that he could, after all, walk in a fashion, or that he

might cause himself to be lifted into the carriage by the footmen. The true explanation never entered my mind—and no wonder!

He was already in the carriage, waiting; at first glance he looked like any other gentleman going for a drive as he sat in the open posting chariot with a rug covering his knees and his gloved hands firm on the reins. The seat beside him was plainly meant for me, and it was not until I had climbed into it that I realized the truth. Mine was the only real seat in the chariot. Mr. Wolfson was still in his invalid's chair, which stood beside me on the same level.

He saw me staring and condescended to explain. (With him, it is condescension.)

"The wheels are locked into position by a simple mechanical device." He demonstrated with his whip. "I had this carriage specially designed. I dislike being touched by servants."

"The chair itself is lifted onto the carriage?"

"No." Again the whip gestured, this time to one of the liveried grooms. The man reached down to the side of the carriage, where the steps would normally be, and unfolded a strange device. When fully extended it proved to be a ramp, hinged to allow being folded, with sliding bolts that held it rigid when in position.

"How ingenious!" I exclaimed. It was also—I thought this, but did not say it—rather admirable. I respect a spirit of independence, and he has contrived matters so as not to rely on other people any more than he must. While I was meditating thus, the groom folded the ramp back into position, Mr. Wolfson lifted the reins, and we were on our way.

He said coolly, "One is forced to be ingenious when one's physical resources fail. I am less handicapped than you might suppose, Cousin."

"I never think of you as handicapped," I said truthfully.

"Then you are unusually perceptive. But then I already knew that."

The statement did not seem to demand a reply so I made none. Instead I looked out at the countryside. It was a lovely day, with white clouds moving leisurely across the sky like scrubbed sheep grazing on a blue meadow. A mist of green surrounded the boughs of the trees. Crocuses and daffodils made streaks of bright color, primrose and purple, along the carriage drive. The lodge gates were open and the gateman stood at attention beside them. Mr. Wolfson acknowledged his timid salute with a wave of the whip. Then we were through the gates and moving at a rapid pace down the main road across the fields.

"Spring is a great event here, after the bitter winter," said Mr. Wolfson cheerfully. "It seemed only fitting that we make an occasion of it."

"Where are we going?" I asked, settling back with a little sigh of pleasure.

"I have business in Middleham. The village itself is ugly, but you like ruins, and there is a castle which may interest you."

"It's wonderful just to be out. I do prefer a comfortable carriage to horseback. Oh—"

"What is it?"

"Your guards." I glanced down nervously at my feet. "Don't tell me you have forgotten them."

He gave me a sidelong look from under his thick lashes.

"I didn't want to distress you," he said, sounding like a worried schoolboy. The change from his usual poised manner was so disarming that I laughed.

"Don't hold my foolishness that first evening against me. I've scarcely seen the dogs since then. It would be ridiculous to be afraid of them when they are obviously so obedient."

"Are you sure?"

"Sure!"

"Then—" This time the whip gestured behind us. I had thought that the back seat of the carriage was filled with articles of some sort, covered with a carriage robe. Now I realized that the shapes beneath the robe were not inanimate. I managed not to gasp or flinch; the immobility of the beasts was a great part of the terror they held for me.

"Very good," I said, turning around again. Mr. Wolfson's eyes flashed approval and—I think—something warmer.

"Very good indeed. You have courage, Harriet."

"Not in this; Ada is the heroine with animals."

"Ada's greatest charm—for a man—is that she completely lacks imagination, which is the mother of fear. To conquer a felt terror is the truer courage."

I changed the subject; I didn't want to talk about my courage, which is strictly limited, or about the dogs. There was much to talk about, for the scenery was new to me and full of interest. Some fields were covered with a carpet of light green crops, but most of the area seemed devoted to pasture, and it was occupied by the most charming sheep—fleecy, gray-white creatures with black faces. The little lambs looked like children masked for a party.

After a time we topped a low rise and I exclaimed aloud. Gone was the rolling pastureland with its cold but pastoral beauty. Before us, reaching to the near horizon, was a great stretch of empty country, covered with a flat wash or rusty brown vegetation. After the homely attraction of the other countryside, this was startling in its barrenness. I knew what it must be, but none of my reading had prepared me for the reality—the emptiness, the deadly color, like the stained floor of an ancient battleground.

"Howland Moor," said Mr. Wolfson. "Try not to lose yourself there, will you, Harriet? Especially not at night."

"I wouldn't willingly go near the place. How horrid it is!"

"When the new bracken and wild flowers are full-grown, it has a kind of austere beauty. But there are dangerous patches of bog, and it is easy to get lost and wander in circles once you are out of sight of the road. There is not a hut or a house for twenty miles."

I pulled the robe up around my shoulders.

"How far are we from the village?"

"Not far now."

The interval passed quickly; he talks so interestingly that I was surprised when the gray stone houses of the village came into sight. Mr. Wolfson drove along the short main street into a small and barren square. He stopped the horses before an inn.

The proprietor was on the threshold before the wheels stopped rolling. He had not even waited to put on a coat, and he stood bouncing up and down like an agitated ball, which he resembled in shape, rubbing his hands together in an effort to keep warm. Two loutish-looking men at once appeared and unfolded the ramp, and I watched with interest as Mr. Wolfson pulled a lever, releasing the wheels of the chair, and propelled himself down the ramp onto the ground. Although the slope was sharp he had the chair under control the whole time, with no undignified rush or bump at the end; even under his coat I could see the great muscles of his back and shoulders stiffen with the effort. Luckily the inn parlor was on ground level with no stairs—I wonder if that is why he goes there?

I was so fascinated by this performance that I had not looked about me. As I turned to go in, however, my attention was caught by the massive walls of a structure which loomed over the humble houses to the right of the square. Crenellated and towered, they announced their identity at once—the dwelling of some prince of the Middle Ages, now abandoned to birds and creepers but still retaining its air of frowning grandeur.

"In, in," said Mr. Wolfson, gesticulating. "It is too cold to linger out here, spring or no spring. I will tell you about Middleham Castle while we dine—if Henry can produce any food fit to eat."

Henry, the host, burst into speech whose rural accent was intensified by his evident nervousness and anxiety to please. He led us at once to a private room—a pleasant, if rustic, chamber with blackened beams across the ceiling and a rough stone fireplace filling one entire wall. The crackling flames made me realize that I was indeed chilled, and I took a seat on one of the rude benches that flanked the fireplace. Mr. Wolfson drew up his chair before the hearth.

I stripped off my gloves and held my hands before the fire; but after a few moments the greater attraction drew me away from the hearth to the window. Through its leaded panes I could see the distorted but overpowering outline of the castle walls.

"We will dine first," Mr. Wolfson insisted, "while I lecture you about the castle. Then, while I transact my business, Dodds, one of my more trustworthy tenants, will go with you and let you prowl the ruins. I'll warrant that even your enthusiasm will not keep you there long; the wind on that height is bitter. We must start back by three; an open carriage is no place in which to spend the twilight hours."

"I know what the castle is," I said, returning to my place. "I had forgotten it was here, that is all. I read about it in the guide to Yorkshire."

"Ah, I see! What a scholarly young woman you are! As soon as you learned you were to come into Yorkshire, you began studying its antiquities."

I sensed at once that I had blundered, and the mocking note in his voice—for I could not meet his eyes—assured me that he had caught it. The man is a wizard; he can read my thoughts as clearly as if my skull were made of glass. He knew I had read the guide in search of information, not about the beauties of Yorkshire, but about him. Probably he also knew what that impertinent book had to say about him.

Fortunately we were interrupted just then by the host, who burst into the room and proceeded to serve our dinner. Mr. Wolfson commands excellent service; within minutes a table was drawn up at his side, laid with silver and linen, and several smoking platters were placed upon it. The *pièce de résistance* was mutton, and the meal was adequately cooked, if not up to Mrs. Bennett's standards.

We were served by mine host himself, with the assistance of a girl who might have been his daughter. These country people are as timid as hares; the child hovered just outside the doorway, handing in dishes but never venturing into the room. The host, for all his cheery rubicund face, said not a word the whole time, except to ask in muffled accents if the food was satisfactory.

Finally Mr. Wolfson dismissed him, rather curtly—his nervousness would make anyone impatient—and said we would wait on ourselves, which we did. Not until the meal was almost over did Mr. Wolfson revert to the subject of the castle.

"Come, Harriet, you shall lecture me instead. Your study of the matter is much more recent than mine."

"It is called Middleham Castle," I began bravely—and came to a dead halt. Staring down at my plate, I tried furiously to think. Surely I could remember something else from that book! A soft sound made me lift my eyes to Mr. Wolfson's face. He was laughing, softly but uncontrollably, and after a moment I joined him.

"Very well, Cousin, I give in," I said, wiping my eyes. "You know why I was reading that book. I don't remember a word of it, except what it said about you."

Our burst of hilarity had brought the host; the sight of his red face and popping eyes peering in the door set me off again, and it was some time before I could calm myself enough to beg, with mock humility, for the promised lecture.

"You mustn't expect too much," Mr. Wolfson began. "The place is a shell; it was badly damaged during the Civil Wars. Before that it was the property of several interesting personalities. One of them was your own ancestor—Richard Neville, Earl of Warwick."

"Warwick the Kingmaker?"

"No less. You know your grandmother always claimed descent from those very Nevilles."

"Yes. But I was not aware that you knew."

"Your grandmother was the one who kept up the feud, not our branch of the family." There was a touch of annoyance in his voice. "I know all about her—and you; it was my responsibility to watch out for her, though she never realized it."

"Please go on," I said meekly.

"Yes . . . Warwick the Kingmaker. He is, to my mind, one of the greatest names in our history. Only imagine it, Harriet—for a few years he did make and break kings, two of them. If he had not been killed at Barnet—"

"In battle with King Edward, to whom he had sworn his oath of loyalty before God."

"Those were rough and barbarous times. An oath meant less than it does today."

"Loyalty is a pure virtue, not a local custom. Oh, I can see why a man might admire our revered ancestor, but to me there is something horrifying in such arrogance and pride. He made a bloody battlefield of England—not because he felt he was right, but just because he wanted power."

"I forget you are a woman, however intelligent," Mr. Wolfson said coldly. "You will never understand ambition.

I suppose the second owner of the castle will be no more to your delicate tastes. He was Richard of Gloucester, later Richard the Third."

"Crouchback? Hardly! I remember weeping for the poor little princes in the tower when our governess told us about their murder by their uncle."

"You have heard only the standard pap taught by semi-literate females," said Mr. Wolfson irritably. "Richard was not a hunchback; the contemporary portraits and descriptions show him without a trace of deformity. Nor is there any proof that he murdered his nephews or anyone else. These were slanders spread by Henry Tudor, later Henry the Seventh, after he defeated Richard at Bosworth. But I suppose you won't take my word for that, either."

"I will take your word on any fact. It is only in interpreting motives that we differ."

"Read Buck's defense of Richard—I have it in my library—and then we will have a good satisfying argument. And take a word of advice—don't call Richard of Gloucester 'Crouchback' here in Middleham."

"Why not, for goodness' sake?"

"He was governor of the North, with his capital in York, for years. After Bosworth, do you know what they wrote in the official archives here? After the battle, understand, when Henry Tudor was in control. 'This day was our good King Richard piteously slain and murdered, to the great heaviness of this city.' "

The words lingered in air, echoing like some ancient dirge. Mr. Wolfson has, as I have mentioned, a beautiful speaking voice.

"I never knew that. But, heavens, it has been four hundred years since Bosworth Field. Do you mean to say that York-shiremen, like elephants, never forget?"

"Precisely. In fact," he added, with a curl of his lip, "if

you mention your Neville ancestry, you will have them fawning at your feet. The Nevilles too were lords of the North."

Lords of the North. What a ring the phrase has—like bronze trumpeting. It kept sounding in my inner ear as I stood on the dry slopes of the old moat and looked up at the overhanging gray bulk of the ragged battlements. I could almost feel a call of the blood, as if I had stood here once before—seeing not abused and battered stones but the bustling life of a long-vanished age.

The wind soon blew that fancy away. It tossed my skirts about, tugged at my cloak and poked inquisitive tendrils under my bonnet. With the aid of my guide, a silent weather-beaten man, I scrambled across the ditch and passed under the frowning portal.

Dodds is as taciturn as all the other true Yorkshiremen I have met. I was grateful for his silence, since it gave me a chance to meditate in peace. Inside the walls the wind was not so strong. I visited the remains of what had been the chapel and stood in the vast but empty enclosure of the keep. The floors had fallen long since, and dried weeds and mud floored the lower chambers.

The place was not ghostly, not in daylight, but as I prowled, dragging my skirts through damp patches and catching them on ragged projections of stone, a feeling of depression crept over me. Ada would say it is a dismal place. Physically, I suppose any ruin must be dismal, but this had an atmosphere of tragedy that had never quite passed away. One could call it an unlucky site; its most famous owners had met violent death and the destruction of their hopes.

At last the brooding silence grew too much for me. I turned to my silent guide and tried to make conversation. But the weather, the castle, and the beauties of Yorkshire all failed; I drew no more than an "Ah" or "Aye" out of the man. His lack of response was challenging. I decided to see if Mr. Wolfson was right about the long memories of Yorkshiremen.

" 'Neville,' " he repeated, and a spark of life animated his rock-hewn face. "Ah. 'Twas tha grandmother that lived here in ma father's time."

That is a rough indication of his speech; at the time I found it hard to follow.

"Yes," I said, after I had puzzled out his meaning. "My grandmother's mother was a Neville. She herself was born a Wolfson. Her father married twice, and Mr. Wolfson of Abbey Manor is the descendant of the second wife."

I feared this might be too complicated for the man to follow, but Yorkshiremen, as I discovered, are fascinated by family history. He nodded.

"That was how it come abaht. How long will tha be visiting, miss, at the Abbey?"

"Until I find a home of my own. Mr. Wolfson is my guardian and the guardian of my cousin."

"Gardeen . . . Tha's *living* at the Abbey?"

"Why, yes."

An extraordinary spasm crossed his face. If it had been summer, I would have thought some insect had stung him. Then his harsh features subsided into their customary blankness.

"We'd best be going back."

Without waiting for a response he stumped heavily back toward the gateway. I followed, in a state of mingled amusement and annoyance.

He waited for me just inside the gate. I hesitated, expecting him to assist me over the fallen stones that littered the portal, and once again I saw the struggle of some emotion on features which were unaccustomed to demonstrate feeling. After a few heavy breaths, he spoke.

"Ma grandsire was groom to tha grandmother."

"Oh, I see."

Another facial contortion followed, worse than the previous ones. I became convinced that the man was subject to fits and was about to shout for help, when, abruptly, he plunged his hand into his pocket, extracted some object, and thrust it at me. I recoiled a few steps.

"Take un," he said in a hoarse whisper, and with an air of such terrified conspiracy that I glanced involuntarily over my shoulder to see who might be spying on us. There was not another living thing in sight, not even a rabbit or a fly.

"Take un," Dodds repeated, wriggling his fingers.

The object lay on his horny palm, almost lost in the vast plain of it. It was a sprig of dried foliage, carefully folded in a bit of cloth.

I took the sprig. It was surely harmless and, at that instant, I was afraid Dodds was not.

When it was in my grasp, his massive shoulders relaxed. He nodded with dour satisfaction.

"Aye, take un and keep un abaht thee. At night, too. Most particalar at night."

I was naturally agog with curiosity, but he gave me no chance to question him; he lifted me down into the moat and propelled me up the farther bank so quickly I had no breath to use for speech. Then he ambled on ahead of me as fast as he could go.

When we reached the inn, Mr. Wolfson was already in the carriage, impatient to be off. He threw Dodds a coin and tugged at the reins, all in the same moment. Big clumsy man that he is, Dodds moved his hand awkwardly and missed the coin entirely. He was still staring down at the dirt trying to locate it when we drove away.

This is a mercilessly long entry. No wonder my fingers are stiff. Perhaps I will become an authoress, like the lady who published that scandalous book under a man's name.

Now that I think of it, she lived in Yorkshire, with her sisters. I must ask Mr. Wolfson about her. The idea is attractive. If I could live by my pen, I could be independent of Ada's charity—or that of some unknown gentleman. I will try writing some little sketches and make my diary entries more novel-like. Not that there will be much to write about; we have no such wild adventures as that poor governess who fell in love with a married man.

Mr. Wolfson said very little on the journey home, except to ask how I had enjoyed my visit to the castle. He seemed amused by my description of Dodds's strange behavior. I meant to show him the little withered plant, but when I looked in the pocket of my skirt I couldn't find it. I suppose I must have dropped it somewhere.

Once a hare bounded across the road in front of the carriage. One of the dogs sat up. He did not bark, but I was rather touched by this sign of—caninity, would one say? Poor creatures, I am getting quite accustomed to them now. I wonder how they exercise those great limbs, shut up all day in the house with their master.

I have yawned four times in the last minute. It is time for bed.

Midnight

The mystery of the dogs' exercise is solved. I have seen them at it.

Tonight was one of my bad nights. I have them, rarely, after a day of unusual fatigue or mental stimulation, and today was full of both. Long after Ada lay breathing deeply—one can hardly use the word "snoring" of such a gentle girl—I lay flat on my back, staring up at the canopy of my bed.

Finally I got up and walked about the room trying to tire myself. It didn't help; I was already tired. After what seemed like hours, I was aching with fatigue and no nearer to sleep, so I went into Ada's room to look for her sleeping drops. She bought the laudanum months ago, just because it was fashionable and because Grandmother would have disapproved. She, of all healthy souls, has no need for such aids to sleep.

Ada's is one of the large front rooms overlooking the entrance to the house, whereas my own windows face the courtyard and stables. She is a creature of light and air; her curtains were flung wide apart and the moonlight spilled in like water overflowing a bowl. I went to the window and looked out.

The moon was full—small at this season, but perfect as a polished silver shilling. Under its light the landscape was an etching in black and white; the shadows of the trees, the tiny branches of shrubs, were as sharp as if they had been outlined by the finest pointed pen. At first nothing stirred to break the illusion of a drawing. Then something walked out from behind a tree toward the steps of the manor.

It was one of the dogs—I can't tell them apart, even now. Its gray coat seemed shaggier than usual; with its pointed nose and pricked ears it looked like nothing on earth except a wolf, but it was as big as a yearling calf. As I watched, scarcely breathing, it stopped and lifted its head toward the window, almost as if it could see me. That was nonsense and I knew it, but I shrank back behind the draperies, clutching them with damp hands. By some trick of the light the beast's eyes looked luminously green—the only spots of color in that gray-hued landscape. Another shadow moved; the second dog came out to join the first. For a long time they both stood staring fixedly at the window where I crouched. Then they wheeled together, like sentries, and walked slowly in step across the front of the house, disappearing behind the far wing.

Of course the poor creatures must get exercise somehow. Many great houses have such watchdogs; they come of a breed which is famous for its devotion to mankind. . . . I cannot imagine why I am so afraid of them!

I will not take the laudanum after all. They say it causes fantastic dreams and visions; heaven knows mine are wild enough already!

May 21

Imagine my surprise when I found on Ada's dressing table this morning a sprig of the same dried plant which Dodds had given me in Middleham! At least I think it was the same plant; it was dried and brown, but the little withered flowers might once have been yellow.

When I asked Ada where it had come from, she looked bewildered.

"Ah, I remember," she said at last. "Elspeth gave it to me."

Elspeth is our maid—a hearty, pretty girl who seems constantly in danger of bursting her stays. She is really a parlormaid of sorts, but she makes up in willingness and good humor what she lacks in the finer skills of the boudoir. Since she overcame her first shyness, she talks constantly; but I confess with shame that, since I can't understand her easily, I simply don't listen.

Ada, her brow puckered, had returned to her sewing. She was trying to mend a rent in a cashmere shawl. Of course this was properly Elspeth's work, but Elspeth's sewing is of the coarse-hemming variety. Not that Ada and I are any more skilled. I have consistently and ostentatiously ignored dear Grandmother's ebony workbox; if I had had any inclination toward needlework, that hateful gift would have destroyed it forever.

"Why did Elspeth give it to you?" I persisted.

"Oh—I don't know. She said it was for good luck or good health or some such thing."

"For goodness' sake, Ada, do listen to me! When did she give it to you?"

Ada gave a little shriek.

"Now I've stuck myself," she said reproachfully. "How you do fuss, Harriet! Let me think. It was yesterday—no, Thursday—oh, me, I can't remember."

She put her pricked finger in her mouth and looked at me wistfully. I laughed and stroked her hair.

"Can you remember anything about it?"

"Well . . . I had given her that gown—you know, the pink muslin that is too large for me. She liked it very much. Later she came back with the flower—she called it a flower, but it is not very pretty, is it? At any rate, she said I must always keep it by me. Why is this important, Harriet?"

"It is not important, I suppose. I was curious."

"Some Yorkshire superstition, no doubt," said Ada placidly. "Perhaps if I place it under my pillow, I will dream of my future husband." She giggled and then sighed. "Oh, dear. I shall never mend this properly. My fingers are all thumbs."

"Let me try—although my efforts are not apt to be much better. Ada, you need some new frocks—and probably another shawl, when I finish running this one. We had so little time for shopping in London. . . ."

"It would be fun to shop." Ada's face brightened. "Just to visit a large town would be a change. We see no one here."

"I'll speak to Mr. Wolfson. Perhaps he will take us to York."

I could not help thinking, as I walked back down the corridor, that she was right. We have no visitors, except for Mr. Wolfson's occasional business acquaintances, and he does not entertain them socially. Of course the Abbey is isolated; in all our rides I have not seen another house. But surely there must be some neighbors? We are not accustomed to society—Grandmother's friends having been elderly ladies and gentlemen—but Mr. Wolfson's abilities and position ought to command a wide circle of acquaintances. I suppose the explanation is to be found in Mr. Wolfson's affliction. I can see him fending off would-be sympathizers with savage remarks and contempt. Julian certainly seems to find life at the manor dull. He is frequently absent on visits to friends. But none of his friends ever come here.

May 22

I spoke with Mr. Wolfson today about a journey to York. To my surprise—for he has acquiesced to almost every whim either of us has expressed—he was not agreeable to the idea. As he pointed out, he cannot travel easily, and there is no one else suitable to chaperone Ada and myself in the shops and inns.

I thought of arguing with him. He can travel quite well when he wishes to—witness our trip to Middleham—but I suspect it is a case of "will not" rather than "cannot." He does not like to display his handicap to the world. I can hardly blame him, and yet it does seem as if some arrangement could be made. Ada and I can hardly spend the rest of our lives here.

He did say, however, that if we would make up a list of what we wanted, he would have William purchase the things for us on his next trip; he visits York monthly to buy commodities which cannot be procured locally. A typically masculine suggestion, I thought angrily.

"A typically masculine suggestion," said Mr. Wolfson, grinning—there is really no other word for that white-toothed smile of his. I thought I was used to his mind-reading abilities, but this time I literally and actually started. His smile widened.

"Now, Harriet, your face is as easy to read as print; you have neither the experience nor the character for dissimulation. You were thinking that it is absurd to expect a butler to choose dress materials for a pair of young ladies, weren't you? But you will discover that William can do anything. Tell him color and type of fabric and he will astound you with his taste. We can find someone in Middleham to make the garments up for you."

"Yes, sir," I said.

"I know—you will miss the fun of choosing the things yourselves. That isn't fair. But just now . . . perhaps later we can manage a shopping expedition. By the way, you will not, I hope, be buying more black? It does not suit either of you."

"It seems hardly proper to abandon mourning so soon."

"If anyone criticizes you, say that I ordered it." He gave me another wide white grin. "Cultivate eccentricity, Harriet, and tell society to go to—blazes. It's much more fun than being conventional."

"It's not very amusing," I said crossly, rising to go, "when there is no one to tell to go to blazes."

He was laughing as I swept out of the room.

Julian is back from one of his visits—this time to stay for a bit, he informed me. He seems sullen and out of sorts; my vanity would be hurt if I were that sort of young lady, for he does not seem to be at all fascinated by our society.

May 29

Wrong again! It is a good thing I am not setting myself up as a student of human nature, for I seem to be constantly mistaken about people. Julian is fascinated by our society; he has been cultivating us assiduously of late. It has made all the difference in our rather dull lives, for he can be absolutely charming. Even his pretended timidity on horseback is amusing, because he obviously is not so inept as everyone seems to think.

It was a beautiful warm morning Tuesday, so we all went riding together. By "all" I mean Julian and Ada and myself. David had four horses saddled, but Julian told him carelessly that he need not accompany us. I was glad to see that Ada seemed not to notice nor care.

We rode to the old abbey ruins and for the first time I had my fill of exploring them. The other two soon tired of this amusement and I left them sitting on a fallen stone, talking. After all, I did keep them in sight for almost the entire time.

The ruined cloisters are quite lovely. Most of the ceiling has fallen in, but there are bits of the most beautiful vaulting still in place. The low building which still seems intact was, as I suspected, the dormitory of the monks. It was at this stage in my explorations that Ada deserted me. She took one look at the gaping black rectangle of the doorway, draped with cobwebs and framed by lichen-smeared stones, and shook her head decisively.

"There will be spiders!" she warned me, as Julian led her off.

There *were* spiders, and I own I am not very fond of them.

But that was not what cut my inquiries short; it was the difficulty of exploring in near-absolute darkness. Only one wing of the monastery still survives; it consists of a long corridor, without windows, upon which the small cells open. The cells themselves have each one window, but these are small and barred and the openings are now almost covered by the rank weeds of what was once an inner courtyard. Since most of the cell doors remain in place—though sadly rotted—the light which struggles out into the corridor is dim indeed.

I ventured into one cell, the one opposite the entrance to the corridor. The fragile-looking but invincible weeds had forced their way up between the stone blocks of the floor, almost obliterating that surface. On one wall I found a patch of plaster, with traces of faded color, but could make out nothing of the design. Popish and un-English as these establishments were, it makes one gnash one's teeth to think of the beauty so wantonly destroyed.

Although I would never have owned it to Ada, I had no intention of exploring that corridor; it was festooned with cobwebs thick as curtains, and the darkness at either end seemed palpable enough to touch. I promised myself that I would come back one day with a lantern—and David. Julian is not the man to ruin his fine shirts and broadcloth with cobwebs, even to oblige a lady.

The tower, which I had planned to investigate, proved also a disappointment. I simply could not gain entry to it at all. The door is a huge structure built of thick planks, which look fairly new. Though there was no visible bolt or lock, I pushed against it in vain. The tower is built right up against the dormitory and may connect with it; perhaps I may be able to enter from the corridor once the cobwebs are disposed of.

When I turned back to Ada, I couldn't help stopping for a moment to admire the picture my two cousins made as they sat chatting. Ada's bright head was dazzling in the sunlight and her black-clad figure was as slim as a child's against the soft gray stone and green grass. Julian was sprawled at her feet, like an effigy of a young knight on a tombstone. He is a graceful creature and his profile—I had not noticed it before—has the true Wolfson look, long-nosed and clean-cut.

As I joined them Julian was in the middle of a description of one of the young ladies at the house where he had been staying. It was malicious but witty; he "did" the simpering young miss, flirting as hard as she dares, to perfection. Ada laughed as much as I did. On the way back Julian showed off. He cleared a wall with such fine form that even Ada was impressed.

May 30

I am so angry I can hardly think, let alone write. But I must compose myself, and I have found this fat old diary a useful means to that end. Of all the stupid, unforgivable, malicious . . . !

I have found out what the mysterious dried plant is. It is St.-John's-wort—*Hypericum*. I remember it now from a course in botany Ada and I once pursued. It is a common-enough plant, though I have not chanced to see any hereabouts. And it is used—

I am still angry! The very thought of it makes my hand unsteady. Let me start from the beginning.

I went down to the kitchens this morning to tell Mrs. Bennett about some change in the menu. Ada had expressed a desire for another apple tart, and I had forgotten to tell the cook earlier. I have a blister on my heel from my exploring yesterday, so I was wearing soft-soled slippers. The kitchen door, at the end of a long flagstoned corridor, stood open for coolness after the morning baking. Inside they were talking as hard as they could—Mrs. Bennett, Elspeth and Mary, one of the other maids. They did not hear me approaching. I was just outside the door when I caught a phrase that held me transfixed. My subsequent eavesdropping, though in poor taste, was unavoidable; I literally could not move for astonishment.

The phrase was:

"He killed one of Abel's sheep last night."

"He," mind you—not "it." I never for a moment thought that they were speaking of an animal.

The voice was Elspeth's. Mrs. Bennett replied (I translate from the broad Yorkshire, which I have come to understand better):

"Aye, it was th' full moon last night."

"It was Abel's telling un that he couldna coom for th' sowing till Moonday."

"Abel should know better," said Mrs. Bennett crisply. "He only—sends th' dogs when summat vexes un."

"Sends the dogs?" It was not a question so much as a sardonic denial.

Mrs. Bennett replied quickly, "Thee's got no call to give way to heathen superstitions. Th' preacher told thee—"

"Ah, the preacher!"

"He's a good mun, is Mr. Ablewhite."

"A foreigner! If he'd been born and bred here, nigh to the wolf's brood—"

There was a little squeak of breath from Elspeth, and another sharp reproof from Mrs. Bennett.

"'T was Abel's own feyther that lamed un," the older maid Mary persisted, but in a lower voice. "He shot th' hound when it joomped at him—shot it in th' hindquarters. He heerd it howl an' saw it drag itself awa'. . . ."

"Aye, I know th' tale. A foolish tale! Hoo could th' beast move, so hurt?"

"Th' dog wa'n't harmed. Next day it was well as e'er. But he—"

"Heathen talk!" The older woman's voice was rock-hard, but I seemed to hear a quiver of marshy doubt under the stone.

"Thee shalt not suffer a witch to live! That's Scripture, that is!"

"Witch. But—"

"Wizard, then." The maid's voice sank to a reedy whisper. "Shape-changers, skin-turners. Old Grannie Price, nigh Ripon—all know she hangs th' hareskin behind her door; didna they almost catch her last Midsummer Day, but for the preacher? If the Wolf—"

I pushed the kitchen door wide open and walked in.

It was the most dramatic entrance I have ever made, I will say that—despite the softness of my movements and the stillness of my face. The three women were stock-still, frozen in the last convulsive movement they had made toward the door: the cook at the table, hands poised over a pot of potatoes, Mary leaning toward her with her head twisted grotesquely over her shoulder to stare at me, Elspeth crouched and white-faced as if she were about to run for her life.

They gaped at me as if I were a bat-winged Fury. I felt like one; the rages Grandmother used to send me into were only pale reflections of the demoniac fury I felt then. When I finally was able to speak, the voice was like that of a stranger.

"The plant on Miss Ada's dressing table. What is it?"

Two younger women sagged simultaneously, like dolls when a child's hand releases them. The cook was made of sterner stuff, but I saw on her disciplined face the same expression that weakened the faces of the maids. The emotion that moved them was relief. It was not my sudden appearance which had petrified them, but the fear that I was someone else.

"St.-John's-wort, miss," said Mary in a gasp. "It's for—for guarding—"

"In Italy they use garlic," I said, a dim memory stirring. The woman stared blankly, without comprehension. "What do you mean by telling such vicious tales? This is England in the nineteenth century, not a ruined castle in the Balkans! I can understand these foolish girls, but you, Mrs. Bennett—you ought to know better. Aren't you ashamed? Your superstitious stupidity is bad enough, but such cruelty toward a man who has been so sadly treated by Providence—"

"Ah, Providence . . ." Mrs. Bennett wet her lips and let the suggestive words linger. "Miss, I'm sorry you heard. You know I tried—"

"Yes, I know. I shall emphasize that when I tell Mr. Wolfson."

The sound that came from Mary's parted lips sent me back a step. It was not loud—that seemed, somehow, to make it worse.

"Nay, nay, thee'll not speak, miss! Please, thee'll not do that—"

She darted forward; before I could stop her, she had dropped heavily to her knees and was pawing at my hand.

"Ah, miss, please, not—"

At first I was too shocked to speak. When I got my wits back, I tried to hush the ugly, pitiful babbling. Nothing moved her, no reassurance would touch her, except the words she wished to hear.

"All right. All right, I promise I won't tell him. Now be still."

She stopped at once, mopping at the tears that had reddened and streaked her face.

"Heaven's blessing on thee, miss."

"Were you really so afraid?" I demanded, incredulity

overcoming my anger. "Does losing your position here mean so much to you?"

"Th' position?"

I realized then the unbridgeable gulf that separated me from these women. I knew what she thought, but I could not comprehend that she really *believed* it.

"What did you think he would do to you?" I demanded.

"Some harm," said Mrs. Bennett suddenly. "Some harm. Now, miss, you know I don't hold wi' superstition. And I'd ne'er ha' said a word to you maself. But since you've heard—it canna be denied, harm does come to them that thwart him or—"

"Then why are you here?" I turned on her, relieved to face a more sensible opponent. "If you fear him so, why do you live in his house?"

Her mouth tightened into a stubborn line.

"When he says 'Coom,' 't is safer to obey. And th' pay is high. I'm not afeard, miss; I'm a good Christian, I am, and evil shall not prevail against—"

"Be still!"

She shrank back from me.

"Thee swore thee wouldna tell!"

"I won't tell. But if I hear any more of such talk—if Miss Ada hears a single word—"

"Na, miss, she won't. We wouldna ha' spoken to you, only—"

I turned to go; the sight of Mrs. Bennett's stupid, self-righteous face was more infuriating than the mindless panic of the maids. I was at the door when a sudden thought struck me.

"But this—this fantastic notion is all over the district, I suppose. Even as far as Middleham. That was why Dodds gave me the plant—"

"Everyone knows," said Mary sullenly.

"And he has heard," I went on, pursuing my own unpleasant train of thought. "Mr. Wolfson knows what they think."

"He doesna' like to have to take notice of it," said Mrs. Bennett. "But, aye—he knows."

"And what does he say?"

"He says naught. He laughs."

I left then; I could bear no more. I am still angry, although the focus of my anger has changed; I keep seeing Elspeth, the younger maid, who did not say a word the entire time but remained crouching, clutching the table with white fingers, her eyes dazed and mindless. They are terrifying that child with their follies, inculcating all the witless hatreds and terrors that I believed were long gone from our modern society. It will be a wonder if they don't frighten her into a fit. And if Ada hears of this—

No, I do Ada an injustice. She would simply stare. Concrete, physical evil might frighten her, but she is too unimaginative and too sensible to be terrified by ancient tales. They are incredible!

These women—and half the North Riding as well— believe that poor Mr. Wolfson is in league with the Devil. They think that, like old Granny Price who turns herself into a hare, he can assume the shape of one of his hounds. (I wonder who is thought to inhabit the second dog!) In this shape he courses the countryside by night, attacking the property of people who have annoyed him; his injury is attributed to a wound inflicted on one of the diabolic werewolves. . . .

Good heavens, it looks even worse when it is actually written down! I could almost laugh, if it were not so bitterly unkind. So he does not "like to have to take notice" of these stories! I can well understand that. They would amuse him, his is too broad a mind to be angered by human folly; but he can hardly appear to condone such stuff.

As I had hoped, writing it all out has calmed me. I must try to have a talk with Elspeth, if I can penetrate that hard shell of Yorkshire dialect. It would be a pity if so young a girl should be corrupted.

June 4

Riding with Julian again today; he captivated Ada by racing with her and—more impressive—he won. I was terrified watching them; the ground here seems dangerously uneven and pitted with holes. But Ada now admits that she misjudged her cousin, and I myself— Well, there was an incident that struck me.

We were sitting, as has become our custom, on a stone amid the abbey ruins, when one of the dogs appeared. That is a fitting word—one never hears them coming; they seem to materialize out of blue air.

It was the first time I had ever seen one of the beasts without his master (*its* master, I mean). Its looks were not alarming; it stood some distance off and regarded us with a grave, almost intelligent, expression. Julian snapped his fingers and called to it, and to my surprise it came to him, stepping sedately through the long grass and coming to a halt beside him. He caressed its rough head and scratched under its chin; and the great hairy thing lifted its jowls a trifle as if it liked the caress. Ada ventured to pat it too; as before, it endured her touch but did not respond at all.

"How do you bewitch them, Cousin?" she asked, a little chagrined.

"No witchcraft." (Julian could not know how I shrank from that word!) "I have known them since they were pups. Poor brutes," he added, half to himself, "they receive little enough affection. They are treated like pieces of furniture. Small wonder they don't respond, even to so soft a touch. Try your wiles, Cousin Harriet."

"Not I. I am fond of those five fingers."

"They wouldn't hurt you. They are perfectly trained."

"I know. I am surprised to see this one alone; I thought they never left your father."

Even as I spoke, I remembered the night I had seen them patrolling, but Julian's prompt, casual answer startled me.

"He is probably somewhere about."

"In the carriage?" I turned to look toward the distant road.

"No, he can get about in a fashion. It is difficult," said Julian, with a callousness that contrasted shockingly with his gentle fingers on the dog's jaw, "but he can walk if he wishes to."

Then he began talking about the old abbey, spinning a wonderful fantasy about the life of the monks in those days. He has a brilliant mind; it is a pity his father does not encourage him to use it.

David came out to take the horses when we returned to the stables. I was shocked by his appearance; he is thinner and looks ill. I must ask William about him.

June 10

I tried to talk with Elspeth today about—how can one phrase such an absurdity?—about the local superstitions concerning Mr. Wolfson. Yes, that sounds better than a bare statement of the facts.

I had not expected her to be responsive, but neither had I expected the abject terror she displayed at even an oblique reference to the subject. She was well-nigh incoherent. I sensed her main concern, however—that Mr. Wolfson should find out that she had gossiped about him. I soothed her with some difficulty—and the gift of a little bead necklace—and sent her away. It is useless trying to combat primitive pagan beliefs with reason. I can only show her, by my own actions, that there is nothing to fear.

It was strange about the necklace. I sensed, somehow, that she regarded it more as an amulet than an ornament. Something belonging to me, who am in favor with the wizard? An object, therefore, which might ward off his antagonism? Good heavens, I am beginning to understand how she thinks, and that is almost as bad as thinking the way she does.

No, there is no danger of my falling into that error. Even if I were mad enough to believe in ghosts and fairies and were-wolves, I would never regard Mr. Wolfson as capable of evil.

Chapter

2

June 21

I WAS COMPLAINING, SOME DAYS AGO, THAT WE SEE LITTLE company. William has returned, by the by, with the purchases from York. Mr. Wolfson was right, his taste is impeccable. There is one pink satin—but I digress. We have another new face among us now; yet, with female inconsistency, I could do without it.

I heard a chaise drive up this morning as I was brushing my hair. It was a beautiful summer day and Ada's windows were open, since she had already dressed and gone down. I also heard the sound of men's voices, but the words were unintelligible—only shouts and thuds, as if some heavy objects were being moved. Then the chaise drove away. The rough exclamations continued, until they were cut off by the crash of the front door as it slammed shut.

It made me realize how quiet the house usually is. Julian glides about like a shadow, and William, the perfect servant, has trained the others to step as lightly as he does. I don't believe I have ever heard that door slammed before.

Naturally I went down as soon as I had my hair up. As I came around the curve of the main stair, I saw a motley pile of luggage heaped helter-skelter on the hall carpet as if it had been thrown there. I hesitated, a trifle wary; then the door opened again and another parcel came flying in, to land with a crash on the top of the heap. A man followed it—in the door, not onto the heap—but I hardly noticed him. The last parcel had, not surprisingly, split at one end as it struck. Out of it rolled an object that almost sent me staggering down the remaining stairs. It was a human skull; it came to rest face (!) up, displaying a set of perfect ivory teeth.

I let out a gasp, or perhaps it was a shriek. The man who had just entered moved, in two heavy bounds, to the foot of the stairs and stood staring up at me. He seemed at first struck speechless at the sight. Then he glanced from my appalled face to the fleshless countenance on the floor and burst into a great roar of laughter.

I descended the remaining stairs with what dignity I could summon up—it was not much. I was trying to frame a scathing remark when this uncouth young man seized me by the waist, spun me up off my feet, and deposited me at the foot of the stairs next to the skull.

"Let go of me," I gasped, plucking at the fingers which held my waist. "How dare you?"

"A most unoriginal comment," said my captor reprovingly. "You seemed interested in Howard, so I brought you down to be introduced. Now, sweetheart, don't be a hypocrite; after Julian's remarkable habits you'll find my embrace like a breath of fresh air."

He pulled me out into the middle of the floor; and I do believe he was about to embrace me when he seemed to see me clearly for the first time, in the sunlight pouring through a side window. He stopped with his face only inches above mine, staring with such intensity that he might have been memorizing my features.

I gave him stare for stare; I am timid about dogs, but impertinent young men merely annoy me, even when they tower over me by a good twelve inches.

Like Julian, this man was fair; but compared with Julian's delicate features, his were coarse and unprepossessing. His nose jutted out like the prow of a ship and his brow ridges were heavy. The lips that were shaped into an odious smile were both full and wide; they displayed a set of teeth as heavy and white as those of poor Howard, down on the floor.

Then the smile faded and the brows drew together.

"By God," said this crude individual, "but you don't look like one of Julian's. You're too—too—" Words failed him; he waved one hand helplessly, and I tried to free myself from the remaining hand that still held my waist. The man tightened his grip absentmindedly, and I gasped with the pain of it. "No," he continued, still staring, "not Julian's. Then why—"

I have read of ugly looks, but I always took this for a figure of speech. It is not. The man's face altered like one of those skin-changers the ignorant servants had spoken of; it darkened and coarsened and flattened. He spoke in a harsh low voice:

"That verminous old—"

I am writing only for my own eyes here, but I really cannot copy that word. I'm not even sure what it means. But I knew enough to recognize the implications. I went first hot and then cold, and my outrage gave me the strength to wrench myself away from him.

"My name is Harriet Barton. I am Mr. Wolfson's ward, the granddaughter of his father's half sister. I intend to tell him what you have just suggested, and I hope he sets both his hounds on you!"

"Harriet," he repeated. His wits are very slow; it was a full minute before comprehension showed on those dull features. They gradually changed back into something which would not frighten a child. "Harriet. But you— Is Ada here too?"

"I am through talking to you. Ask Mr. Wolfson."

"I will." He turned on his heel and stamped off toward the library. The heavy pictures on the walls rattled in their frames as he passed.

I was left in the middle of the hall staring helplessly at Howard. (I wonder why the name seems so ridiculously appropriate for that fleshless bit of mortality?) His grin was too like that of his owner; I had to repress an unladylike impulse to kick him clean across the room. By that time I had a pretty fair idea of the identity of the offensive young man; the reality was even worse than I had anticipated. I turned and looked down the hall. I couldn't see the library door, which was around a turn in the corridor, but I could hear echoes of significant sounds in the distance. I hesitated only a moment, not even long enough to give my conscience time to clear its throat.

Unfortunately the doors in the manor are heavy oaken panels. Even when I stood outside the library, I could not make out the conversation—though conversation is hardly the word for the shouting match that was going on inside. A few phrases were clear; I caught the word "female" several times, spoken like an epithet. Mr. Wolfson's voice was lower and quite incomprehensible, but that he was as angry as his antagonist I had no doubt.

They gave me no warning at all; I was still standing there, with my ear not quite pressed against the panel, when the door flew open. Luckily it opens inward, or it would have sent me sprawling. Out came Howard's owner, in such a passion that he seemed not to notice me. I had a glimpse of Mr. Wolfson crouched down over the desk, and what I saw sent me flying down the hall after the other man, who, at that moment, seemed less terrifying. Thus I happened to be entering the hall from the corridor just as Julian came in from outside.

He wore riding clothes, and Ada was with him. He was smiling down at her and she was laughing, apparently at some sally of his; she was hatless and the breeze from the open door lifted her curls so that they seemed to flash in the light.

None of them saw me as I stood back in the shadows of the corridor, but I had a good view of the newcomer's expression. His eyes went from Ada's face to Julian's. He has none of the discipline his father has had to cultivate; his contempt for Julian and his instant admiration of Ada were plain to read.

Poor Julian! The other man's sheer size and animal vitality seemed to shrivel him. But I had to admire the way he recovered from the initial shock. He straightened his slight form to its tallest and said quietly, "Hello, Francis."

"Julian." Francis' glance dismissed his brother and lingered on Ada's interested face. "Don't bother to introduce us—Brother. I know this is Cousin Ada. Don't believe what you've heard of me, Cousin; I'm not so bad. In fact, I think we're going to be very good friends."

I don't know how he did it, but somehow he and Ada were moving off toward the drawing room, her arm in his, and Julian was standing alone in the open doorway. Our eyes met. No words were necessary; we were allies at once. If he only knew what terrible things his brother had hinted . . . but

I expect he does know. Francis is not the man to spare anyone's feelings.

I foresee a long and unpleasant summer.

Late that night

I know now why Mr. Wolfson keeps to his chair. Poor man—poor man! I wish I had not seen what I saw, and yet it was bound to happen.

I was unaccountably restless tonight. Long after Ada was asleep and dreaming I writhed and tossed in the big bed. The fire had died to red coals and the room was chilly; I slipped on a wool dressing gown and walked up and down the room trying to tire myself enough to sleep. I did think of the laudanum drops in my table drawer and got them out, but I have a foolish reluctance to take the stuff, even though it is so commonly used.

A sound outside in the corridor drew me to the door. Only the idlest of curiosity moved me to open it; the hour was so late that I was surprised, I think, to find anyone else in the house out of bed. The corridor was dark except for the light of a single candle, and it wavered and shook so badly that the area seemed lighted by a lost streak of lightning.

Mr. Wolfson was carrying the candle. He was walking down the corridor, on his way to his own room, and he—

It was like a giant crab; that is all I can think of, horrible as it sounds. One leg must be much shorter than the other. He lurched from side to side, and the candle he held jerked up and down, shedding that poor, distorted light; yet he covered the ground very quickly. Above the twisted, warped limbs his magnificent head and torso looked like those of an antique statue being transported by clumsy porters. . . .

I was so shocked that I committed the final, unforgivable error. Instead of withdrawing at once into my own room, I stood still, and as he opened his own door, he glanced back over his shoulder. He saw me.

He too stood motionless for a long, long moment. Finally—oh, God, the horror and pathos of that movement!—he flung himself through his door and slammed it after him. How can I face him tomorrow? I will never speak of it unless he does. I will do everything I can to show him. . . . Sleep is impossible now. I will take the drops and I hope I do not dream. A crab. A giant crab . . .

June 28

Some people, they say, improve with acquaintance. Cousin Francis is not one of them.

There are a few social errors which he has not yet committed—but then he has only been at home for a week!

That week he has spent cultivating Ada. He treated her like a man with a new kitten or puppy—amused, patronizing, and quite infuriating. At least he infuriated me; Ada is impervious to anything short of direct insult. At first, I think, she was attracted to him. His vitality, crude as it is, naturally appeals to her vivacious spirit. But—alas for Francis' hopes—he fell, forever and irretrievably, when Ada discovered that he was but an indifferent horseman.

I use that word "hopes" calculatingly, but I am not sure, upon consideration, that Francis really meant to court Ada seriously. She is pretty and rich, so any sensible young man might want to marry her, but there were times when I thought Francis' attentions were exaggerated, intended to irritate Julian rather than woo Ada.

I have been very careful to accompany Ada wherever she goes. Not that I believe Francis would dare offend her here in his father's house, but he is really quite unpredictable. This afternoon she admitted after dinner that she was rather tired and would like to rest. After tucking her up, I wandered down to the drawing room and found Francis there alone. I would have retreated at once, but he saw me. He was seated before the small inlaid table where the chessmen are always set out, and he was toying absently with the black king. His face was unusually thoughtful.

"Come in, Cousin," he invited, without rising. "Unless you're afraid of me."

I couldn't resist that challenge. I wonder if he knew it? I came in, with my nose in the air, took up a book, and sat down in a corner of the couch. It was an error. Francis immediately took a seat next to me.

I realized again how big he is. When he looked down at me I felt as if I were being surveyed from the top of a mountain.

"Where is Ada?" was his first question.

"Resting," I said, looking intently at my book.

"I'm glad to hear she sometimes tires. After that ride this morning I felt ready for a week in bed. Is she always so cursed energetic?"

"I should think a strong young man could keep up with a fragile girl like Ada," I said crushingly.

Francis refused to be crushed. He laughed and stretched out arms that looked like tree trunks.

"Ada fragile? She looks so, I'll admit, but she has the energy of a monkey."

"I'm sorry you find her so exhausting. You mustn't put yourself to so much effort being kind to her. I assure you, she can manage to exist without you."

"Damn my eyes," said Francis admiringly, "that was

straight through the liver. Withdraw your blade, Cousin, I give up. But be honest now, you aren't terribly keen on these active sports yourself."

"I am just another fragile female."

"While I am—what did you say?—a strong young man. Very true, Harriet darling. But I've been working like the very devil this winter and I need amusement. What the hell do you find to do with yourself in this tomb?"

"I doubt if my amusements would entertain you," I said tartly, without removing my eyes from the page—of which I had not read a single word.

"Probably not. I expect you don't even play chess."

"Why shouldn't I play chess?" I demanded, looking up.

His eyes were narrowed with laughter and I realized that he had been baiting me. They are brilliant blue eyes—very like his father's, except that the golden lashes are untarnished by time.

"No reason at all," he said patronizingly. "Except that I thought it was considered too intellectual for young ladies."

"I played often with Grandmother."

"And lost—if the stories I hear of your grandmother are true."

I bit my lip and Francis, grinning fiendishly, went on:

"I'm just a stupid male, Harriet, surely you can defeat my plodding brain. Come, I'll give you a knight."

"I'll give you one," I retorted, slamming my book shut with unnecessary vigor.

"Make it even, then." He reached out with those long arms and lifted the whole table, setting it down before us without so much as shifting a pawn. "But you may have white. That's the least I can do to prove my gallant manners."

I took white, in silence. Fencing with him was like hurling rubber balls at a wall—the missiles bounced right back into my face.

Grandmother used to tell me, frequently, that I would have made a passable chess player if I played with my brains instead of my emotions. I am rather reckless, but I expected Francis to be even more so. To my astonishment he proved a slow, calculating player. His caution increased my daring; after fifteen minutes of play, I cornered his queen and swept her off the board.

"I *am* sorry," I murmured, lowering my eyes to conceal my triumph.

"Don't apologize," Francis said, moving his king's pawn.

I still don't comprehend how it happened. Three moves later and I was staring incredulously at the corner of the board where my poor beleaguered king huddled, quite defenseless.

"Check," said Francis cheerfully, while I examined square after square in a vain search for a safe move. "And mate."

I couldn't believe it. Francis leaned back in his chair and lighted a cigar. I continued to search for the nonexistent—a square which was not already covered, fore and aft, by one of his pieces.

"You shouldn't have taken my queen," Francis said mildly. I think he went on to explain the subsequent moves, but I did not hear him; my ears were ringing with chagrin. I heard only the last sentence: "Always watch out for the black knight."

If I had remained in the room I would have done, or said, something quite unladylike. As I swept out, I could hear him chuckling. And he didn't even ask my permission to smoke!

July 2

I wrote, a few days ago, that Francis had committed most of the social errors. Tonight he added another—the worst so far. It was a dreadful evening.

Yet I must admit, it had its amusing moments.

We have been dining with both cousins most evenings, except when Julian is absent or ailing. (I suspect that his illnesses arise from boredom or self-pity, but that is, after all, his own affair.) They have not really been pleasant dinners, for the enmity between the brothers is barely concealed; I constantly expect their animosity to flare into open combat, and I would have excused myself from these delightful meetings except that I hesitated to excite Ada's curiosity. Bless her, she is oblivious to atmosphere; it soothes my nerves to watch her placidly devouring mutton and gooseberry tart while a battle of innuendos and insults rages just above her head.

This evening we met Julian in the drawing room as usual, but Francis was not there. When William announced dinner I asked after the missing brother. Julian only shrugged.

"I've no idea."

Nor any interest, I thought, watching him offer Ada his arm. Francis has been taking her in, usually with an odious grin at Julian, who is too wise to battle over such a trivial matter.

Our first surprise—a pleasant one—came when we found Mr. Wolfson waiting for us at table. He has taken to being already seated when we come in; no doubt he prefers this to making a ceremonious entry in his chair. But this was the first time he has dined with us since Francis came home, and almost the first time I have seen him for some weeks. He made his apologies for that as we were being seated.

"This is pleasant," he said, smiling. "I have been so preoccupied with business of late that I have had to forgo dining with you. I would apologize if I thought my absence caused you as much grief as it does me."

His glance traveled around the table—rather deliberately, for there were not that many of us present, after all.

"Where is Francis?"

The ensuing silence, for some reason, was distinctly uncomfortable. Ada murmured something, and Julian said, "I don't know, sir."

Mr. Wolfson's blue gaze turned to me. I smiled, shaking my head a little, and he grinned back at me.

"Very well, I'll not make an issue of it, Harriet. William, Mr. Francis is delayed. We won't wait for him."

We had proceeded to the meat course before Francis made his appearance.

It was quite an entrance—precisely the sort I would have expected him to make. It reminded me of the day he arrived.

The doors at the far end of the room burst open. One leaf hit the wall with a crash that must have knocked off bits of plaster. In the open doorway, silhouetted by the candles in the drawing room, stood Francis.

He remained still for a moment, hands braced on either side of the doorframe, head tilted as if he were studying us. Then he came forward with a slow deliberate walk which was quite unlike his usual bounding stride. He was dressed respectably in a tweed suit and boots, but his hair was unkempt and his cravat askew. I wasn't happy, either, about the glitter in his eyes. But he bowed correctly enough to me, to Ada, to his father, to Julian—and then I realized that even the first bows had been exaggerated.

"I do beg your pardon, ladies, Father, Brother." The drawled tone puzzled me at first; then I understood, and in spite of my growing annoyance I almost laughed. It was an imitation—and not a very good one—of Julian's voice.

"Leave the room," said Mr. Wolfson.

"Now, Father, don't excite yourself. It isn't good for you." He shook an admonishing finger at his father's reddening face and let his gaze travel slowly around the table. Julian was in the chair Francis usually occupied, beside Ada. Francis shook his head.

"Unsporting, Brother," he murmured. "No sooner gone than forgotten, eh?"

For all his bulk he can move quickly when he chooses. This time his action left us all gasping. He picked up chair, Julian and all, and deposited them six feet back from the table. Then he picked up one of the empty chairs and sat down in it, next to Ada.

"William," he announced to the staring butler, "I see I am a bit late. I shall omit the soup, William. I shall have the beef, William, if you please."

It was dreadful; it was incredible. I put both hands over my face and shook—with laughter. I couldn't help it; the sight of Julian's face as he sat there up against the wall, holding a knife and a fork in his lifted hands, was too much for me.

Mr. Wolfson's voice sobered me at once. It almost lifted me out of my chair.

"Leave this room!" he shouted. "How dare you come here in such a condition—and before your cousins!"

I *am* a simpleton. It simply hadn't occurred to me. But then I have had little experience with such habits. I lowered my hands and stared at my elder cousin's flushed face with, I own, more interest than abhorrence.

He didn't *look* intoxicated. No, amend that—he didn't look as I had thought an intoxicated man should look. They staggered, I believed, and spoke incoherently. Francis' voice was peculiar but quite clear; he walked steadily. In fact, he behaved as he always does, except a little more so. Then a new idea struck me. Could he possibly—does he always . . .

Well! I thought and pressed my lips hard together to achieve a suitable look of disapproval.

Francis paid no attention to his father's bellow. He was

smiling—rather fixedly, now that I noticed it—at Ada. Poor William, quite transfixed by the horror of it all, stood like a statue with a platter of beef poised on his hands, looking just like a hierophant making an offering.

William's face almost sent me off again, but then I caught sight of Mr. Wolfson and the situation lost all its humor.

In his fury he had tried to rise. He stood now half-crouched, clutching at the edge of the table with whitened hands. From where I sat I could see that the lap robe which was always carefully tucked about his lower limbs had slipped and fallen to the floor. I was on my feet at once.

"Francis," I said urgently, "you had better go to your room. William, help him. He is—unwell."

I would like to believe that my words turned the balance (always the little peacemaker, as Francis would say!). But I don't believe for a moment that Francis would be affected by any plea of mine. No, he simply realized that he had gone too far. He rose, knocking the chair over, swept Ada a graceful bow and me another, ignored William's proffered arm, and walked quickly out of the room.

Mr. Wolfson sat down with an audible gasp. His face was ashen as he reached for his wineglass. His other hand—

His other hand was groping futilely, under cover of the table, for his fallen lap robe.

A stab of—something—pierced me to the heart. The emotion couldn't have been pity; it was too sharp for that. I moved without thinking.

Kneeling at the side of his chair, I picked up the robe and draped it across his lap. My head was bowed; I presume that it, too, was below the level of the table, for his hand moved slowly and deliberately down the back of my hair in a caress as gentle as it was concealed.

"Thank you, Harriet," he said in his normal voice, and I rose and returned to my place.

Julian came back to the table, carrying his chair. We went on eating. But it could hardly be called a success, the rest of that meal.

I could forgive Francis almost everything else if he did not hurt his father so terribly.

July 8

The gypsies have arrived—the ones Mr. Wolfson mentioned as spending part of the summer on his estate. He told us of it tonight at dinner. Ada at once asked if we might see them.

No, that is not quite right. Ada was not much interested at first. It must have been I who suggested it—or perhaps Julian, I really can't remember. At any rate, the important thing, Mr. Wolfson consented readily. I confess I was a trifle surprised, considering his earlier comments on their habits. But he feels we will be well guarded with both our cousins in attendance—yes, Francis too. There has been an uneasy truce since that last ridiculous episode, and Francis volunteered to come with us. I don't think Julian was much pleased.

It is silly of me, but I am quite excited. I must be more desperate for society than I realized, so to anticipate seeing a band of dusty, disreputable Egyptians!

July 9

I am to marry a tall dark man and travel across the water and become quite rich!

How pleasant it would be if one could believe in such

things—especially the last clause. I don't much fancy dark men, in fact. But I fear my fate is settled; a gypsy, as everyone knows, is part witch. Certainly the old hag who told my fortune this morning looks the part.

When we came down to breakfast this morning, we found that it had all been settled, somehow, the night before. We were to visit the gypsies at once, this very day. We set out as soon as the meal was over, I, by Mr. Wolfson's particular orders, ignoring my duties for one day. We let the horses take a leisurely pace, for the day was already growing warm. The north meadows are some distance away; for all his tolerance Mr. W. does not let the vagabonds too near his chicken houses and stables. During the ride, which must have taken us an hour, Julian amused us with predictions and imitations of the gypsies. Francis, slouched over his horse's neck, was his usual self; he is sullen and silent in the mornings.

The encampment is not in the meadow itself, but in the fringe of the patch of woods that stretches from the abbey ruins to the northern pastures. I can see why shelter from rain or sun would be desirable, for the gypsy wagons are cramped and ramshackle affairs.

From a distance the scene was colorful and picturesque—the gaily painted wagons, the horses cropping the grass of the meadow, a tin kettle suspended over an open campfire, and dark, strange people sprawled on the grass around it. Some of the men are a hard-looking lot; they might be London thieves save for their dark skins and the occasional bright kerchief or golden earring. I suppose the women are just as brutish, but they did look quite charming from a distance, with their green and crimson and purple skirts, their strings of copper and gold ornaments, and long black hair. They seem to have extraordinarily white teeth, or perhaps it is only the contrast against their brown faces. The children are as gay and shy as young puppies, and as alike as members of the same litter: black hair, sparkling black eyes, slim dark arms and legs barely covered by tattered garments. And over it all was a babble of sound—singing, cursing, shouting—in a strange tongue that flowed like music.

For a moment it gave me an uncomfortable feeling, especially when one young urchin darted out from behind a tree and flashed me an impertinent white grin as he sought the safety of his mother's caravan. It has been a long time, but I remembered a hot, shadowy Roman street. Surely there was once a boy like that. . . .

The babble ceased as soon as we were seen. The brightly dressed figures stiffened and forty pairs of hard black eyes fixed themselves upon us, the intruders. Only for a moment, then they all relaxed, a woman laughed, a man's voice took up its song again. They returned to their previous occupations, but I sensed that they continued to watch us, slyly, from the corners of their eyes. They are a hunted people—deservedly, perhaps—but it is uncomfortable, that sensation of being watched, not by human eyes, but by the bright unwinking stare of an animal calculating the next move of the hunter.

How my fancies have led me on! I wasn't aware of having such thoughts at the time; I simply enjoyed the color and sound of it, and tried to ignore the dirt. Not the dirt of the ground which was their floor—that was unavoidable—but the gay wide skirts had not seen soap and water for too long a time, and the women's hair was oily looking.

When the old woman came down out of the caravan, the noise stopped again briefly. I knew at once she must be the queen or chief personage. Her caravan was bigger and more ornate than the others, but her manner alone would have told me her rank. She was bent with age, and one foot dragged as she came toward us, but she carried her head arrogantly.

She came up to where we sat, still on horseback, and curt-sied four times, slowly and deliberately, to each of us in turn. I could see now how really old she was, though her hair had hardly a trace of gray. (I suppose it is artificially colored.) The bright black eyes peered out from a mass of wrinkles. They went at once to Ada's face and never left it. When she spoke, her voice was a harsh cackle.

"Ah, the pretty lady," she said crooningly. "Have you come to old Marian to find what the future holds? Only joy for one so sweet and beautiful, only joy. Come down, pretty dear, and let Marian tell you the future."

Ada's face was a study. She had been prepared to pity the old woman; her enormous compassion flows out to the poor and injured, to the very young and the very old. But despite the gypsy's obsequious manner, she did not command pity.

Then Ada laughed and nodded. Without waiting for as-sistance she slipped down off the horse's back, leaving the reins dangling. One of the gypsy men stepped forward to take them. He passed quite close to Ada, staring at her boldly.

"Wait a moment, Cousin," said Julian, frowning.

"Why? This is why we came, is it not?"

"That's right, that's right." The gypsy woman chuckled. "Don't listen to the men, little lady, let them follow you. They'll follow, never fear. Come now, come into the caravan with Marian. The ball is there, the magic ball given me by the pharaohs long ago, the ball that tells what was and is and will be."

Julian laughed, his good humor apparently restored. But he was, I noticed, quick to join Ada.

"Lead on, Macduff," he said cheerfully. "Or, no—surely one of the witches, eh, Cousin Ada? Did you ever see a more hagridden countenance?"

Ada frowned at him warningly—she does hate to hurt

even a beggar's feelings—but the old woman seemed not to mind. Her cackling laugh mingled with Julian's chuckle.

"That's right, a witch I am, one of the wisewomen who know the future. Come, lady, and you too, Master Julian. Don't you trust old Marian with your pretty mistress?"

They walked off together, making a very oddly assorted trio: Julian, half in jest, held the old woman's elbow and supported her limping steps. Then Francis, who had not moved, grunted and dismounted. He came to me and held up his hands, without speaking; in equal silence I let him lift me down. We followed the others toward the caravan.

It had a half door at the back, with a flight of steps leading up to it. Ada was already seated at a table, with the old woman seated across and Julian lounging behind her. The table was draped with a piece of draggled black velvet, and on it sat a ball of glass or crystal, foggy with dust and cracked along the side.

Marian was already studying the ball, one hand on either side of it, head bent. She looked up, frowning horribly, as I mounted the steps with Francis behind me.

"Come in, lady, come in. There's room, yes, room enough, beyond me. Squeeze past me here, so. That's right. Master Francis, you'd best stay there. You're too large for this little place."

Francis obeyed, leaning his elbows on the half door, while I pushed by the old woman and squeezed myself into a chair between her and Ada. The caravan was certainly small; it was just long enough for a person to lie down in and only half as wide. A heap of ragged blankets in a corner represented the old woman's bedding, now rolled up for the day. The table and chairs were the only furnishings, save for a few garments hung on hooks along one side and a corresponding row of pots, pans, and utensils on the other. Calico curtains of varied and hideous colors hung at both ends of the wagon and at the window; the latter curtains were purplish with a yellow flower, the ones at the door were blue-and-green checked. It was a sickeningly poor place, almost too poor. I had a sudden sense that it was deliberately designed to appear that way.

When I looked back at Marian she had already begun her trance, or whatever it is called. A ray of sunlight slanted through the high window above Ada, lighting her hair and holding a positive army of dust motes. It left Julian completely in shadow, but his pose, head tilted and arms folded, was so suggestive of amusement that I fancied I saw him smile. The old woman was also in shadow. Her dark, sharp profile might have been cut out of wood, but her hands, around the crystal, were in the heart of the beam of light. Every vein and tendon in them stood out; they were bird claws with nothing but skin stretched over the brittle bones. Yet in their clawed pose there was an unpleasant suggestion of strength.

Ada sat quietly, hands in her lap, looking at the old woman with the air of a well-bred child at a grown-up tea party. The interior of the cart was cool, being sheltered from the sun; yet the air seemed oppressively still. I could hear a fly droning away somewhere. The babble outside seemed lessened.

Sunlight glanced off the crystal surface of the ball without lighting it; it seemed opaque, perhaps because of the dirt that coated it. No object ever looked less like a source of occult mysteries. Yet the glancing spark of sunlight tended to hold one's gaze. The droning of the fly grew louder in my ears. . . .

"It comes now," said the old woman, in a tone so like the fly's buzz that it startled me. "It comes. I see. I see . . ."

Her voice faded. I stared intently at the crystal. For a moment I fancied I saw something stir, down in the fogged heart of it. But it was only suggestion. The ball remained a dusty cracked globe of crystal, nothing more. I leaned back in my chair.

"I see her," said Marian suddenly. Ada started. "I see her with her head of golden curls and her light quick step, coming across the floor. White she wears, and white flowers—flowers in her hands and on her hair. The pretty lady, dressed for her bridal . . . Her face smiles, her face shines with love for him. . . . His face will not come. I cannot . . . Tall he is—oh, very much the gentleman—a fine strong hand he holds out to take her hand. Fair hair, shining like a cap of gold on his head. His face—no, it is hidden, he turns toward her. Now the other gold comes, the golden, golden coins, they rain down, they fall in heaps, they cover her feet. Wealth, love, happiness . . ."

The veined hands clenched. The old woman's body gave a convulsive jerk.

"Wealth, love, happiness," she said, in her normal voice. "It is gone now, the vision. Never does it last. . . . But I saw, I saw! Did you see, pretty lady? Did you see yourself in your bridal flowers, hand in hand with a tall, fair lover?"

Ada shook her head. Her mouth was slightly ajar with fascinated interest, but her hidden core of common sense had not quite deserted her.

"No, I didn't see," she said regretfully. "What a shame! Is it really true?"

From Julian, behind her, came a soft affectionate laugh, but Francis, leaning over the half door, made a more emphatic sound. The old woman grinned unpleasantly, first at one brother, then at the other.

"Ah, they're unbelievers," she said indulgently. "The one laughs, the other scoffs. But never mind, never mind. The future will come, for all of them."

"It was very exciting," Ada said. "Harriet, you must try. Please, Miss—Mrs. Marian, will you tell Harriet now?"

"Ah, the other lady." The dark glance flicked obliquely toward me. "To be sure, it's her turn now. Come, lady, and sit where she is sitting."

"Don't you want your palm crossed with silver once more?" Francis demanded harshly, as Ada and I exchanged seats.

"Oh, yes, oh, yes, the ball won't speak without the precious silver."

Julian threw a coin; it bounced, ringing, on the table till the withered brown fingers snatched it up.

I'll not repeat what she said; it was a formula and she delivered it in a bored voice. I presume she had exhausted her dramatic talents with Ada. What nonsense it all is! And yet it has its amusing aspects—partly, I suppose, because of the spice of adventure involved in visiting so strange a place. I would really feel rather nervous going there without an escort. That is nonsense, too, because these people would never molest anyone who is related to Mr. Wolfson. The old woman asked after him as we left, with the same touch of fear I had seen in the villagers. No doubt, as a qualified witch she respects his superior influence with Satan!

One other thing happened. After we had mounted and were ready to go, Julian addressed the old woman.

"Have you seen David yet?"

Then—then I saw the empress reveal herself. Old, ragged, poor, lame—for an instant I seemed to see her in a high, wide place with fire at her feet.

"No!"

"I'll convey your love," said Julian, laughing. "To your devoted grandson, eh?"

Ada glanced at me and I shrugged. David must be the child of the queen's daughter. I wonder what that makes him in the tribal hierarchy? Well, but we knew he was of gypsy blood and that he had repudiated his heritage. Now we know that his people resent him for denying them. But what is that to us?

A tall dark man . . . such nonsense!

July 15

I have just left Ada. She is calm now, and sleeping. I wish I were.

There is no reason for my distress, I know. I can't imagine why I was so upset.

Francis has proposed to her.

I expected it. I knew it was bound to happen. Did I not write, in these very pages, that a marriage between Ada and one of her cousins would be of all things the most suitable? And the gypsy spoke of a tall, fair man. . . .

I didn't think it would be Francis.

But he is the elder son. That, too, is just as the real, fashionable world would have arranged the matter. She is so desirable—"such a fine match"—that they must both want her. Then the firstborn should have the first chance to win her.

I happened to be in Ada's room tidying her toilet table—she is such an untidy little thing and I don't like to have the maids touching her trinkets and toys—when she came bursting into my own chamber in search of me. Not finding me there she came at once through the connecting door. She was not crying then, but her cheeks were unnaturally flushed—not a delicate pink but a bright crimson. As soon as she saw me, her blue eyes overflowed.

"What is the matter, Ada?" I demanded. But I wasn't much concerned; Ada can weep over a wounded puppy or a trampled flower.

The tears increased from a trickle to a flood; in a series of gasps and sobs she poured forth the tale of the proposal.

"What did you say to him?" I demanded.

"Why—" Ada peered up at me from between her fingers. "Why, I said No, of course. That is, I said, 'I am deeply honored, Cousin Francis, by your expression of affection, but at the present time . . .'"

She learned that speech from a book of etiquette. I never thought, when we practiced it together amid gales of laughter, that I would hear it repeated under such circumstances.

"Very well," I said, folding her in my arms. "Don't cry, Ada. Was he angry? Is that why you are distressed?"

Ada sniffed.

"No," she said after a moment. "He wasn't angry. He just tweaked my nose—"

"Your *nose*?"

"Yes. He wasn't disrespectful, Harriet, truly. He was very nice about it. He was laughing when I ran away."

"Why did you run away? If he wasn't angry, why are you crying?"

Ada thought. The tears continued to flow, as casually as rain sliding down a windowpane.

"I don't know," she said at last, and subsided, wailing, into my embrace.

"Oh, Ada, do hush! Was he unhappy?"

"No, I said he was laughing." Ada sat up and fumbled distractedly at her skirts. I supplied her with my handkerchief—she can never find hers—and continued to pry.

"Are you sorry that you refused him?"

"Of course not! Harriet, how can you question me like a—like a nasty governess when I am so upset?"

"I am trying," I said patiently, "to ascertain why you are upset. He was not angry; he was not sad; you are not unhappy at refusing him. You are not weeping from sympathy or fright or regret. Why on earth *are* you weeping?"

It was silly of me; hard enough to make sense out of Ada when she is composed, impossible when she is distracted. I still don't know why she was crying. Just because she is Ada, I suppose.

By the time I left her she was feeling fairly cheerful again. I had her sitting up in bed, looking less like an invalid than any damsel I ever beheld and holding one of Miss Austen's charming tales, which she will not read. That was all I could do for her.

I wonder if, after all, she is regretting her hasty refusal. Julian would be a much better husband—kind, gentle, courteous—but what if she is drawn to Francis' vigorous strength without knowing it? She may yet reconsider.

I hope she does not. Julian is much more suitable. I do not trust Francis. A man who behaves as he does would be capable of anything. He might even beat her. Men who drink to excess often beat their wives, I believe.

Later

Francis is impossible!

I wonder how often I have written those words? And how many more times will I be driven to write them? The man surpasses himself; each time he commits some enormity, I think, "He cannot possibly do anything worse," and then—he does.

I went in to look at Ada a short time ago and found her asleep, looking as placid as a wax doll, with *Pride and Prejudice* lying flat across her lap, still opened at the first page. I decided to take a turn in the rose garden. The house was stuffy and warm; I needed fresh air.

Francis was in the rose garden.

I hadn't thought to ask Ada where and under what circumstances her first proposal of marriage had occurred. I didn't ask if it were romantic, gracefully phrased. Knowing Francis, I knew it would not be. But as soon as I saw him, I sensed that he must have spoken to her there, among the roses. It suggests more sensibility than I gave him credit for.

He was sitting astride one of the marble benches, his arms folded along its back and his chin resting on his wrist. I turned as soon as I saw him, prepared for headlong flight, but he was too quick for me.

"Cousin Harriet!" (I am learning to hate my name, as he pronounces it.) He unwound his long legs from under the bench and rose, coming toward me with one hand outstretched.

"Cousin Harriet, will *you* marry me?"

The emphasis on the "you" was unmistakable. I am always, I fear, too ready to prefer combat to retreat. I turned on him in a fury.

"Francis, you boor! What have you done to Ada?"

"Done?" His eyebrows went soaring up.

"She is up there in her room sobbing her heart out," I said indignantly—suppressing my memory of Ada's peaceful face as she slept. "You must have said something—done something—"

"Ada cries when she doesn't know what else to do," said Francis coolly. I stood stock-still in surprise. He was right. I had never thought of it.

"You don't believe me," he went on sadly. "No, wait. I must clear myself. I can't let such unjust suspicions cloud my impeccable reputation. Here, sit down. I'll run through the entire performance, and you shall judge whether or not I did it nicely."

The wretch took me by the shoulders and sat me down on the bench with a thud that jarred my teeth together. His hands went rapidly down my arms to my hands and captured them. At the same time he dropped heavily to one knee.

"Dearest Cousin Ada—I beg your pardon, Harriet—it cannot have escaped your attention that my warm regard for you has of late deepened into an emotion sweeter, warmer, than cousinly affection. Forgive me, in your modesty, if I offend—but I cannot control my heart any longer. Ada—Harriet—I love you! Will you make me the happiest man on earth by consenting to be my bride?"

He knelt staring up at me with wide eyes. I pulled my hands from his.

"Francis, don't be an idiot," I said irritably. "You didn't really say that."

"I did." He sat down beside me on the bench, his arm along its back, behind me. "Nothing in that that you could take exception to, was there? It doesn't seem to have been very effective, though. Perhaps I should have proceeded further."

He took me quite by surprise, but even if I had known what he was going to do, I doubt that I could have stopped him. One arm was already in position. It wrapped around my shoulders like a rope, his other arm encircled my waist, and before I realized what was happening, I was being thoroughly and efficiently kissed.

It was the first time, except for that boy at Mrs. Palmer's musicale in the conservatory. And he only kissed my cheek.

I can't possibly describe that kiss. I'm not sure I want to.

I liked it.

Liked it! Good heavens, what an inadequate phrase!

Grandmother was right. I must be a true child of my deplorable mother. I don't love Francis; I don't even *approve* of him! I must be—like that—about men in general, or I could never have responded so shamelessly to an impertinent embrace from a thoroughly despicable man who had just been refused by my cousin not an hour before!

It was that thought that brought me out of the glory. I couldn't breathe, but breathing seemed quite superfluous. My ribs were being crushed and the buttons on his coat were embedding themselves in my skin, but I didn't notice. Then I remembered Ada—and my ribs hurt, and I panted for breath, and I pulled myself away and sprang to my feet.

Francis came up with me, as if propelled by a spring. Even in my confusion I saw that he looked just as wildly startled as I felt, and a mean joy added itself to the other uncivilized emotions that raged within me. I took my time about what I did next. And he just stood glaring down at me, while I lifted my arm and drew it back, stepped carefully backward one step in order to get the proper force, and slapped him as hard as I could across the face.

The sound echoed through the peaceful garden like a pistol shot—and my hand dropped, numbed, to my mouth. It was like striking a rock. Francis wasn't even jarred. His mouth opened a bit, and his expression changed to one of intense concentration. He reached out for me.

For once in my life, common sense prevailed. I turned neatly out of the closing circle of his arms and walked away. He did not follow me.

July 16

Francis was at the breakfast table this morning when I came down. That is unusual, and I was at once on my guard, expecting a possible repetition of yesterday's impertinence, or at least some mocking reference to it.

He greeted me with calm, distant courtesy. No one could have objected to his words or his manner.

Unless I am mistaken, he had been drinking heavily last night. I am beginning to recognize the symptoms.

If he isn't going to mention the episode, I certainly will not. A dignified silence is, after all, the best thing.

July 17

Sometimes I really think Ada's emotions are quite shallow. She has completely forgotten her distress over Francis' proposal; when I referred to it today, she had to think for some moments before she realized what I meant.

I was concerned to discover whether she entertained any regrets. Although I haven't the faintest intention of telling her about my encounter with our cousin, I thought perhaps . . . if she indicated any warmer feelings for him . . .

Well, there is evidently no necessity for telling the story now. Her affections are certainly not engaged. Not only did she refuse Francis, she informed him that she would not accept his brother either!

"Really, Ada," I remonstrated mildly, "there was no reason to refuse the entire family, *en bloc*."

"He asked me if I cared for anyone else," Ada said defensively. "That was natural, was it not? And Julian is the only possible person."

She is the strangest mixture of common sense and innocence! I keep forgetting how young she really is. (And I keep forgetting that I am only two years older. But I feel very elderly in Ada's presence.)

July 22

Mr. Wolfson called me into the library this afternoon. We talked of household matters for some time, but I could see that he was not really concerned with them. He is not looking well. A casual observer might not see a change in his well-cut features, but I noted the subtle signs of strain and the slight darkening of the skin under his eyes. He must not be sleeping well.

"Harriet," he said abruptly, cutting me off in the midst of a report about bed linen, "has Francis annoyed you in any way?"

For a moment I felt sure that the *tête-à-tête* in the rose garden was painted in bright colors across my forehead.

"Why, no," I said as casually as I could. "Not personally."

"What do you mean?"

"Well, he—he certainly is not a peaceful person to have about the house, is he? Mr. Wolfson—very well, Wolf—you mustn't let him distress you so. I'm sure he doesn't mean half the things he says."

He did not take offense at my frankness, but smiled at me most kindly.

"He has distressd me all his life," he admitted gravely. "No control, no direction . . . Heaven knows what he intends doing with himself."

"But he is studying medicine. Surely that argues purpose and determination."

"I don't know what he is doing in Edinburgh. It is a city which offers other occupations than medicine."

I hadn't even thought of that. Francis' profession was the only thing about him that had given him some stature in my eyes. Now I realized that, once again, I had been overly naïve.

"Never mind," Mr. W. went on more briskly. "I just wanted to be sure he was behaving himself. He'll be returning to Edinburgh in September, Harriet. Just grit your teeth—if that is a proper gesture for a lady—and hold on till then."

I assured him again that I had no need of teeth-gritting, and he turned the conversation to pleasanter topics. We had one of our old discussions, a habit which has lapsed since Francis' arrival. He read me part of Buck's spirited defense of King Richard, and though I argued vigorously with the conclusions, it was more because he seemed to enjoy our debate than because I really disagreed. An hour passed before we noticed it, and I think we could have gone on but for William, who came in with the post. It must have contained bad news, for Mr. Wolfson's manner at once changed, and when I excused myself he let me go. I took Buck's book upstairs with me; I must read it over again when I am alone, for, I can't possibly judge it impartially when it is being defended by Mr. W. He could persuade me that there was something to be said for Satan himself.

Perhaps there is, come to think of it. The only report we have on that affair comes from a biased source.

Blasphemy, Harriet, blasphemy!

August 1

I am still shaking—and it happened hours ago. To think I once complained of insufficient stimulus for literature! This will read, I fear, like a scene from one of the sillier novels for weak-minded ladies, and the plot is more far-fetched than

anything Miss Brontë (that is the name of the lady I was trying to recall) has ever imagined.

I try to make light of it now. But it was a very unpleasant
experience, and the implications may be worse than unpleasant.

It began, casually enough, when I knocked on Ada's door
this morning after breakfast. We have a new upstairs maid—
Mary has taken herself off with, they say, a traveling
tinker—and I was showing the girl her duties, one of which
is to tidy Ada's room.

Ada's gay voice bade us enter. She was standing before
the mirror adjusting her hat, which has a long plume, and
she was humming. She can't carry a tune from A to B, but I
didn't blame her for trying. The windows were wide open
and the air that poured in was heavenly—aglow with golden
light, perfumed by wild roses and thyme.

"I can't get the pin in," Ada said, frowning at her reflec-
tion. "Help me, Harriet, please."

I adjusted the pin, which was at the back, and couldn't
resist stroking the springing golden curls.

"But, Ada, where are you going? You promised not to
ride without me. I am occupied just now, but if you will only
wait an hour—"

"Wait? On such a heavenly morning? Come as soon as
you can, dearest. I'll meet you at the abbey ruins. But I can't
waste a moment of this."

It was in my mind to remonstrate, but I glanced at the
maid, standing there with her arms piled high with household
linen and her mouth wide open with interest in the doings of
the gentry. So I said only, "You aren't riding alone?"

"No, no." Ada turned and gave my cheek a playful pinch.
The maid's presence didn't bother her at all. "Don't turn into
a fussy old lady, Harriet; you are too young and beautiful.
How can you be sensible on such a day?"

She opened both arms, embracing the air, and twirled around the room in a waltz step. The little maid's eyes widened and she stared in delight. Ada circled me, dropped a curtsy, and added, "Julian is going with me."

"Oh. Well, then . . ."

"At the ruins, in an hour, dear Harriet."

The room seemed darker after she had gone.

It took me more than an hour after all, and the time seemed even longer because I had caught some of Ada's summer madness. I am not so old and wise that I am impervious to that! The maid—her name is Agatha, and her mother must have been in service in York or London to produce such an unsuitable name—did not know how to do the slightest thing. After I had told, and demonstrated, how to make a bed, sweep a floor, and dust, I was tired and would have preferred to enjoy the summer weather curled up in a pile of heather reading. But—but! We have grown very casual here—and rightly so, I deplore many of our worn-out conventions, especially the ones that reduce women to the position of dull children—still, it is not proper for a young lady to spend so much time alone with an eligible young man. (Quotation: *Mrs. Primm's Book of Manners*, page 1.) So, with a sigh, I put on my riding habit. The heavy folds felt horridly hot and stuffy.

When I went down to the courtyard my temper was not improved by the sight of Francis, bent on the same errand as myself—although you would never have guessed it from his attire. He was dressed in his usual untidy fashion, without so much as a coat covering his wrinkled white shirt. His sleeves were rolled clear up above his elbows and his collar was open at the throat. All in all, he exposed an unseemly amount of tanned skin. In this day and age we are supposed to admire a pink-and-white complexion, but I confess I find this golden brown attractive—not on Francis particularly, although it does contrast strikingly with his fair hair and lashes, just in general. He looked like a day laborer instead of a gentleman. He also looked maddeningly cool and comfortable. I felt my collar choking me.

His eyes widened in exaggerated surprise at the sight of me, and he sprang up from the carriage block where he had sprawled himself.

"Cousin Harriet, as I live and breathe! What tears you from your household tasks so early?"

"I'm riding, of course," I said shortly, nodding at old Adam.

"How fortunate for me. I had anticipated a long, lonely ride."

"You may have it yet."

He came closer, looking down at me with his infuriating grin. In a lower voice he said, "Watch your language before the servants, my dear. Do you want half of the North Riding gossiping about our quarrels?"

"I can't imagine why you should care."

"Oh, I don't. I was only thinking of you. They have a proverb in these parts, you know: 'Hate is the cousin to love.' They'll have us betrothed if you don't stop berating me."

"Bah," I said. I had never imagined that people really said "Bah," but Francis would drive a saint to clichés.

"As a matter of fact," Francis went on coolly, "I am looking for Ada. Where has she gone? Do you know?"

I was half minded not to answer or to turn the question off with a sarcastic comment. But it was really absurd to continue sparring with him; I could be calm and reasonable even if he were not.

"She is out with Julian," I said. "I am meeting them at the ruins. Come if you like."

"With no chaperone? Will I be safe, Cousin?"

Really, he is impossible! I turned my back on him, biting

back a hot retort. Adam had finished saddling a tall roan and was putting the bridle on my little mare. His shaking old hands moved so slowly that I wanted to shout at him, but of course he can't help being old and infirm.

"Where is David this morning?" I asked him.

The old man muttered something, and Francis interpreted:

"His day off work, as they say. I suppose he is with his wild relatives, on the moor. Oh, yes, had you not heard? He made overtures to his grandmother and was amicably received. Touching, is it not?"

Almost as if he sensed my impatience, he stepped forward, and in a few moments his big hands had buckled the saddle girths. I swung up into the saddle, ignoring his proffered hand—a bit of childishness for which I was immediately sorry—and in silence we rode side by side out through the gate. When we were out of Adam's hearing, Francis said, "I'm worried about David. Have you observed that he does not look well?"

"I had noticed," I said, glad to find a sensible topic of conversation, without overtones. "I can't imagine what is wrong with him."

"You can't?"

"No. What do you mean?"

"Nothing at all, nothing at all. Why must you always suspect me of innuendos?"

Not for the first time I wished that ladies were permitted to use those sharp, short words that gentlemen find so satisfactory for relieving their feelings. I know several, mostly learned from Francis. But I controlled myself magnificently, saying, in a mild voice, "I gave him a bottle of tonic last week. It does not seem to have helped."

"A bottle of tonic! Had you forgotten that there is a physician in residence, or don't you trust my skill?"

I had forgotten! Or rather, I never thought about him in that way. My picture of the medical practitioner comes from Dr. Bellows, Grandmother's physician, who had whiskers down to *here*, and gray ones at that.

"It never occurred to me, Cousin, that you would be interested in the health of the servants. Perhaps you might examine David."

"I have already offered to do so. David insists that there is nothing wrong with him. We grew up together, you know."

The comment was made in a flat, expressionless voice, but something in the words touched me. The horses were jogging at a gentle walk, side by side; I turned toward Francis.

"I didn't think—"

"You don't think about a good many things."

"Why must you always—always—"

"Bait you?" His frown vanished, and the familiar mocking smile destroyed my tentative sympathy. "But you are so responsive, Cousin. Ada is not at all entertaining, she just opens those vacant blue eyes wider and stares at me."

"Ada's eyes are not vacant!"

"Compared with yours, they are. Your eyes mirror your soul, Cousin—and I must say that you ought to be ashamed of some of the thoughts those flashing black orbs express. Or perhaps I tease you because you look so handsome when you are angry. Your eyes fill half your face and your cheeks are the color of a poppy."

I looked at him sharply, prepared to rein up; but he was not even looking at me. Tone and expression alike were calm, almost bored, and I decided that the seeming compliment was just another of his tricks to rouse me.

"What do you think is wrong with David?" I asked, returning to a neutral subject.

Francis shrugged. I couldn't help but notice how the muscles of his back and shoulders moved under his thin shirt, and I marveled anew that such a stalwart specimen of manhood should be so lazy and indifferent.

"How should I know without examining him? He's always been as stubborn as a mule, damn his eyes. The only way I could get a look at him would be to wrestle him down and sit on him while I took his pulse—and that's hardly good medical practice." His hands lifted the reins. "Come along, Harriet, don't dawdle. I'll race you."

His mount leaped into a gallop, glad to have the restraint lifted. I followed, but more cautiously; he couldn't dare me into racing with him. We were at the ruins in a matter of minutes, having covered half the distance during our conversation, and I was surprised to see no black-clad figures anywhere in sight. Ada and I usually sit in the courtyard where fallen blocks of stone make clean, if not comfortable, seats. But today the grass-grown wilderness was deserted.

"Not arrived yet?" Francis asked, as I joined him.

"It would seem so. . . . Yet I am late myself."

"Then where can they be?" He was strangely concerned, and I wondered if, despite his pretended indifference at her refusal, he was really in love with Ada.

"What does it matter?" I demanded curiously. "Nothing could happen to them."

"You're a fool," said Francis impersonally. "An accident can occur to anyone. Where do they usually ride? You know their habits better than I do."

"Why . . . nowhere in particular. But we would see them, the fields are so open. Ada likes to visit the stallion, in the east pasture—"

"What stallion?"

"The black, Satan. Your father had him moved from the stables after he tried to trample one of the grooms. David is the only one who can handle him, but he allows Ada to touch him."

"We're wasting time. The east pasture is next to the ruins; we would have seen or heard them. Where else?"

"I tell you I don't know! Why are you trying to frighten me?"

"For God's sake, girl, I don't give a damn whether you're frightened or not. Could they have gone to the gypsy camp? Ada seemed fascinated by the grubby old witch."

"I suppose they might have. Ada would be afraid to go alone, but with Julian—"

"My brother is about as much use as a babe in arms. Come along."

I caught at his arm as he turned the horse.

"Wait, Francis. What is it that you fear? The gypsies?"

"I don't fear anything," he said impatiently. "But Ada is punctilious about time. If she is not here, something must have happened to detain her. I'm trying to think what, and it is only reasonable to consider all possibilities. Are you coming with me or not?"

I had no time to reply; he was off at a gallop across the fields. I went after him toward the little woods which led to the gypsy camp. We had almost reached the first trees when we heard a woman scream.

Blurred as it was by distance and terror, it was Ada's voice. I recognized it immediately and my horse bolted in a gallop as my hands urged it on. For a second I was ahead of Francis, but he soon caught me up, riding with his usual ungainly slouch. He shot into the woods like a cannonball. I had to slow up; the tree trunks were too close together for such derring-do, and I have sometimes suspected that my mare is nearsighted as well as gentle.

So, when I came upon the tableau in the little clearing, Francis was there before me. The sunlight trickled down through the thick leaves, casting a wavering greenish light over the players. There seemed to my frightened eyes to be an army of them, but I suppose there were not more than half a dozen ragged, dark-skinned men. I saw Julian, doubled over, his fair hair hanging over his face, his arms bent high behind him and held by two of the villains. Ada was struggling in the clutches of two others, who sought to lift her and carry her toward the cart that stood nearby.

I tugged at the reins, bringing Fanny to a quivering halt, and Ada's teeth flashed as she sank them into the dirty brown hand that circled her arm. The man threw his head back with a howl, the golden hoop at his ear glittering with the movement. As I struggled to dismount, entangling my feet in the folds of my skirt, I realized that Francis had not moved. The others had not seen him; he was partially hidden by an ancient oak tree. He was still mounted, his hands relaxed on the reins, his face set in a meaningless half-smile. The oddity of it stopped me in an abominably awkward position, half on and half off the horse, and in that moment a new factor entered the play.

It was David, but I did not recognize him immediately. He was simply a thin dark streak as he hurled himself from among the shadows of the trees straight at Ada. One of the onlookers was bowled over and sent sprawling by the fury of his rush and then his hands were tearing, in a kind of frenzy, at the two gypsies who were holding Ada.

It happened so quickly, and his passion was so intense, that he succeeded in detaching one man and throwing him to the ground. The second fellow, a man almost as big and burly as Francis, with a scarlet kerchief twisted about his head, was not so easily disposed of. He had to release Ada in order to deal with David, however. She went staggering, to fall in a heap on the ground. The gypsy's head jerked back, the ends of his kerchief flying, as David's fist struck his chin. His hand went to his sash, and I shrieked a warning. But instead of the knife, whose handle was so evident to me, he pulled out a stout cudgel from his sash and brought it crashing down on David's bare head.

As the boy slumped to the ground, Francis finally moved. He loosened his reins and rode out into the clearing, and that was enough. The tall gypsy in the scarlet bead scarf rolled dark eyes toward the mounted man. Moving with blurred speed, he scooped up the fallen gypsy, threw him over one broad shoulder, and, shouting a command, made off between the trees. The others followed; they seemed to melt into the underbrush. In a second the clearing was empty except for us. Julian had fallen forward when his attackers released him, and the soft mossy ground was strewn with limp bodies, like a battlefield.

I finally got my feet untangled and ran to Ada. Before I could reach her she was up, winded and disheveled but apparently unhurt. She seemed not even to see me. Her wide china-blue eyes were fixed on David, where he lay facedown with a patch of sunlight on his dark hair.

"Don't touch him, Ada," came Francis' voice, as she reached out. His tone was sufficiently peremptory to penetrate Ada's daze. She turned a white face toward Francis as he came striding toward her. He dropped to his knees beside David and his hands began to explore the boy's head.

When they came away, the fingers were stained with red; I turned away, swallowing the illness of fear and horror.

"He's all right," said Francis calmly. "Just a lump on the head. Damn it, Harriet, what are you standing there for? The silly little ninny is swooning, catch her, can't you? I'm busy."

I ran to them, wonderfully relieved by his diagnosis, and took Ada's limp body from Francis' hands—or hand, rather, for he was holding her half-erect with one arm while the other hand continued to probe at David's head.

"Lay her flat," said Francis without looking up. "She'll be coming around in a minute. Give me a hand here."

I straightened Ada's limbs and arranged her skirt, noting with relief the return of color to her cheeks, even though her eyes remained closed.

"What do you want me to do?"

"Haven't you got a handkerchief or a petticoat or something to tear up? These scalp wounds bleed copiously. Hurry up, damn it, or I'll have to rip up my shirt."

His hand actually went to his collar, and I said hastily, "No, no, just a moment. Here's my handkerchief."

Francis regarded the small white square with unconcealed disgust.

"That will last half a minute. Here's my pocketknife. Rip up your underskirts, or Ada's."

I started to turn up my skirts—after turning my back, of course—but Ada was too quick for me. She sat bolt upright and flung her skirts up as if there weren't a man in sight for miles.

"Give me the knife!" she said and snatched it from my hand. In a few moments she had reduced her upper petticoat to a series of rough strips and Francis, without so much as a look or a thank-you, was binding them around David's head. He turned David over and, with a sudden, seemingly effortless heave, stood up with the thin young body in his arms.

"He can have my horse," whispered Ada, still on her knees.

"How do you propose to put him on it—hanging across the saddle?" Francis scowled at her; then her white-faced misery softened his look into a reluctant smile. "We'll put him in the cart. Climb in, Ada, you can hold his head and keep it from banging about."

Ada climbed into the cart in a tangle of torn skirts. I opened my mouth to remonstrate—I don't believe I knew why, but I sensed somehow that what Francis had suggested was the wrong thing to do. By then it was too late, and in any case there was no use arguing with Francis. Once he had decided to do something, he did it. Seeing that neither of them was paying any attention to me, I got slowly to my feet, feeling dizzy with the shock of it all.

And it was actually not until then—unforgivably—that I remembered Julian.

Sick with remorse, I hurried to him. He was sitting up, his head bent, cradling one elbow in the other hand.

"Did they hurt you?" I asked unnecessarily. "Julian, I'm so sorry. Francis, come here! He's injured—"

Francis, standing by the little donkey which was harnessed to the cart, turned and looked at us over his shoulder. He stood still for a moment. Then he dropped the donkey's lead rein and sauntered toward us. He stood with his hands at his sides, looking down at Julian's bowed blond head.

"What's the matter, Brother?" he asked blandly.

"My arm—" came from Julian, half-inaudibly.

"Broken? Dislocated?"

"For pity's sake, Francis, do something, don't stand there discussing the problem!" I exclaimed.

"Do you want me to do something, Brother?" Francis asked.

His voice was—well, all I can say is that, if anyone made me an offer of help in such a voice, I would have rejected it if every bone in my body had been broken.

I always knew Julian had resources that no one else suspected. His head came up until he was staring directly into his brother's mocking eyes. His face was white and streaked with dirt where it had rested on the ground, and his lips were drawn back over his teeth in a grimace of pain. But his eyes looked like those of his father when Mr. Wolfson was in a rage.

"No, thank you, Brother," he said. His voice was a whisper—with anger rather than weakness, I am sure.

I looked incredulously from him to Francis, from the latter's smiling face to the hands which hung, deliberately lax, at his sides. I remembered those hands moving with swift, knowing precision on David's injured skull. They were not surgeon's hands, as I had always pictured them; they were too big. But they knew what to do.

"You aren't going to help him?" I demanded.

"He doesn't need my help." Francis turned precisely on one heel and went back to the cart. Over his shoulder he called, "You'll have to lead my horse, Harriet. Julian can take Ada's. His own seems to have bolted."

I couldn't think of anything to say.

No, that is incorrect. I thought of a good many things to say, but I was so choked with rage that my voice would not function.

"Never mind, Harriet." Julian, still holding his arm, smiled at me. "No doubt I will be better off with old Dr. Garth in Middleham. If you could help me up—"

"You can't ride back to the house in that state."

"Yes, I can. Don't worry. I'll take the carriage to Middleham."

He tried to rise and sank back, biting at his lip, as the movement jarred his hurt arm. I pulled at the scarf around my neck. It was tucked well under my collar and I had to unfasten the top buttons of my bodice before I could remove it. It was thick, wide white silk and made an admirable sling. Julian bowed his head so that I could knot the ends at the back of his neck, and as he lifted his head again, smiling at me, I couldn't resist brushing the tangled hair off his forehead. He turned his head so that his lips touched my fingers.

"Thank you, Harriet. Now let's try again."

The cart creaked past us on its way to the manor. Francis was leading the donkey; it needed such inducement, for it obviously would have preferred not to move at all. As I glanced around, Francis gave us a mocking grin and a salute with one upraised hand. Ada did not even see us. Her head was bowed and her hands were cupped around David's face. His eyes, I was relieved to see, were still closed.

Julian waited until they had passed into the trees and were out of sight. I suppose that he didn't want his brother to observe his struggles to rise, and I admired him for it. It was a struggle, certainly; I thought once that he was going to topple over upon me, and by the time he had gained his feet I had both arms around him, trying to brace him without hurting his poor shoulder.

"That does it," he said, through clenched teeth, but sounding fairly cheerful. "Now if we can get me onto that horse . . ."

All at once, for no reason, my eyes filled with tears. They were hot, salty tears, and they stung my eyes. I didn't want Julian to see them, so I didn't raise my head to answer him but stood staring blindly at his cravat. Despite my efforts the tears overflowed; two of them landed on Julian's coat lapel. I don't see how he could have felt them through the thickness of coat and shirt, but he seemed to know at once.

"Harriet . . ."

His fingers touched my hair. They were very gentle, not at all like those other, large hands which had refused to relieve suffering.

"That devil," I muttered, and my voice broke in a thick, ugly sob.

Julian's hand moved from my hair to my cheek and then lifted my chin. I couldn't see anything except a white blur through the water that fogged my eyes, but I sensed that he was smiling.

"Your heavenly compassion," murmured Julian.

It sounded like a quotation—and, illogically, it jarred me. Before he spoke, it had all seemed quite natural; I was not even aware of the impropriety of what I was doing, standing so close to him that I could feel his heartbeat. Now I was suddenly and unpleasantly conscious of the weight and size of him in my arms and I stepped back so suddenly that he staggered. The warmth of my cheeks dried most of the tears. I brushed the rest of them out of my eyes with the back of my hand.

"You'll do better with Dr. Garth," I said firmly. "I don't believe Francis could mend a blister properly. Come, Julian, and let's get it over with. I fear it will hurt you."

After all, he mounted more easily than I had expected. His good arm pulled him lightly into the saddle. He must be stronger than anyone suspects—except myself; there was good solid muscle under that fine coat of his. But he landed in the saddle with a rather undignified thud, and it took him a moment to get his breathing under control. His color seemed better, however, and I was no longer so concerned for him.

We went back at a walk; the slightest jar sent Julian's teeth digging into his lower lip, and I had to lead Francis' roan. It was during that slow ride that Julian sowed some seeds in my mind which have already grown into rank, ugly thoughts.

"I want to tell you what happened," he began, after we had left the copse and were heading across the field.

"Don't talk until you feel stronger."

"Oh, I'll do well enough. Harriet, I may be laid up for a few days. I want you to promise to watch over Ada."

"Of course. I always do. But why—"

Julian's face was grave.

"Those men were, of course, from the gypsy camp. I recognized Tammas, the leader, and two of the others, if there could be any doubt. Don't you see what that means?"

"No—"

"This band has enjoyed my father's hospitality for years. They do not find a friendly welcome often, not with their thievish, filthy habits. They are not stupid; they know they can expect short shrift from him for molesting his ward, even if he were not inclined to punish them for injuring me. Why would they risk such unpleasantness?"

"Why, I suppose ransom . . ."

Julian snorted, sounding for a moment just like his brother.

"Ransom, with half the population of Yorkshire on their trail? Not to mention my father . . . He's not—er—an easy man, Harriet. There isn't a peasant in the North Riding that would dare shelter them, and they know it. Think again."

The horses had gradually slowed as we forgot to guide them. Now they came to a halt, and I studied Julian's face in mounting worry. The subject was of grave concern to him. He stared back at me in bright-eyed intensity, forgetting the pain of his injured shoulder.

"Tell me, Julian."

"I had hoped you would arrive at the same conclusion. Perhaps I'm being absurd. . . ." He shrugged. "They could, possibly, elude pursuit for a week. In that week they would have time to marry Ada to David and make sure the marriage was—er—consummated."

I felt as if I had been struck across the face.

"But—but your father would have any such marriage annulled and David imprisoned," I cried.

"If he could find them, yes. But suppose Ada were not a prisoner but a willing accomplice—"

"Oh, no, Julian!"

"She loves that lout. Didn't you see her face just now? I've seen it coming for weeks. The way he looks at her . . . Harriet, I'm not blaming her; she is young and foolish, easily led; in that lies the danger."

"She would not do such a thing!"

"Ah," he said, "you are not so sure, are you? I don't say that she would cold-bloodedly decide to elope. But if she had been carried off, if David came to her as she huddled in terror in some filthy gypsy caravan . . . Then, you see, with a simple disguise the two of them could elude pursuit indefinitely. And the old hag Marian could shrug her shoulders. 'A kidnapping? Ah, what a pity, but the men who took Ada were renegades; they have run away; we promise to punish them if they dare to return. The girl is not here—search, gentlemen, all you like. . . . '"

"Ada could not live that way," I argued frantically. "Spend the rest of her life in a dirty gypsy camp?"

"She wouldn't have to," said Julian grimly. "In a year or so she could reappear, with her husband, and my father couldn't have the marriage annulled. It would be too late."

I understood what he was too delicate to say, and a wave of horror washed over me. I grasped desperately at the one mitigating fact.

"But it was David who rescued her! He was injured in trying to save her!"

"Trying—precisely. He did not succeed, did he? And what could be more romantic than a wounded hero? That would be the one sure way to win her confidence. He wasn't badly hurt—you heard Francis say so."

I sat in silence, my last hope demolished. Julian gave my horse a gentle slap on the flank. We rode on.

"I may be wrong," he said softly. "But watch Ada, Cousin."

As soon as I had seen Julian tucked comfortably into the carriage ready for the journey to Middleham, I went in search of Ada. She was in her room, sitting before the dressing table. She still wore the crumpled riding habit. Her poor little hat lay on the floor beside her, the plume bent beyond repair.

"Ada," I cried, "why didn't you call one of the maids to

help you? You ought to be in bed after such a shocking experience."

"Francis says he will be all right," she said. "He opened his eyes and knew me."

"He—" I ought to have been more gentle, but this, coming on top of what Julian had just told me, frightened me out of what wits I normally possess. I fell on my knees beside her and shook her till her hair flew about her face.

"Ada, you are out of your senses! This boy is nothing to you! A servant . . . Has it not occurred to you that he may have planned the whole conspiracy?"

"He? David?" Her eyes focused on me. A spark lighted in the blue depths. It ought to have warned me, but I was too distraught to notice.

"Yes, David. Why would the gypsies risk Mr. Wolfson's anger?" And I went on to pour out Julian's theory, in almost the same words he had used. I never finished. Midway through, Ada turned from a frightened little kitten into a full-grown cat, spitting and ready for battle. She sprang up from her seat, knocking me over backward.

"How dare you!" she shouted. "How dare you say such things? When he is lying there injured because of me? When he risked his life to save me? Don't ever say such things to me again, Harriet, or I—I hate you! I hate you!"

Sprawled on the floor, supported by my elbows, I stared up at her in consternation. I had seen her angry once before, when she flew at a carter who was abusing a horse, but never like this. I hardly recognized her—and yet she still managed to look beautiful.

"Ada," I said weakly and at the sound of my voice her face crumpled and fell back into its soft pink-and-white contours. She flung herself down on the floor and put her arms around me, and for some time the two of us sat there holding one another and weeping, like two silly children.

"Harriet, dearest, darling, I am so sorry," mourned Ada. "How could I speak to you so, when I love you. . . . Forgive me, dearest Harriet. But—you didn't mean it, did you?"

"I—I don't know."

One great load had been lifted off my mind by Ada's reaction. She, at least, had no knowledge of any such plot. Julian had not hinted at this, but he would have too much delicacy to do so to me.

"He would not do such a thing," whispered Ada, against my shoulder.

"I want to ask you something, Ada. Look at me."

She raised her head obediently, but, after all, there was no need to ask the question. As our eyes met, she began to blush. The color, an exquisite rose-pink, spread slowly up her throat over chin and cheeks, till it vanished into her hair. With a little sound, half gasp and half sob, she hid her face against my breast.

"Promise me one thing," I said, in the calmness of despair. "You would not leave me, Ada? You would not go away with anyone and not tell me?"

"No." The answer was muffled but prompt; I could not doubt its sincerity. "Harriet, darling, I'll never leave you. But—oh, dear, I am so unhappy!"

I held her in my arms stroking her tumbled hair, while she wept. She knew the truth, and knew its hard corollary that spelled death to her hopes before they had fully bloomed. And I knew I must crush those hopes, if she lacked courage to do so herself. I don't know which of us was more miserable.

I left her finally tucked up into bed, bathed and comfortable, her bruises tended. I wanted nothing more than to climb into my own bed and pull the covers over my head. But such escape was not for me. I sat down at my writing desk and began recording this day's events.

Now that I am out of Julian's presence I am not so sure that his theory is correct. He has a good deal of the Wolfson power of persuasion. Of course David loves Ada; I was willfully blind not to see how it has affected him. And she, thanks to the unfortunate events of today, has discovered that she returns his love. But that he could have planned such a fiendish thing—no, I cannot believe it any more than Ada could, and I lack her strong emotional faith in him. He is not an evil man. Surely I could not be mistaken about that.

Yet, still, the gypsies' unaccountable daring remains unexplained.

Oh, there is another possibility. I thought of it when I was holding Ada, trying to calm her sobs. There may well have been a plot, but David need not have been the villain.

I cannot forget the look on Francis' face as he sat in the half-shadows of the trees and stared out at Ada struggling with those abominable men, and at Julian, helpless and twisted in their hands. *He knew.* He was not surprised or horrified. He had expected something to happen. And how could he have known unless he had planned it?

But we did arrive in time, we did stop them.

Julian's cursed habit of argument has infected me. I can think of difficulties—and the explanations of them.

If Francis had meditated some harm to Ada, an excuse for his morning actions—an alibi, I believe they call it—would be useful. He took me with him as a witness. Good heavens, was he not waiting for me in the courtyard, lounging lazily about until I appeared?

He may have heard Ada arrange to meet me. In any case, it was important that I be kept from her until the deed was done, and at the same time I could serve as a witness to his own innocence. But his plan went astray. We arrived too soon. Perhaps Ada's struggles caught them all by surprise, for she can be a wildcat when she chooses; or perhaps Julian put up more of a struggle than they expected. That—yes, of course! If Francis blamed his brother for foiling his pretty plot, that would explain his cruel hostility toward Julian.

So we arrived at the wrong moment. And as Francis hesitated, not having decided quite what to do, he saw David approaching. The odds then were too great for his confederates—David and himself and Julian, not to mention Ada and myself—so he decided to play the hero himself.

Yes, it could have been that way. Francis hates his brother. He may desire Ada, not for her charm and sweetness—he is too coarse to appreciate those qualities—but simply and crudely for her money. When she refused him, he sought this means of winning her. His father would storm, but he would not be so quick to annul *that* marriage, and that difficulty was one of the strongest objections to David's part in such a plot.

Oh, God, I can't go on thinking this way! It is inexpressibly painful—as painful as Francis' brutal refusal to assist his injured brother. I don't *know* that anyone planned this, and I won't believe that they did. The gypsies were stupid. Men often are. They acted without thinking of the consequences. Men almost always do.

But I shan't take my eyes off Ada from now on.

August 19

I have not written in my diary for some time. I have not had the heart to do so. As I look back through these pages, I see that the whole summer has been a failure insofar as literature is concerned. And it surely has been a failure in other ways.

I overheard today not one but two conversations. I was not eavesdropping—I say that truthfully, for if I had been, I would admit it here. This just was my day for overhearing other people's affairs.

The first incident occurred this morning. Mr. W. was closeted in his library with a visitor who had arrived early from Middleham. I did not realize he had a guest. I came down the corridor, quite unsuspecting, to make one of my infrequent requests for additional household supplies.

The visitor was just leaving; he had opened the door and was standing with his hand on the knob. Thus it was that I happened to hear the final remarks that Mr. W. addressed to him, and his replies.

Mr. W.: "Nothing can be done yet. Extend the note till November."

Visitor: "It will cost you dear."

Mr. W.: "Devil take you, I know that. The young fool won't suffer, I assure you."

Visitor: "But how do you propose—"

Mr. W.: "That's my affair. Now get out and do my bidding."

The visitor emerged, without further parley, catching me standing there in the middle of the hall. He seemed taken aback at the sight of me, but recovered himself at once and passed me with a slight bow. He was tall and fashionably dressed, but the sidelong glance he shot at me gave him an appearance of shiftiness which, I feel sure, is undeserved.

I went on to the library and transacted my business. Mr. W. was his usual smiling self. Naturally I made no reference to the snatch of conversation I had inadvertently overheard, though I was mildly curious. Apparently Mr. W. holds some poor young man's note for a sum of money and is willing to give him additional time to pay it, even at the risk of losing the whole. How like him that is!

The second conversation destroyed all the pleasant glow the first one gave me.

My household tasks certainly afford me ample scope for prying, if I were so inclined. I may need to wear heavier shoes; my thin house slippers are too quiet. I was in an upstairs corridor later this morning, going to Julian's room to make sure that Agatha (that most unsuitable name!) had cleaned it properly. She is improved, but still far from perfect. I assuredly did not expect to find Julian indoors at that hour, for I had seen him at breakfast dressed to go out.

His door was not ajar. I heard what I heard because both men were shouting at the top of their lungs.

They had been talking for some time, for the first sentence I heard was obviously in reference to a previous statement. I wish desperately that I had come five minutes earlier and heard the remark which prompted such a violent reaction from Julian:

"You can't do it! I won't let you do that!"

Yes, the passionate shout was Julian's normally gentle voice. I recognized the answering voice more readily.

"And how do you propose to stop me?"

The ensuing silence rang with tension. I braced myself for another shout from Julian; but when he finally spoke, it was in a lower voice. Even though my ear was by then (I may as well admit it) flat up against the door, I heard only the words "not alone." To this Francis replied with a series of exclamations which I need not repeat; they expressed extreme annoyance, to put it mildly. He added loudly, "I've given you fair warning, Julian. You're a sniveling, degenerate coward, but you are my brother."

Luckily his walk is as noisy as his voice. I heard him coming, even across the soft carpet that covers Julian's floor, and I knew I had less than a minute in which to hide myself. The corridor was long, its only furnishing a small table with a vase of flowers on top; my only hope lay in one of the adjoining rooms. As Francis' feet thudded toward the door, I seized the handle of the next door, flung it open, and darted inside, closing the door in the same movement.

I had forgotten, in my panic, that the brothers had rooms side by side.

It was Howard that told me I was in Francis' chamber—from the frying pan into the fire indeed! The skull sat on top of a pile of books on Francis' bureau. I was in no mood to appreciate Howard, though his white teeth gleamed in a grotesque but not unfriendly smile. All I could think of was what Francis would say if he found me here.

Julian's door opened and crashed shut. I looked wildly about the room. Could I pretend that I had looked in to inspect Agatha's cleaning? I could, but that would not spare me Francis' sarcasm, and I could imagine only too clearly the tenor of his comments. I thought of hiding. There was ample room for me in the big wardrobe or under the bed. But what if he spent several hours in his chamber? What if he found me, with my nose in the dust (Agatha does not always dust under beds) or buried in one of his shirts? Imagination quailed at the thought.

Then I realized that the danger was over. The footsteps passed the door without pausing.

I waited several minutes before venturing out and fled, with undignified speed, back to my own room.

Julian's speech—or threat—might have referred to any nefarious scheme of his brother's. Francis is capable of almost anything, and I know little of his private affairs.

Then why do I have the feeling that they were talking about Ada?

I suppose I have not been able to dismiss my suspicion of Francis' involvement in the gypsy episode. And I have no proof of that.

But something is wrong. I can feel it, like the heaviness of the air before a thunderstorm—a hot, breathless oppression, a tension of the nerves. It is not new; I have felt it before and set it down to temporary depression. But it is not my nerves. It is external, in the house and the air around it. This house, which seemed like a haven, has become a source of infection. What has happened to change it?

One change is obvious. Francis came home.

September 10

Alas for my poor diary. I really must reform my writing habits. Events have occurred, but they are not of the sort one wants to record. There is no doubt about it, the atmosphere grows increasingly uneasy, and I am not the only one to feel it.

Ada's unhappiness is understandable. She has tried; I will give her credit for that. We went once to visit David—a proper, formal call from the ladies of the house to a faithful servant who is ill. The encounter was not pleasant. The easy, though respectful, camaraderie among the three of us was gone. David lay propped up in his bed. He looked at me occasionally but never gazed directly at Ada. And she, who normally bubbles with talk when she is in congenial company, said hardly a word.

David is back at his duties now. He still wears a picturesque white bandage, which only adds to his romantic looks. He lost weight during his illness and is pitifully thin. He spends a good deal of time with the wild stallion, Satan; I overheard one of the other grooms saying that he has done wonders with the beast but goes about it so recklessly that he is sure to have his neck broken yet.

I don't know how long this can continue. Even with David's hours in the pasture with Satan, he and Ada see each other almost daily. It would be better for both of them if they were apart. But I can't bring myself to tell Mr. Wolfson of the difficulty. Wise as he is, he would never understand; he would be angry, and the poor young things have had enough misery without that.

When Mr. W. first heard of the gypsy attack, he was furious. I have seldom seen him so angry. He swore all sorts of dire revenge against *him,* meaning, I suppose, the leader of the group. I was surprised when I heard from one of the maids that the gypsies had been sent on their way—abruptly and in disgrace, but with no legal action being taken. When I asked him about it, Mr. Wolfson shrugged ruefully.

"There was nothing to be done, my dear. The participants in the assault had disappeared, and the old woman swore that they had fled her anger as well as mine. You ought to have seen her, Harriet. It was as good as a play—she wept, knelt at my feet, shook her fists, and swore by all her heathen gods. She might even be telling the truth; it would be folly for her to antagonize me. And I can hardly punish the innocent along with the guilty."

Julian? He recovered quickly from his injury, but seems unusually silent and subdued, even for him. He has not spoken again of the matter which concerns me so, but he watches Ada with a new intensity. I think he is falling in love with her.

Francis is drinking steadily.

Several times a week he goes to Middleham and returns in the small hours. He keeps a bottle of spirits in his room; the maids gossip about it. I stay as far away from him as I can, and I must admit that he makes no effort to see me or Ada. If I were romantically inclined, I would think he is trying to drown his sorrows, but it would require a greater imagination than mine to attribute such motives to Francis. Day by day I keep expecting him to announce his departure; it is September, and he must be gone soon. I look forward to that event as to a deliverance from illness. Once he has left, we can settle back into our old comfortable ways.

September 15

Francis is still here. I begin to think he means to stay forever. If he does, we shall all go mad.

He had another terrible quarrel with his father today. There may have been other encounters that I did not hear, but this time their voices were audible all over the house. I had no desire to eavesdrop. I ran away. A conflict between those two has the elemental fury of a hurricane. He will kill his father if he goes on. Why doesn't Mr. Wolfson send him away?

Can he send him away?

September 18

An alarming bit of intelligence from Julian today. He says some of the gypsies are still in the neighborhood.

He mentioned it casually at dinner. (Francis was not present.) I could not hold back an exclamation of dismay.

"There is no cause for alarm," said Mr. Wolfson, with a terrible glare at poor Julian, who looked as if he would like to bite out his tongue. "Probably a tinker or solitary beggar."

"Oh, undoubtedly," said Julian, too enthusiastically. "The servants call any dark-skinned vagabond a gypsy."

Mr. Wolfson changed the subject, and I glanced uneasily at Ada. She did not seem alarmed; indeed, I wonder whether she even heard. She is so wrapped up in her misery that very little touches her.

September 21

This time he has gone too far! I must take action now.

But how?

I cannot go to his father. There would be an explosion which would shake the family to its foundations.

Tonight after dinner I went to walk in the gardens. I have not been out of doors after sunset for some time; I am still ridiculously nervous about the gypsies. But this evening the house seemed unusually oppressive. We had one of those ghastly dinners, with Francis glaring and making obscure remarks which kept his father and brother on the edges of their chairs. Ada sat in dumb misery, as she always does nowadays. William's eyes kept rolling nervously from Francis to Mr. W. It was frightful. Afterward I fled out of doors.

The air was balmy, with a soft breeze. In the west the last shades of sunset lingered, pale gold and mauve and rose below a vault of sky that deepened from clear watercolor blue to indigo. One bright star hung over the black shapes of the fir trees.

I walked up and down while the shadows thickened and the deep blue of night spread down the sky. Gradually my nerves relaxed. He will go soon, I thought. I am becoming unnecessarily perturbed. All this will pass.

My heart rose up and almost choked me when the shadowy figure of a man moved out from the shelter of the pines. The terror was so sudden, after the peace which had surrounded me, that it held my limbs motionless and froze my voice. Then I turned to flee and opened my mouth to shriek, but that moment of paralysis had lasted too long. The man reached me in one long leap. His arms enveloped me and his hand came down hard across my lips.

As soon as he touched me, I knew him. I went limp with relief for a moment—before I realized that now I had even more reason to be afraid. His hand had loosened its hold when I relaxed, but as I drew breath to scream, it tightened again. There was no air in my lungs or in my throat; I could not breathe; his grip crushed my ribs. I did not faint, though I lost all power to struggle; I felt myself being drawn, still held erect but helpless in his grasp, across the grass and into the darkness of the firs. I could not distinguish the blackness of approaching unconsciousness from the heavy shadows of the night.

He stood for a moment as if undecided. Then he started to lower me to the ground, and I discovered that I had not, after all, lost all capacity to struggle.

"Damn it," said Francis, in a slurred whisper, "if you go on like this, I shall have to hurt you."

I tried to say that he was already hurting me, but his fingers still blocked my voice. Hearing me gurgle, he lifted his hand a cautious inch.

"One scream and I'll put it back. Harder. Talk nicely now."

"You—you are intoxicated," I said stupidly. I was not going to scream; the air felt too good.

"Drunk, you mean. Shun euphemisms. But not drunk enough, more's the pity."

"Are you out of your senses?"

"Wish I were."

"Francis, what are you trying to do?"

"What the hell do you think—" His voice broke off. There

was a silence that lasted for half a dozen heartbeats. (I could hear mine only too clearly, and they were abnormally quick.) Then Francis laughed.

"I'll be eternally damned. You would think— Well, it's a cursed fine idea. I had planned a quiet little talk, but that's not going to work, I can see that now. So I shall proceed to abduct you, my treasure. Fling you over my shoulder and carry you off to my lair. We can come back for Ada," he added.

"Ada? What on earth—"

Francis started to laugh again, so heartily that I could scarcely make out his next words.

"I'm something of a Turk, you see. Fond of variety."

"Francis—please— You don't know what you are doing. You are intox—drunk. Let me go, and I—I'll not tell anyone of this."

"Not my father?"

"Not of all people. It would hurt him so."

"Hurt him, eh? And you wouldn't want to do that?"

"Never."

"Touching . . ." Again he was silent, and hope slowed my racing heart to something like its normal rate.

"No," he said abruptly.

"Francis—"

"No. If I don't take you now, I'll never do it. It will be too late. I've given myself away; you won't let me near you another time. . . ."

He was holding me, with his careless strength, several inches off the ground. I could not even stand on my own feet; I could only lean helplessly against his breast, pinioned by his great long arms. The change in his voice, now humorless and shaking with pent fury, told me that I had lost all hope of reasoning with him. I could only conclude that he was mad.

"Harriet."

I started, looking up, trying to see his face more clearly in the darkness. There had been another change in his voice—one that set my heart pounding anew.

"Harriet, come with me. I can't drag you screaming—and I don't want to hurt you. Come with me. I promise you won't regret it. I'll explain everything—"

His lips were on my cheek, moving clumsily. I could smell the strong reek of spirits on his breath. I was completely helpless; I could not move even my head, for it was pressed against his shoulder. Knowing it was useless to resist, I resigned myself. . . .

At least that is how I ought to have behaved. What liars we women are!

Mind, I am not ashamed of how I felt. Despite Grandmother's horrid hints, I cannot believe that it is wrong to respond to the touch of the man one loves. But I do not love Francis—I loathe him. That is what I am ashamed of, the object of my feelings, not the feelings themselves.

I did object—a trifle.

"Francis, don't— Give me time—"

"No time," he said, against my ear. "Now or never. He won't let me. He'll stop me somehow—"

"I'll stop you," said another voice in melodramatic accents. "Now."

I could hardly see him except as a darker shadow, but it had to be Julian. Who else would come to look for me when night fell and I did not return?

"That will be enough, Brother," said Julian coldly. "Harriet—you are not hurt?"

Still suspended from Francis' grasp, I managed to squeak a reassuring negative. Under my breath I hissed, "Let me go at once, Francis!"

I could almost hear him thinking. He would have made two of Julian, but he could hardly attack his brother without releasing me. And I would immediately run screaming for help. He reached the only possible conclusion at the same moment I did.

"I *beg* your pardon, Harriet," he exclaimed, setting me down on the ground. "Dear me—I fear you misunderstood my little joke. My sense of humor—"

"Is abominable," I said, between my teeth. "And I do not—"

"You don't what?" inquired Francis politely.

"I—nothing."

Francis was trading, quite unscrupulously, on my reluctance to cause trouble. How much Julian had heard I do not yet know, but he could not have seen very much—it was too dark. Yet the younger brother's waiting silence was as sharp as a shout. If I had wept or shouted accusations, heaven knows what he might have done. If Francis were attacked, he would fight back; in his present frame of mind, which I knew only too well, he might do the slighter man serious harm.

I went toward Julian with unhurried steps—but my knees were shaking.

"Thank you, Julian," I said calmly. "Let's go back to the house, shall we?"

I left my rescuer in the hall, where the light was dim; I did not want him to see me clearly. But when I inspected my image in the glass in my room I was surprised to see how few signs there were of those terrible moments. There was a small cut on my lip, but it was on the inside so did not show. It was not until I undressed for bed—which I did at once, being weak with reaction—that I saw the bruises on my upper arms. Luckily they are in places which are not normally

visible. I will have to take care to keep Ada out while I am
dressing.

What *shall* I do?

September 22

I shall do nothing. Perhaps I am the one who is mad. Could
it really have been only one of Francis' "jokes"?

When I met him this morning at breakfast, he looked me
straight in the eye and greeted me as if he had absolutely no
recollection of his insane behavior.

I cannot fathom what is happening here. Perhaps all I can
do is try to forget it.

September 26

Today was our first intimation that summer is over. The
weather has been clear and warm, unseasonably so for this
part of the country, I understand. But when I woke this
morning, it was to gray skies and a keen wind that whipped
the yellowing leaves off the trees. The day suited my mood.
I wish some spiritual wind would come and blow away the
dead leaves that clutter my brain!

When I went in to Ada I found her still abed. Her looks
alarmed me, but she was cool to the touch and insisted she
felt no pain, only weariness. This increasing apathy frightens
me. If she would only speak to me of what troubles her! But
she hugs her sorrow to her as if it were a kind of comfort.

I decided to go out; the house is becoming increasingly

uncomfortable to me. We have heard no more of the gypsies, but they are only one of my worries. I decided to ride only as far as the ruins; the ruined cloisters would, I thought, restore some of my peace of mind.

The ride did me good—the first part of it, at least. The cold air seemed to blow some of the cobwebs from my mind, and I became more cheerful. Sooner or later Ada's absurd attachment would fade; soon Francis must leave for Edinburgh. Then Mr. Wolfson and I could resume our pleasant hours together, and perhaps Ada and Julian . . .

I was dreaming, happy and only half aware, as my mount picked its way daintily through the thick grass to the entrance of the court. It knew its way; this is my favorite ride.

The intelligent beast stopped in the gateway, and when I looked up, I saw that someone was there before me. Francis sat on a stone at the foot of the opposite wall. He was deep in thought and, since he faced away from me, it was no wonder that he did not see me.

His manner toward me of late had been impeccable—almost gentle, in fact. But I still had no intention of meeting him alone.

A movement among the grasses attracted my attention and that of Francis. He raised his head alertly but did not rise; perhaps, I thought, he is expecting someone. Then a patch of gray moved among the yellowing green of the weeds and one of the dogs came into view.

I really am not afraid of the dogs. I have been with them many times now, and I know they would never harm me. However, I feel no great affection for them!

I could not see Francis' face but his actions left no doubt as to his reaction to Fenris or Loki, whichever it was. As the dog came toward him, stepping slowly through the drying grass, he bent and picked up a stone.

"Get away, you brute," I heard him say.

The dog stopped. I suppose any animal can recognize a threat, particularly an animal as unpopular as this one. He has probably been stoned before. But there was an uncanny, almost human look on the shaggy thing's face as its eyes traveled from Francis' face to the stone in his hand. The fanged mouth opened wide and the red tongue lolled out. Some dogs look as if they are laughing when they do this. The wolf-dog seemed to sneer. It turned without haste and made its way off, through the doorway that leads to the cells.

I was trying to think of a way of retreating without attracting Francis' attention when something else moved. And this movement froze my voice and my limbs.

The wall of the ancient courtyard is well preserved. In some places it is ten or twelve feet high. The stones are roughhewn compared with those of the church, and presumably they did not make such attractive building material, so they were left in place when the other buildings were looted. Only the vandalism of wind and weather has marred the courtyard walls, and though the old masonry is crumbled away in many spots, the very weight of the stones holds them firmly in place.

Now a section of stonework three or four stones wide, just above Francis' head, was beginning to move.

It happened very quickly. My vocal paralysis broke; I let out a shriek that brought Francis to his feet and whirled him about in my direction. I will never forget the look on his face when he saw me; heaven knows my own expression must have been wild enough. There was no time for comment or movement—the center stone was poised and ready to drop. One of my frenzied gestures must have told him the truth. He looked up—and the whole top of the wall seemed to collapse.

He moved with a speed I had never thought possible,

throwing himself to one side in the only movement that could have saved him. But the movement was simultaneous with the crash of the stones, and the dreadful thunder of their fall and the cloud of dust that rose where they struck momentarily blinded me. I fell off the horse—my newly acquired equestrian skills desert me completely in moments of stress—and ran toward the spot, expecting some indescribable horror.

I found him on the far side of the tumbled pile of rock. He was sitting on the ground. He glanced at me, and at first there was no recognition in his eyes. The shock, I thought; and thanked heaven that there seemed to be no mark of injury.

Then he struggled to his feet, steadying himself with one hand against the nearest block of stone, and I saw that his left arm hung at an odd angle from his shoulder.

"I'm here," I said quickly; my voice was shrill with relief. "It is Harriet, Francis. I'll help you to the house."

I thought he didn't see me. He was glancing wildly around as if looking for something. But when I put out my hand to touch him, he snatched at my arm.

"Here, take my wrist in both hands and hold steady," he said.

I obeyed automatically, but when he pulled away from me, I let go his arm for fear of hurting him.

"God damn you," he said hotly, "hold on, don't let go. Pull."

"No—how can I? You must go to a physician—"

"I am a physician, remember? Hold on, damn you, and pull."

After that I didn't mind hurting him.

Not at first. When I saw his face whiten and the drops of perspiration break out on his brow, I almost let go. He saw my intention and opened his mouth in a wordless snarl, and

I dug my fingers in tighter. I heard the sound when the bone went back into place. It made me feel ill; my fingers dropped their hold. Francis went staggering back, fetching up against the wall, and slowly slid down to a sitting position. He sat there with his long limbs absurdly extended before him, nursing his shoulder and swearing.

I knew by his language that he was better, and for the first time I had leisure to think over what had happened.

It frightened me half to death.

"Francis," I said, sidling closer to him. "Someone must have pushed those stones."

"Indeed?"

I paid no heed to his sarcasm; there were more serious matters on my mind.

"We must get away from here!"

"Give me a chance to catch my breath, can't you?"

"No, no, there isn't time! He may come back—he may try—"

"Not with you here." Nevertheless Francis got to his feet. He was still white around the mouth, and it was with some difficulty that he thrust his bad arm into the breast of his coat for support.

"I'm sorry," I said. "Do you want my scarf?"

"No. Thank you. Let's be off."

He found his horse, which was placidly cropping the grass outside, and mounted. The effort left him absolutely gray in the face, and I was furious when he insisted on inspecting the area behind the wall from which the stones had fallen. No one was there. The grass was too thick to retain footprints.

"Did not Julian tell you that the gypsies have been seen in the neighborhood?" I asked, as we rode toward the manor.

"No. But I knew."

"Then it was careless of you to go about alone."

"Why, in the devil's name?"

"Revenge—"

Francis snorted.

"Why?" he asked again.

"You thwarted their plot to kidnap Ada."

"Nonsense."

"But, Francis, if not the gypsies, who else could it have been?"

"Harriet—" He caught at my sleeve, halting his horse.

"What is it?"

We sat gazing at one another. The frowning intensity of his look set my heart pounding. I felt that I was on the brink of discovery, that in a moment he would tell me the truth about the mysteries that surrounded his actions.

"My father," he began.

"Oh, Francis, you are breaking his heart. Why can't you be kind to him?"

For a long time he sat without speaking, his face hard. Then he grimaced unattractively and let go of my arm.

"It's cold," he said flatly. "Why are we sitting here?"

I feel badly about it now, but I don't really see what I could have done; all the way back to the manor he made no sound or complaint. But when we were dismounting in the courtyard, he had no sooner set foot on the ground than he fell over in a heap. He would have struck his head quite badly had not David managed to break his fall. The servants got him to bed and I sent someone to Middleham for the doctor. They tell me he is resting comfortably now.

It is extremely farfetched to think that the gypsies had anything to do with this. Francis must have some private enemy. Or else it was an accident. The stones look solid, but, after all, they are very old. I saw no one and heard no one; the horse gave no warning, which it ought to have done at the sight of a stranger.

It must have been an accident. If not—then what I saw today was a deliberate attempt at murder.

October 1

The plot thickens, as the novelists say. Oh, it is no use trying to treat it lightly; what happened this evening is only another source of discomfort.

It was Julian this time. He chose the rose garden too. I wonder if he knows that that was where Francis made his proposal?

Poor Ada is completely overcome. She wept when she refused Francis; Julian left her in a state of hysteria.

The difference, I imagine, lies in the attitudes of the two men. Francis really did not care. Julian, said Ada, was crushed. "He felt so miserable," she sobbed.

I feel miserable too. I had hoped— But then perhaps it is too soon. She is still in the grip of this silly infatuation of hers, and as long as David is about the place . . . It is time I did something. If this goes on, Mr. W. is sure to hear of it. I fancy he would approve of a marriage between Julian and Ada. But, gentle as he is, he might be unkind if he discovered that Ada has a fancy for one of his grooms. (It sounds quite ugly, phrased so, but that is how he will look at it, and really it is the truth!)

I can't go to Mr. Wolfson except as a last resort. I will speak with David first. With his abilities he surely can secure another post, and he must see—he must!—that he cannot stay here. I will be very kind but very firm.

Julian, too, might be encouraged by a bit of advice. I need not tell him to be gentle and patient, for he is always that. But perhaps he has given up hope entirely, and I cannot believe that he need do so yet.

Yes, I shall certainly speak to both of them. I feel quite encouraged. Some good may yet come out of all this.

October 2

When will I get over being such a childish, silly optimist? None of my schemes has succeeded. In fact, the situation is as bad as it could be. The fat is in the fire with a vengeance.

I had no chance to speak to David or Julian today. Ada kept me fully occupied. I have rarely seen her so distressed, and I had to sit by her holding her hand before she would fall asleep. Dusk had fallen, and I was preparing for dinner when the summons came.

William brought it. That is not unusual; Mr. Wolfson almost always sends him to me when he wishes to see me. But a summons at this time of day was out of the ordinary. And it was for Ada as well as myself.

I told William that Miss Ada was indisposed and would not go down. He nodded gravely; but five minutes later he was back, with the news that Mr. Wolfson insisted on seeing Ada. If she was not well enough to come to him, he would come to her.

I cannot even say that I had a premonition. Of course, with the love affairs of my poor cousins uppermost in my mind, I naturally wondered if Mr. Wolfson had gotten wind of what was going on. But common sense made me dismiss the idea. Julian might possibly report his proposal and Ada's refusal, but he would never be cruel enough to tell his father of Ada's fancy for David.

I told William to wait and went in to Ada. She woke at my touch and listened apathetically while I explained.

"Certainly I will go," she said, so I went and reported the result to William.

Ada never takes long to dress. Why should she, when she looks charming in anything she wears? Tonight she was totally disinterested in her appearance, so it was not long before we were ready to go down. As we approached the library, I confess I was curious. But I had no idea of how bad it was going to be.

Mr. Wolfson was, as usual, seated behind his desk. His manner told me nothing; he was pleasant and calm, and he gave Ada one of his most charming smiles as he inquired after her health.

Again as usual, it was some moments before I realized that Julian was also present. Why is he so colorless? If he would only assert himself more, his chance of winning Ada would be immeasurably improved. But then most men would fade into dullness beside his father's magnetic person.

Julian's expression gave me my first pang of alarm. He looked like a whipped dog. As I caught his eye, his brows lifted and his mouth moved as if forming words. He was trying to convey something, but the sense of it was too complex for miming. Then Mr. Wolfson spoke, and I turned my attention to him.

"I am sorry to hear, Ada, that you are unwell."

She murmured something without looking at him. She is generally inarticulate in his presence, and in her recent state of apathy she hardly speaks at all.

"I know something is troubling you," Mr. Wolfson went on. "It hurts me to think you would not confide in me. You know my desire is to make you happy, Ada. May I not help you?"

Still she would not or could not answer. I sat twisting my hands together in an agony of uncertainty. I was tempted—how I was tempted!—to speak. But I could not humiliate Ada by telling her secret. She had to do it herself, and I could not imagine how she could resist her guardian's tender but firm appeal.

Mr. Wolfson waited a moment. Then he said gently, "I am sure Harriet and Julian will understand if you wish to speak with me alone."

Ada roused at that, but in the wrong way. She shook her head violently and reached for my hand.

"Very well." Mr. Wolfson moved a paperweight on his desk. "Then I will proceed. You are almost eighteen, Ada. It is time you thought of marriage. I confess to a father's partiality; I had hoped you might learn to care for one of your cousins. Had you considered the matter at all?"

"No!" Ada exclaimed.

We were all startled by the violence of her tone, after her previous silence. She seemed startled herself; as soon as the word left her lips, she hung her head and squeezed my hand hard.

"Do you mean that you have not thought of it, or that you have decided against it?"

"Against . . ." She did not look at him. "Please, Cousin John . . . I cannot . . . I don't wish to marry now. . . ."

"Now or later, it is your decision. But you must consider, Ada, that I am not a young man, nor am I in the best of health. What is to become of you when I am gone? To be sure, your lawyers will look after your fortune, until you marry; but who will look after you? You will marry one day; it would relieve me inexpressibly to have you settled before I must—leave you."

There were tears in my eyes when he had finished. I looked at Ada, expecting to see her equally moved and more responsive. She sat like a stone and said nothing.

"I don't mean to press you, Ada," Mr. Wolfson went on, more firmly, "but I must know. Could you learn to care for one of your cousins?"

"No—no!"

Mr. Wolfson's face was no longer so kind. I could hardly blame him; he had been very patient, and she was as sullen as a small child.

"You force me to a most unpleasant task, Ada," he said.

He touched the bell on his desk, the one he used to summon William. When the butler appeared, he said only, "Fetch him in." By then I knew what was going to happen. I was not surprised to see David, hat in hand, propelled through the door by William's heavy hand.

Ada looked at him and quickly looked away. I could have groaned aloud. That one look was as good as a confession. Mr. Wolfson could not have missed it even if—as I no longer supposed—he had been unaware.

"Let's be quick about this," said Mr. Wolfson, his lip curling. "Ada, you are suffering from one of the most distasteful infatuations I have ever encountered. I am dismissing this servant at once. But first I want him to tell you that he has never had the effrontery to think of you in the way in which you evidently think of him."

His eyes, glacially blue now, turned on David.

The boy looked like a cornered fox. His eyes shifted unattractively from side to side, and his fingers crushed his cap. Once out of his own milieu, thrust into that other world to which Ada belonged, he was graceless and ill at ease. I felt sure Mr. Wolfson had more or less bribed him to administer a quick, merciful *coup de grâce* to Ada's folly, and for one hopeful moment I thought the sight of him must bring her to her senses.

Then Ada looked him full in the face—and the miracle happened. It supported every insipid poet who has ever written about love. The boy's shoulders straightened and his thin hands were still. His eyes met Ada's, and the air between them was almost luminous.

"I—I canna say that, sir, and speak th' truth. I wish I could, indeed, sir. I see 'twas wrong, and I'll be going away. I wouldna do her a hurt for a sure place in Heaven," he added, in a burst of eloquence. "I pray happiness for her, sir."

It was the wrong thing to say, from any practical point of view. But as I saw Ada's face aglow with the first sign of animation it had shown for days—as I watched the answering glow light up David's young face—sentimental female that I am, I could have cheered.

In the ensuing silence the tap of Mr. Wolfson's fingers on the desk sounded like thunder.

"You wish her happiness, do you," he said in a mild voice; and suddenly, in a burst of fury: "You insolent young dog! You'll go, right enough—in disgrace, with no recommendation from me. If you show your face on my property again, I'll set the hounds on you! William, thrash this—this scoundrel and put him out the door. At once, do you hear me?"

With a cry of protest Ada rose to her feet. We were all standing now; even Mr. Wolfson had raised himself, supporting his weight on his muscular arms. If he had been able, I think he would have snatched up his stick and pummeled the groom personally.

I was just in time to capture Ada as she darted toward David, and he, discretion forgotten, was struggling ineffectually in William's huge embrace. It was a horrid, painful scene. The only ones who seemed unmoved were Julian, pale and silent in his corner, and William. The butler's face did not alter, not a single line. He lifted the boy as if he had been a puppy and propelled him out of the room. He was even able to use one arm to close the door.

The sound of its closing broke Ada's resistance. With a little gasp she slumped in my arms, and I lowered her to the floor. Mr. Wolfson sank back into his chair, panting; his face was an ugly red, and I feared he was about to suffer an attack. Julian's quiet voice seemed the most soothing sound I had ever heard.

"I'll take her to her room, shall I?"

I had thought the situation was as bad as it could be; I had forgotten that he is always about when trouble is brewing. The door opened and in walked Francis. I could smell the liquor on his breath from ten feet away.

He surveyed us all with owlish amusement, nodding his head gravely.

"Met the gladiators coming out when I came in," he announced. "Unsporting, Father—William would make two of him. And here's Ada in a faint. Must have been a pretty scene. Sorry I missed it. Give her to me, Harriet."

For once in his neglected life, Julian was before his brother. He bent and lifted Ada, not with Francis' ease, perhaps, but without strain.

"You are too late, Francis," he said quietly.

With an ostentatious shrug Francis moved to one side. I followed Julian as he bore Ada up the stairs and into her room.

The tears and tantrums I had expected from her did not materialize. She is too still. Even as I write these lines I know she is lying awake, staring up at the bed canopy with eyes that do not see it. I wish she had never seen him. I wish it were a year from now. I wish—oh, I don't know what I do wish, except that we were happy again.

Next day

When I awoke this morning, my first thought was of Ada. It seemed heartless of me to have slept at all.

I was slightly surprised to see the connecting door, which I had left ajar, now closed. But that was nothing to my astonishment when, upon trying the handle, I found it would not turn.

I pounded on the door with my fist and shouted to Ada to open. I supposed, naturally, that she had locked me out. She had never done such a thing before, but grief can drive people to strange actions. . . .

As that thought passed through my mind, I grew sick with sudden fear. There was no sound from the next room. I dropped the handle and ran to the table, pulling out its drawer so hurriedly that it came out completely, spilling the contents onto the floor. I dropped to my knees and began sorting through them. Weeks before I had put Ada's drops in that drawer.

The laudanum was there. Of course I never expected it would not be, but . . . ! I put the drops carefully into my reticule. From now on I would carry that bag with me wherever I went.

I went back to the door and lifted my hand to pound again. Then I heard a voice saying my name. It was not Ada's voice; I recognized the tones of the upper housemaid Agatha.

"Miss Harriet?"

"Who else? Let me in at once."

"I canna, miss. I doesn't dare."

"Why not?"

"Mr. Wolfson's orders, miss."

I flew downstairs with my hair unbound and my dressing gown hastily thrown around me. I burst into the library without so much as a knock. As always, the sight of my guardian stilled the complaints that were on the tip of my tongue. His face looked as sad and careworn as I felt.

"I'm sorry you discovered the truth in this manner, Harriet," he said, before I could speak. "I meant to tell you myself. I forgot you would go to her immediately upon arising."

I sank down in the chair he indicated—my usual chair, next to the desk and within reach of his hand. That hand now caressed mine as it lay, trembling, upon my knee.

"Ada is perfectly well," he went on, going at once to the aspect of the situation that concerned me most. "She feels very sorry for herself, of course, but one of the maids is with her at all times, and we will take care that her health does not suffer in the slightest. You must agree, Harriet, that some form of confinement is necessary?"

"I don't see why—"

"Yes, you do; your tender heart is interfering with your considerable intelligence. In her present state of mind Ada is capable of any folly. Would you say that there is no danger of her eloping? I know, I know—you would guard her, be with her constantly. But you cannot sit up all night. Even if she is not contemplating such a scheme, she may try to communicate with that insolent boy. A sad, romantic love affair can be perpetuated interminably by means of hidden notes and secret meetings. Ada must come to her senses. She will do so more quickly if she is isolated from the source of the contamination."

"Yes, I see that," I murmured wretchedly. "But why cannot I see her?"

"Because she must realize that she is hurting all of us, not only herself, by her stubbornness. Why, Harriet, do you think I enjoy doing this? I love her as my own daughter—and I am doing precisely what I would do if a child of mine behaved in this way."

His voice was so kind; I think I could have controlled myself, except for that. I felt like a wretched little urchin as I sat sniveling and wiping my eyes on my sleeve since, for once, I had forgotten my handkerchief. Mr. Wolfson gave me his and completed my demoralization by raising my hand, kerchief and all, to his lips.

"Poor Harriet," he murmured softly. "Your unhappiness distresses me more than Ada's, because it is purely unselfish. It won't be long, my dearest girl. She will give in soon. And the moment she gives me her word, you shall have the key to her room."

I fled from his sympathy as quickly as I would have fled from his anger. What the servants must have thought of me I cannot imagine, for I went stumbling up the stairs, blinded by tears, not caring who saw me. I have been in my room all day—listening. He did not ask me to promise not to speak with Ada, but I feel bound all the same—all the more because he did not ask. He is right, of course. He is always right. But at least I can stay here, near the door. Just in case.

October 15

Ada is still confined to her room. I never thought she would hold out so long.

I see her almost daily, from outside the house. She comes to the window and looks down, and I brave the now chill winds, sometimes walking up and down for an hour or more, to obtain that one glimpse of her. It is worth it to see her wave and smile. Agatha assures me that she is perfectly well. She seems to be eating. I prepare her trays myself and inspect them when they come out of her room.

Francis is still here. I hardly see him. He avoids me as I avoid him.

With Julian I have achieved a companionship of shared misery. He does love her; he has never said so directly, but his pale, strained looks and his restless wanderings about the house are sufficient testimony. Bad as I feel, I suppose that his sufferings must be even greater—for he knows that her present unhappiness comes from love of another man.

Surely this must end soon.

October 29

I accused poor Agatha today of eating part of Ada's meals, in order to keep me from fretting over her untouched trays. To such nonsense has worry driven me!

I never thought she could hold out so long.

Yesterday I asked Mr. Wolfson for permission to talk with Ada. I feel sure that I could make her see reason. He was kind but firm; he feels she is weakening—in purpose, not in health—and will soon give in, and that seeing me would only strengthen her resistance anew.

In this I think he is mistaken. After all, he cannot know her as I do. But I could hardly insist, especially when he himself is so obviously distressed by what he must do. He looks most unwell and has developed a nervous habit of fingering all the objects on his desk as he speaks.

When I left him, I said despondently, "I hope you are right. It is so hard to wait."

His agreement was quick and vigorous:

"Waiting is the hardest thing in the world."

Chapter

3

October 31

THE DATE MUST BE WRONG. IT CANNOT BE ONLY TWO DAYS since I wrote last. The calendar lies; it is winter here. The trees are leafless, bending under a chill wind. The sky is gray and bleak; there are flurries of snow, white against the sullen darkness of the firs.

I have been pacing the floor of this room for what seems like hours. I do not know what to do. Or rather, I know, but the performance of what must be done is almost beyond my powers. I must wait, and waiting *is* the hardest thing in the world.

I turn to my diary in the hope that it can, as it has in the past, calm my nerves and strengthen my will. It seems an absurd occupation at a time like this. But there is nothing else I can do—not yet—and someday it may be important to have a record of the incredible things that have happened.

Incredible. Events are precisely that; I wonder why I am not, really, stunned by disbelief. Perhaps in some hidden part of my mind I saw this coming. Perhaps I know that it is not uniquely villainous but only too common. Are not a woman and her fortune the legitimate prey of any man who can take them?

Matters came to a crisis this afternoon. I have been so distressed about Ada; all these weeks, and no weakening of will, no sign of surrender. It was as if she were bewitched. I knew she was not the frail blossom she appears, but I feared that even her healthy constitution must be undermined by confinement and lack of the exercise on which she thrives. A breaking heart? I'm not sure I believe in that.

I have tried to see her, from a distance, at least once a day. Sometimes I have tapped cautiously at her door, just to hear an answering rap. The panels are so thick that nothing less than a shout could penetrate, so I didn't try to speak. This morning, when I tapped, there was no answer. I thought nothing of it. She might have been asleep. I suppose she has slept a great deal. There was little else for her to do.

I went for my morning walk as usual, along the front of the manor. Her curtains were open, but today there was no small face looking down at me, no hand waving a forlorn good morning. It is not the first time this has happened, so I don't know why I should have become uneasy. Perhaps instinct is stronger than reason.

This afternoon I tapped again. When there was no answer, I ventured to call her name—quite loudly. No answer, no sound. There was, I repeat, no reason for the sudden terror that gripped me. I certainly did not think that any harm had come to her; the worst thing I imagined was that she had fallen ill and they had not wanted to tell me.

I applied my eye to the keyhole, as I have done before; as before, the hole was filled by the big iron key, on Ada's side of the door. Now I took a pen and pushed the key out. By then I had quite made up my mind that she was ill, dying. I pictured her lying pale and still in the big bed. I almost wish, now, that that picture had been true.

When the key fell, under my awkward but determined prob-ing, it hit the uncarpeted floor inside with a crash that sounded like a rock falling. I expected someone to rush to the door.

No sound! No movement! I leaned back on my heels, afraid to apply my eye to the keyhole. I was sure, now, of what I would see.

And, after all, there was nothing. The bed was out of my line of vision. I saw only the front windows, the dressing table, a stretch of carpet, a chair. And I knew that my worst fears were justified. Something was seriously amiss.

The room was too tidy. Ada is not neat; her belongings strew every room she occupies, even briefly. Shawls, slip-pers, ribbons, little trinkets and ornaments . . . The dressing table was bare. Her brush, her mirror, her little bottle of scent, all were gone. The room was an unoccupied room, cleared and ready for the next tenant.

For a brief time I lost my head. Crying and shouting, I beat on the heavy panels with my hands. The obdurate si-lence that followed my violence was confirmation of my fears, if any had been needed. She would have heard my voice even if she had been sleeping. If she were ill, there ought to have been someone with her, someone who would have run to the door and bade me stop my rude noises.

After my first panic had spent itself, I tried more rational methods. It was useless to fish for the fallen key. The door (why had I not noticed it before?) was thick as a prison door, fitted as nicely as a secret panel. There was not the smallest crack at side or bottom.

I ran out into the hall, heedless of noise or staring eyes. The outer door to Ada's room was also locked; the key was missing. I dropped to my knees and applied my eye to this keyhole. Now I could see the bed. Empty—unoccupied—made up with counterpane and pillow cover, curtains neatly drawn back and tied.

I knelt there with closed eyes, my cheek pressed against the cold hard wood of the door. When I finally arose, my limbs were almost too weak to support me; I leaned against the wall like a feeble old woman.

I knew what I must do. I was afraid to do it. Not afraid of him—not then—but afraid of facing a truth which would war against everything I had come to believe. I hoped even then that there would be some explanation. But I must have known that nothing could explain this.

He was in the library. I stood outside the door pressing my hands together in an effort to stop their shaking. Whatever happened, I knew I must not seem afraid. That would have put me at an impossible disadvantage. My first knock was a pitiful effort, barely audible, like a servant's timid scratching. The thought of that comparison stiffened my courage somewhat. I raised my hand again and banged on the panels.

The familiar deep voice bade me "Come in." It was a shock to hear him sound so normal after finding that eloquently deserted room—even harder to see him look up with the warm smile that had so often welcomed me.

The smile faded when he saw me, rigid as a statue, white-faced and staring.

"What is it, Harriet? Are you ill, my dear?"

I had tried to think what I must say, tried to form in my mind tactful phrases which would convey my composure. But when I opened my mouth, a single blunt phrase came out:

"What have you done with Ada?"

If he had raged at me, I would have raged back. If he had put on a look of astounded innocence, I would have flown at him. Instead, he laughed. It left me shaken and foolish, feeling like a silly child.

"I might have known you would find out, despite my orders that you were not to communicate," he said calmly.

"Come and sit down, Harriet. No—here, next to me. Pull the chair closer. I have a feeling that I must be able to touch you physically in order to reach you mentally, to make you understand. You must understand—nay, you will; we have been too closely attuned to one another for you to fail me now."

I did as he asked, for the last time. That strange mesmeric look compelled me as always; there was a sense of some invisible cord connecting us. My skirts brushed the arm of his chair as I took my seat.

"Ada is perfectly safe," my guardian continued in the same cool voice. "Even if you should think me capable of harming a woman, you must realize that her welfare is as important to me as it is to you. It was for her own good that I had to remove her from the house. You know how she has behaved. Not a sign of weakening or remorse or sense; she clings obdurately to her infatuation in a way I would have believed impossible for her."

"She loves him," I said, somewhat to my own surprise—I had not intended to speak.

"She does," said Mr. Wolfson dryly. "A child loves a bright shiny knife, but we do not put such a weapon into its infantile hands. You do agree, do you not, that it is preposterous to allow Ada's love—as you call it—to achieve any consummation?"

"Yes . . . I suppose so . . ."

"Suppose?" The blue eyes blazed at me. "Would you welcome this gypsy's brat as your cousin? See an illiterate, ill-bred clod the husband of Ada, the master of her fortune and her person?"

"Is it the fortune or the person that concerns you most?"

"Both." He added, with a look that made me draw back, "If any person but yourself had asked me that question, I would have struck him. Harriet, Harriet—I want your intelligent, willing consent to what I have done. Show the sense I have always admired in you, and tell me you agree with my first premise."

The look, the smile, the compelling voice—I felt myself weakening.

"Of course I agree. She cannot marry him. But—"

"Good, so far. Then will you admit the next logical step? That the best possible husband for Ada is one of her cousins?"

"I've thought of that too," I said wretchedly. "But she has refused them both. How can I agree to making Ada miserable? She is so young! There are other young men in the world, men whom she might come to love. . . ."

He took my hands in his. I let them lie in his hard grasp, too miserable and beaten to resist. His arguments were unanswerable. And I knew what he would say about my last feeble, feminine suggestion.

"Love. It is a big word, Harriet. Are you sure you know what it means?"

"No. That is, I have never—"

"Haven't you? I forget how young you are and how inexperienced. Harriet, there are so many kinds of love. The kind you are imagining doesn't exist, except in the minds of naïve young girls. Ada fancies she is in love. Do you think this love would survive a year of marriage to a man who has nothing in common with her, no breeding, no knowledge of the world in which she has been brought up?"

His voice was low. It echoed oddly in my ears, as though he were speaking from far off. I sat with head bowed, looking at the long muscular hands that held mine; my heart was pounding so hard it seemed to shake the ruffles at my breast. When he stopped speaking, I muttered a "No" that was as meaningless and involuntary as words spoken in a dream.

"No. Of course not. Love between husband and wife is

based upon communality of class and background. It develops after marriage. Ada is incapable of a genuine passion, Harriet. She is not like you."

Heaven help me, I think I was half mesmerized by the voice and the hands. They still held my hands; now I was aware of a pull, gentle but persistent, that drew me toward him. I was as limp as a stupid stuffed doll, I could feel myself swaying toward him, held erect only by his hands and by a terrifying, vital current that ran through my veins like fire. The voice went on, murmuring and musical, lulling me farther into the spell. . . . And then one phrase caught my failing senses and brought me back to awareness.

". . . after she has been with him for a night or two . . ."

It struck my brain like a dash of icy water. The world fell back into place around me, the dreamy, languorous spell of his voice was broken. I seemed to return from some distant place to find myself bolt upright in my chair, my hands straining to free themselves.

"With him?" My voice was almost a shriek. "Where? With whom?"

"Certainly not with the groom," said Mr. Wolfson, eyeing me keenly.

"With your son. Francis . . . My God, are you mad to do such a thing?"

"Language, language, my dear."

"I wish I knew words enough to tell you how vile you are. Dear heaven, this will kill her! She is only a child, she doesn't know—"

"She thought she knew—enough to yearn for the arms of the stable boy. My son's embraces are surely preferable to *that*. Damn you, Harriet, will you stop struggling? You will only hurt yourself. I'm not planning to ruin the wench, after all. A few days—and nights—with my obedient offspring, and she will be happy to settle for a respectable marriage.

They will make a charming couple, don't you think? And the great gossiping world need never know that they anticipated their wedding night by a few days."

He meant it. Sincerity breathed in every line of his face—sincerity and genuine impatience with my blindness. If he had looked and acted the villain, if he had shown any awareness of evildoing, I might have been able to control myself and fight cunning with cunning. As it was, I lost my wits completely. I think I was crying—there were tearstains on my face later—but I was unaware of that or anything else, even the pain in my wrists, as I struggled against the iron fingers that held them like fetters. I felt myself being pulled out of my chair. My knees struck the floor with a jolt that left bruises, even through the thickness of skirts and petticoats; I was kneeling at his feet, held motionless by a grip that had shifted from my wrists to my arms and pinned them across his knees. He lifted one hand and deliberately slapped me twice across the face.

"Good," he said calmly, as my incoherent voice stopped in the middle of a shout. "A sovereign remedy for hysterics, that one. I had thought better of you, Harriet. But I must confess I find your spirit more attractive than Ada's whining. Are you calm now, or shall we try another dose of the same?"

I shook my hair out of my eyes; it had completely escaped its pins and net and was falling in heavy masses over my shoulders.

"Let me up!"

"No, no, not yet. I'm afraid you might do me some harm."

"If I could . . ."

"You would, of course. Haven't you forgotten my little pets, Harriet?"

"Yes. No. I don't care about them."

He laughed—a queer, choked sound quite unlike his usual chuckle. I have never heard such a sound before; I pray I never will again, for I know, now, what it means. Even then I realized that something new and dangerous had entered the quiet room. I blinked frantically to clear my vision and looked up at his face.

Then I saw it—the face of the wolf. His lips were drawn back in a travesty of a smile, and the long white teeth seemed, impossibly, to have grown longer and sharper. There was no color in his blazing eyes. The old wives' tales had been correct when they whispered of him as a beast. But their poor imaginations had turned into a harmless fairy tale this reality which was worse, because it was true. I made no effort to resist when those abnormally developed arms and shoulders lifted me like a child, off the floor and into his embrace.

It was physically painful, but I hardly felt the force of the arms that held me or the rocklike muscle of his shoulder against the back of my head. Had he but known it, there was no need for duress; if he had taken his hands away, I would still have lain there across his knees, staring up into his face like a mesmerized madwoman. I saw the contours of his face quiver, as if in some internal struggle. I tried to close my eyes to shut out his distorted features, but they would not close, not even when the face came nearer and nearer, till at last it filled the whole of my vision.

I wonder how long it will be before I can remember that embrace without feeling it again, in every nerve of my body. . . .

But the worst . . .

I *will* write it! I must face the truth in order to fight it. The worst was that, though part of me cried out in dumb but violent protest against his embrace—another part did not. It was the conflict within myself that shook me most, disgust and repugnance warring with my own baser instincts. . . .

I must get away from here. Not only for Ada's sake, but for my own. No one can protect me from him; he can do whatever he wishes. And I know what he wants. When his lips left mine, leaving me gasping and limp, he made his intentions clear.

"Harriet," he said thickly. Then in a more normal voice: "Always you surprise me, my dear. Is it your Italian blood, perhaps? If I didn't know your grandmother so well, I could fancy that this was not your first experience. . . . What a pity you aren't the heiress, sweetheart; we could solve my problem without all this fuss. And I wouldn't let one of my feeble sons deputize for me, you may be sure of that."

Again he bent his head. I turned my face so that his lips only touched my cheek. His embrace had loosened; he held me with one arm while his free hand stroked my hair and face and throat. Perhaps it was the insulting sureness of his touch that roused me. I would prefer to think it was some lingering remnant of decency. I moved so quickly that his hands missed their grasp, and then I stood facing him from several feet away.

"You flatter yourself," I said, trying to keep my voice level. "I won't have you or one of your sons. Nor will Ada. You think me helpless. . . . But there are laws in this country for the protection of the helpless."

"Certainly," he said blandly. "All you need to do is find someone who can apply them. There may be a magistrate in Ripon, but probably York is the better place."

"Then I will go to York."

"On foot? Without money?" He laughed. "Why fight your own nature, Harriet? Do you take me for a fool? Do you think I have no experience of women, that I can't tell that you—"

"Stop it!" I retreated as he came out from behind the desk, his hands on the wheels of the chair. The movement

gave me more courage; he could not pursue me that way, and
his vanity would keep him from trying to walk.

"Wait a moment," I said. "Why must Ada marry Francis?
Why can't we be reasonable? You don't need her money—"

"Ah, but I do. All this"—he waved a comprehensive hand
around the richly furnished room—"all this is facade, my
dear. My fortune is gone; my wife's dowry is spent—in fact,
the funds of a certain young gentleman, for whom I have
been acting as trustee, have also melted away. Since the esti-
mable youth reaches his majority in a few months, it is not
even a question of luxury or poverty for me, but one of prison
or freedom. Do you think"—the words were a snarl—"that
I'll let the whims of a silly girl stand between me and secu-
rity? I must have Ada's money. When she marries—my son,
it will be under my control."

The words were like a sharp knife severing the one strand
of rope that had held me from falling into an abyss. His villainy was not the abstract, storybook affair it had seemed; it
had a concrete, practical motive. There was no possible hope
of his relenting.

At that moment I did not think of that or of plans of escape; I only knew that I must get away from him, away from
the chill gleaming eyes and merciless hands, away from the
invisible cord of unwilling sympathy that drew me to something I hated. With one sudden powerful movement of his
arms he sent the chair rolling toward me, and I turned and
fled, slamming the door behind me, holding my skirts high
as I pounded along the corridor and up the stairs. I did not
stop until I was in my own room with the door locked, and
for a long time I crouched on the floor with my ear to the
panel, waiting for sounds of pursuit.

It did not come. Of course he would not follow me. Why
should he trouble himself? All he needed to do was wait,

and no doubt his monstrous vanity convinced him that he would not wait long.

When at last I got unsteadily to my feet, I felt as if I had just arisen from a long illness. The lightening skies outside my window shocked my sight; it seemed incredible that my whole world had been overturned in such a short space of time, or that the sun could shine on such black villainy. The light drew me; I went to the window and sat down, staring out at the courtyard below.

The normalcy of the scene was a second shock. The horses were being exercised; old Adam had just come out of a stall with one of the grays that drew Mr. Wolfson's carriage. I thought of David and could have beaten my fists against the windowpane in frustrated fury. I had thought him not good enough for Ada!

Mr. Wolfson had said that David might try to communicate with Ada. Yes, but that was part of his lie, to convince me and keep me stupid and quiet a little longer. Perhaps the boy did try to reach Ada, but he cannot have succeeded. He would need a confederate among the servants, and I know only too well how much they fear their employer. I knew, also, that they could not help me. I would only betray myself if word of any such appeal reached Wolfson. He must think me cowed and frightened. He would have me imprisoned too if he thought me capable of defying him.

In a sudden panic I flew to the door. Perhaps he had already locked me in! But, no—the key was on the inside. I withdrew the key—somehow I felt more secure with it in my hand—and went back to my seat at the window.

As I watched, William came out of the manor door into the courtyard. He went to Adam and stood talking, giving him directions of some sort, for the old man's head kept nodding. William. How much did he know of the secret affairs of Mr. Wolfson? He was his master's right-hand man, and yet I suspected that William was too clever to be mixed up in such a business. No, Mr. Wolfson would keep him unwitting if he could. Might I then appeal to William for help?

I looked at the man's stiff back and emotionless face and decided—no. William might believe me, but he would never admit it. Belief would involve him just as thoroughly as complicity, and he was not the man to be involved in what he would call "unpleasantness." And there was always the chance that he *was* Mr. Wolfson's tool, in which case an appeal would only betray me.

I could trust no one. It was an unpleasant truth, but one I had to face.

The knowledge should have cast me into utter despair. For some strange reason it had precisely the opposite effect. If I could trust no one, I must rely on myself.

So I turned to this diary, and, as I hoped, it has helped me settle my mind. I must get away from the manor. That is the first, the immediate step to be taken.

The first thing I will do after that is look for Ada. I think I know where she may be. There are not many places, near or far, where a girl may be kept an unwilling and protesting prisoner. Places where screams and cries for help cannot be heard . . .

I saw her yesterday morning. She has only been gone for one day—and night. But that is enough.

I must find her! Surely he cannot be with her every moment; there must be a chance to let her free. In my present mood I could even face him—Francis—big as he is, and fly at him with any weapon that came to hand, a rock, a stick!

But . . . if I cannot find her quickly, or if I cannot free her, then I must go on without her and get help. I, or we, will try to reach Middleham. If David is there—he has an aunt living in the village—he will take care of Ada. How gladly, now, would I entrust her to his hands!

For I see now the meanings of so many little incidents that I ignored or misinterpreted. The gypsies were not David's tools; they were Wolfson's. Dear heaven, he flung it in my face time and again, their dependence on him! David must have overheard some allusion to the plot while he was visiting the gypsy camp—and I wonder, now, whether his reconciliation with his kin might not have been prompted by suspicion. If so, he was not alone in his mistrust of Wolfson. To think that the whole countryside walked in darkest fear of him while I sat and simpered under his flattery! The landlord in Middleham and his timid daughter; old Dodds, shrinking even from the coin that had touched Wolf's hand . . . they were afraid, all of them—and rightly. Heaven knows what oppression and cruelty he has visited upon them.

So, even if we can reach Middleham, we may not find shelter. The whole village is terrorized; if Wolfson drove into the square and demanded his fleeing wards, we would probably be given up to him.

From that same square a coach leaves daily for York. I—we—must catch the coach. Surely in the great northern capital there must be someone to whom we can appeal for sanctuary. There must be some law in enlightened England against what he is planning!

Dear heaven, it is all so hopeless. . . . For the coach we must have money. I have none. For our escape we will need horses; we cannot walk that distance. And how am I to obtain mounts here, where every servant may be a spy? How am I even to leave the house unseen?

In the novels I have read—surreptitiously, through the lending library—the threatened heroines steal forth from the haunted castles by night. It seems to me a poor choice in any case: doors are locked and bolted, watchers are alert, and any movement is conspicuous. In my case, nighttime is out of the question. There are the dogs.

So I must leave by daylight, the moment a suitable chance presents itself—now, today. I wish I could run this instant, straight out the door, down the road, through the gates. . . . But that would be folly. I will wait, for a time at least, in the hope that Mr. Wolfson may go out. Perhaps he will wish to call on his first victim, to see how matters are progressing. . . .

I can't let myself think of that subject; it conjures up visions which make me boil with fear and fury; it weakens my will, which *must* be cool and calm. If he should leave the house my chances of escape increase one hundredfold. I might even venture to try for a mount—without which, let us admit, I stand little hope of reaching any place. When he is in the house, I feel—surrounded. As if there were a thousand eyes watching my every movement.

I will gather my few possessions together—a warm cloak, heavy shoes, my few jewels—and, of course, my diary. It would hardly do to have him find that! But first I am going to try to break into Ada's room. She may have money.

Later

Success! I am a successful burglar. That small venture has buoyed me up; it is a good omen.

It was very simple after all. I was stupid not to have thought of it before, but then there was usually someone with Ada who would have prevented my entry. The key to my door fits the connecting door between the two rooms.

A sobering thought—other keys may fit my lock. I must leave here soon. It is growing late.

Something has just happened which gives me hope. I have been sitting here by Ada's front windows, hidden behind the curtains. It is an excellent vantage point which commands the entire front of the house and the drive. A few minutes ago a hired chaise rolled up and stopped before the steps. A man got out. He had the look of a lawyer's clerk or small broker. He was admitted at once and has presumably been closeted with Mr. Wolfson ever since. The chaise is waiting; that suggests that he plans to return soon to wherever he came from.

I was tempted at first to try to communicate with this man. But it was only an impulse, born of my realization that my plans of escape are almost futile. He would not believe a mad tale like mine, poured out in breathless haste. He may even be an accomplice of my guardian's. I must remember—I can trust no one.

The minutes drag by and race by—agonizingly slow when I think of my anxiety for Ada, frighteningly quick when I remember that I must be gone before dusk. If that chaise does not go soon . . .

I found Ada's pearls and three pounds in change. A help, but not enough for a good solid bribe. If I had fifty pounds and a horse, I would feel confident of success.

Most of her belongings are still here. Her gray merino dress is missing and her sable cloak; at least she is warmly dressed. I cannot tell what else is gone, perhaps some under-garments. . . .

Wait.

The visitor is coming out. He turns, hat in hand; he speaks to someone. . . . Yes, it is Wolfson himself, in his chair. He says—what? Good-bye, no doubt, for the visitor is getting into the chaise. It drives off, in a spurt of gravel. The York coach leaves Middleham at seven; perhaps that is where he is going.

Someone else has come out—William. Wolfson is speaking to him. Can it be? I hardly dare hope. . . . William goes back into the house, following his master. Now to the side windows in my own room.

I can hardly believe it, but it must be true—William has ordered out the master's coach. I see the ostlers harness the grays. I am back at the front window now . . . and here it comes, around the corner of the house.

He is here—Wolfson—still in his chair, dressed in caped cloak and tall hat. His gloved hands propel the chair forward; the groom lets down the ramp. . . .

The dogs are with him. I shrank back at the sight of them, almost as if I had been warned—for at that moment, just as he was about to get into the coach, Wolfson looked up, directly at this window. Those eyes of his! Hidden as I was by the curtains, it was all I could do not to drop to the floor and cower. At last he looked away; I am still breathing heavily.

He is off—in a hurry, too. I never saw him use the whip before, but the horses seem to know it well. Now is my chance—this moment—before my spirit fails me.

I wonder when—or if—I will write in this book again.

That night

It is settled now. Over—done—finished. There is that much consolation—the end of an effort which was always too great for me. I am, after all, "only a woman." And he—he seems, just now, more than a man.

The great escape began well enough. As I went down the stairs—boldly, cloaked and hooded as if for an afternoon stroll—I was still thinking about the money I needed so badly. With a leap of the pulse I realized that Wolfson's study was empty. He had money; I had seen it often, in a tin strongbox. Petty cash for household expenses, but enough for my purposes. The strongbox did not worry me, I felt I was capable of wrenching it open with my bare hands.

The poker sufficed; one strong blow and the hasp broke, displaying a heap of bank notes and silver. I gathered it up pell-mell, like a child scooping sand in its fists, and thrust it into my reticule. For all my bravado I was nervous in that room—silent and serene with its shelves of mellowed old bindings and its smell of cigars and oiled leather; it still breathed of his presence and of the scene that had transpired there earlier that day.

I would have fled at once had it not occurred to me that I might delay discovery of my absence a little longer by leaving the room apparently undisturbed. A broken money box on the hearth could hardly escape even a servant's eye. I picked the box up and thrust it back into the drawer, and then I saw what else was in that drawer—concealed before by the box which had been on top of it.

It was a letter, long and stiff, with a blob of red sealing wax on it. But what stunned me was the fact that it bore my name—Miss Harriet Barton.

For one mad moment I thought that the epistle must be from Wolfson, that he had anticipated even this insane action and left a jeering note to tell me that all was in vain. I knew, at the same instant, that the handwriting was not his bold black scrawl; the cramped script looked familiar but not in that terrifying way. As I picked it up, I saw something else. The seal had been broken.

In the wonder of the discovery I had momentarily forgotten my fear. A sound, seemingly just beside me, brought me back to awareness and to terror. I never discovered what the noise was—the fall of wood in the fireplace or something equally harmless no doubt—but it sent me flying from the room as if pursued by demons. I had just sense enough to snatch up the reticule with its precious contents before I fled.

I had to pause for a moment in the hall to quiet my pounding heart. I meant to avoid the servants if possible, but if I did meet someone, it was vital that I appear calm and unconcerned.

After a time I felt ready to risk the next and most dangerous step. I must take the risk; without a mount I was doomed to almost certain failure. Swinging my reticule nonchalantly I walked through the corridors to the side entrance that opened onto the courtyard. The house seemed strangely silent; I did not meet a single servant.

In the stableyard, though, were Adam and another groom.

They did not see me at first. This was the worst moment of all; I would know, as soon as they looked at me, whether they had been given certain orders. I was almost afraid to find out; in uncertainty there is at least hope.

But I had no time to waste. Taking a deep breath, I strolled out into the flagged court, letting the door slam behind me. Adam looked up.

There was not much of his face showing between the shaggy gray hair and the tangle of gray beard, and what little showed had the typical dour blankness of the countryman. Yet something—his manner, his very lack of response—told me that I was one step ahead of Mr. John Wolfson. In a daze of relief I heard my voice say casually, "Saddle the mare, please, Adam," and I couldn't help but admire my own histrionic ability.

Since David left, the other grooms have made no attempt to go with me on the rare occasions when I ride out. I did not even have to think of an excuse to avoid an escort. My pulses were pounding—with excitement and hope, for a pleasant change—as out of the corner of my eye I watched Adam put the harness on the horse. He was old and horribly slow; internally my mind was screaming at him to hurry, my hands itched to push him aside and do the job myself. But I showed no outward signs of my frantic haste.

At last the girths were tightened and the bridle in place; I was actually strolling toward the mare, and Adam was bending his rheumatic knees to give me a hand into the saddle—when it happened.

The gates of the stableyard were open, as they always were during the daylight hours. The horseman must have come around the south corner, for I did not see him until he was passing through the gateway. For one appalling moment I saw only a silvery cap of hair and a familiar, jutting nose; it was a horrid shock, like being thrown and having all the breath knocked out of one's body. I realized at once that the rider was not Wolfson but his son—not Francis but Julian, whom I had believed to be away on another of his interminable visits.

My first reaction was one of joy. Why had I not thought of Julian? He had been away; that was the pathos of Julian's life, I thought, that one did tend to forget he was alive unless he was actually present.

He came toward me, his face glowing with one of the rare smiles he kept for me. The cold wind had whipped color into his normally pale cheeks and his slight frame, in the saddle, had a look of ease and vigor. The candor of his smile was marvelous. I *knew* he was unaware of his father's villainy. I almost spoke. With his help I was sure of success—I was safe. I don't know what stopped me. . . .

Yes, I do. It was the fact that he too was a Wolfson—one of the sons of the wolf. I could trust no one, no one at all.

My face was not so controlled as I thought. When he was

near enough to see me distinctly, Julian's smile faded into a look of concern, and he quickly dismounted.

"What is it, Harriet? Are you ill?"

"Why, do I look as bad as that?"

"No . . . Only pale and—distressed. What is wrong?"

"I do have a bit of a headache," I muttered. "I thought a ride in the fresh air . . ."

"Too fresh for comfort," said Julian positively. "You'll be chilled to the bone, Cousin, and have a cold to add to your headache."

"I—I never take cold."

"I think you are making a mistake. But if you insist, I'll go with you."

For the life of me I could not help shooting a quick, suspicious glance at him. His eyes were clear and calm. Surely, I thought, he is not that good an actor; there is genuine interest and concern for me in his look. So much interest, in fact, that I wondered . . . A shiver ran through me.

Julian's hand went out to pull my cloak more tightly about me.

"There, you see, you are cold already. Lie down for a bit, Cousin. I'll send one of the maids to you with a nice hot cup of tea. That is a sure panacea for a lady's ills, is it not?"

"Perhaps I had better. Thank you."

"My dear . . . It must be a frightful headache, you look really ill. Come along."

He put his arm around my shoulders and led me toward the house. He had done this before, to me and to Ada. His embrace was impersonal; no one could object to it. . . . He reminded me too much of his father. It was all I could do not to pull away from that supporting arm.

As we walked through the corridors toward the stairs Julian continued to talk, expressing concern, suggesting remedies. He had some drops a doctor had given him once. I must take them. A hot brick, too, in the bed . . .

I scarcely heard him. I was trying to decide whether to run as soon as he left me or wait until after the maid had tucked me up, presumably for the day.

The second alternative was, on the face of it, more sensible. It would give me hours, perhaps the whole night, before anyone looked for me. Yet when he left me, at the foot of the stairs, to go in search of the servants, my brain stopped functioning. The moment he was out of sight I walked to the front door and went out.

The only inhabited rooms at the front of the house belonged to Ada and to Wolfson. Unless some servant was in one of them, cleaning, I was safe from observation there. Julian's rooms were in the south wing. I went north, around the long side of the house, creeping on hands and knees through the shrubs until I reached the copse of trees that stood behind the manor. They were bare and leafless now, but they gave some cover. As soon as I reached them, I took my skirts in both hands and ran.

It took me nearly an hour to cover the distance between the house and the old abbey, although I ran until I got a stitch in my side. The ground was rough; I fell twice, scraping my hands rather badly the second time. It was necessary for me to double back on my tracks, since the ruins were to the south, and I went as cautiously as possible, concealing myself between rocks and trees. Perspiration ran down my body and immediately chilled. Julian was right, I thought hysterically; I shall have a cold—if not something worse.

From the time I left the house until I reached the ruins, I was moving like an animal, by instinct; I do not recall a single coherent thought. Fear drove me; anxiety filled my brain; I did not even pause to wonder what Julian would do when he found me missing or try to plan what steps I would take next. But at last I stood behind one of the tall willows, now desolate and bare, that overshadowed the roofless walls of the ancient church; and necessity brought back some measure of sense.

With an unpleasant, if minor, shock I realized that time had passed too quickly. It was late afternoon; the clouds were clearing and the sun was far down the west. Although the day was bright, it was bitter cold, and the sunlight did not warm me mentally or physically; it had a chill, pale-yellow light that outlined every blade of grass with merciless clarity. I would have preferred clouds and fog.

I knew that, even if I abandoned a search which might well prove fruitless, I would not reach Middleham before dark. It would take me all night to walk there—but I could not walk all night, not in that bitter cold. My stomach was empty too. I had forgotten to eat dinner, and there had been no way of packing food even if I had had the sense to think of it.

Resolutely I thrust despair away. I would go as far as I could; perhaps I might find a cottage where shelter or transportation could be procured. If not, I would simply walk until I dropped. That fate was preferable to the one that awaited me at Abbey Manor. And since an hour could make no difference now, I would spend that hour searching the ruins. They were, as I had realized, an ideal place of concealment for a captive girl.

And among the ruins the most likely place was the block of rooms which had once been the cells of the monks. I knew from my explorations that they were still solid. One of them could easily be made habitable, for a short time at least.

As I stood behind the trunk of the tree, peering out at the ominous piles of gray stone, the only sound was the beating of my own heart. No wind moved the chill air; the birds had long since gone south; crickets and insects and small animals slept snug in their burrows. I told myself that the silence was good for my purpose; I could hear any human movement, however slight. But I did not like that abnormal hush. It seemed as if something had cast a spell over nature itself.

So I hesitated, afraid to delay, yet afraid to step out onto the last stretch of open ground that separated me from—what? From the picture I had been trying all day to keep from my mind. It would no longer be denied. It leaped up, fully limned and detailed, before my inner vision—a picture of Ada struggling in Francis' arms. Wolfson always misjudged her; she was no terrified rabbit; she would have fought her seducer tooth and nail. But her girl's strength was useless against Francis' bulk. He was a man of violent temper; her resistance might anger him; he might have struck her or even—

"No," I said. I said it aloud, though there was no one to hear. He would not do that. He would not hurt her. But wasn't that precisely what he had set out to do? I put my hands to my head, as if I could reach into my skull and obliterate that vision.

And, after all, I told myself, after all my dramatics I might find nothing. Ada might not be here. I looked out again on the ruins. Nothing moved. I might have been gazing at the engraving in the guidebook.

I was about to venture forth when I heard the sound. It felled me to the ground, flat as a fallen pillar, and sent the breath rushing from my throat in a soundless gasp. It was only the distant neigh of a horse—but I thought first of Julian, then of Wolfson speeding homeward in his carriage. . . . The sound was repeated, and then those hours spent with Ada in her favorite pursuit came to my rescue. I thought I knew that particular neigh. Cautiously I raised my head.

Beyond the ruins, behind a row of trees, there was a flash of black—a black so complete that it gleamed like a raven's wing in the pale reddening sunlight. I dropped my head onto my clenched hands and breathed again. The horse was not Julian's or one of Wolfson's grays—it was Ada's beloved, vile-tempered Satan, exiled to a far pasture since David's departure.

Then I saw the smoke. It was no wonder I had not seen it before; pale gray against a graying sky, it was more a quiver in the air than a shape. But the sight of it set the blood leaping in my limbs. Someone was here. Fires are not built to warm chilly rabbits or cold stone.

The grass was brown and brittle, but high. I was already prostrate on the ground, so I stayed there, crossing the yards that separated me from the cells on hands and knees. A watcher might have seen movement, might even have seen the black of my cloak through the pale-dun stems, but somehow I felt safer close to the ground.

The empty doorway that gave entrance to the cells gaped dark and forbidding. I saw that the cobwebs which normally hung across the frame were gone. That meant someone had entered—or did it? Do spiders die in the winter? It was a ridiculously irrelevant question, but it cheered me enough so that I stepped into the darkness without hesitation.

There was a faint light inside—light that was weakened by its long journey through small barred windows, across empty rooms, through half-closed doors. I waited until my eyes adjusted to the darkness. There was no one in the corridor which stretched out to right and left. The doors of the cells looked just as they had the last time I was there. It would be necessary for me to check each door in turn.

I started out to my left and had not gone ten feet before I did encounter cobwebs—a thick mass of them, right across my face. Ordinarily I would have gasped and retreated; now

I clawed them away absently, more concerned with the message they gave me. Nothing had passed this way for a long time.

The right-hand portion of the corridor was now my goal. The first few cells were obviously empty. The doors were either missing altogether or crazily ajar, hanging by the rotted shreds of hinges.

The fifth cell was different.

I knew at once this was what I had been looking for. The door was solid and firmly in place. More—a bolt and catch, shining in the gloom with the look of new metal, closed it from the outside.

There was a small barred window high up in the door. I stood on tiptoe to peer through before touching the bolt. If Francis was within, I had to come upon him without warning. As I strained to see through the high window, my hands were already searching through my reticule for a possible weapon—a silly performance, for I had nothing which would serve that purpose. I would have to go back outside, find a rock or heavy stick. . . .

The room was as dim as the hour before dawn. One small window admitted a beam of sunlight, but it was masked by creepers and weeds and by thick bars, and the light died before it reached the corners of the small stone cell. In one of those corners was an object which drew my straining sight. A low bed. On it lay a huddled form hidden by blankets.

My hands tugged frantically at the bolt. No one else was in the room; Ada was alone, ill, unconscious, perhaps dying. I forgot that Francis might be somewhere about. The bolt slid smoothly; I flung the door open and rushed in.

The huddled form was covered, even to the face, with blankets. But on the pillow there was a gleam of golden hair. I snatched at the blankets and pulled them down—and then I dropped to my knees, staring and staring and staring. . . .

The occupant of the bed was not Ada. It was Francis.

His face was masked by dirt and dried blood; long scratches marred cheeks and forehead, as if he had been dragged, face down, through brambles. One arm was roughly splinted and bound to his body by filthy bandages. A faint growth of beard covered cheeks and jaw. His eyes were closed and his breathing shook his whole body.

I saw it all in one comprehensive glance, but my mind quite refused to take it in. I watched with vague interest the movements of my own hands as they brushed the tangled hair off his brow, settled the blankets up around his shoulders, touched his cheeks.

My body knew the thing my stubborn mind had refused to see. The wonder of that discovery drove everything else out of my head. Ada was gone as if she had never existed; even Wolfson's menace was forgotten. I never thought, until much later, of one possible explanation for Francis' situation. The scratches on his face might have been made by fingernails. If Ada had been able to lay hands on a weapon, such as a poker, she might have broken his arm, and then—it would be like Ada—bound up her enemy's wounds before fleeing out onto the moors—anywhere except back to the house.

I never thought of this. I did not think at all. I only knew he was here, hurt and ill, and that was the only thing in the world that mattered. I said his name and bent over to touch his lips with mine.

He stirred and I drew back, alarmed by the heat of his skin. His eyes opened, but they did not see me. His uninjured hand reached out, groping; I took it in mine.

"Ada," he said, so faintly that I had to bend close to hear. "Still here? Run . . . little fool. Before he comes . . ."

The effort exhausted him; his heavy lids drooped and fell. I knelt by his side, rubbing his hand mechanically, but I felt as if the winter chill had penetrated my heart. He loved Ada. How could he help it? Those few words, spoken in the truth of delirium, had cleared him even as they betrayed his feelings. His injuries had been incurred in her service. He had tried to save her—save her from his father, from—

It was beautifully timed; but then he has, as I ought to have realized, an innate sense of the dramatic. The truth came to me just as I heard the gentle, deliberate cough from the doorway behind me. I turned, knowing full well what I would see.

Alone, Wolfson could never, for all his strength, have spirited Ada away and forced her into a hidden prison. He had spoken of his son. I was the only one who had mentioned Francis by name, and it had amused Wolfson—oh, it would amuse him!—to let me think that. Perhaps he meditated some plan whereby Francis would take the blame and Julian get the credit for a noble rescue. God knows what he had in mind; only a devil could plumb the depths of that devious brain.

Of course it was Julian, all along.

He stood smiling at me, leaning in that graceful girlish way of his against the doorframe.

In the next seconds I created, and discarded, three desperate plans. He stood barring the only exit from the room. I am bigger than Ada, but no stronger; certainly I was no match for Julian. There was no use pleading with him, no threat I could conceivably make. . . .

Of course it was Julian—with his love of the little luxuries that made life worth living, his "gentlemanly" disinclination for honest labor, his fear of his dominating father, even his sympathy for those abominable hounds. Everything had pointed to him; everything I knew about Francis should have absolved him. After the incident with David, after watching the sure, gentle surgeon's hands at work, I should have known that he would never refuse to assist an injured man. Julian had not been injured; he had been pretending, just as he would have pretended, later, to come to Ada's rescue. No doubt he had some scheme in mind to persuade her that marriage with him was the only way of escaping from the gypsies' plot.

With his pleasant, meaningless smile Julian extended one hand to me. I hesitated, but not for long. A struggle would have been degrading and useless.

I put Francis' limp hand on his breast and rearranged the blankets. It was an act any humane woman might have performed, yet Julian's smile widened, and I knew with a stab of terror that I had made a dangerous mistake. How long he had been standing there I did not know, but if he realized the truth . . .

Well, if it was done, it was done, and any decent person would have said what I said next.

"Let me stay here, Julian. He needs care. The room is not even heated. He will die if you don't—"

"It is chilly, isn't it?" said Julian cheerfully. "No place for you, Cousin—with your nasty headache."

He laughed. I stopped several feet away from him, contemplating seriously one of the plans I had already discarded as impossible. It would have been a great satisfaction to claw at his face.

He saw my intention—I was making no serious effort to conceal it—and he straightened. As his right hand came into view, I saw that he was holding his riding crop.

"Why, Cousin, how badly you think of me." Julian's eyes followed mine; with an ostentatious gesture he dropped the whip and showed me his empty hands. "I won't hurt you, Harriet, even if you fly at me. I shall simply enfold you in a firm but painless embrace. Come, do fly at me. It might be fun."

"Julian. For the last time, let me do what I can for your brother. I won't fly at you or try to run away. I'll do anything you say."

"Would you?" He stared at me speculatively, his smile no longer pleasant. "We'll discuss that possibility later, Cousin. Just now, you have a long wait. You shall be comfortable whether you want to be or not."

The peremptory hand was as white and well tended as a girl's, but I knew its strength. There was nothing to be gained by further speech; I had lost enough ground as it was. In a silence I hoped was contemptuous I went toward him. At the last moment he moved aside and I swept through the doorway, my head high and my heart aching.

What a feeble figure of speech that is! It was not my heart that ached, but an area lower down—and it was not so much an ache as a churning sickness.

Sickness or ache, it is a weakening sensation. Yet I was alert for any possible chance of escape. There was none. He never touched me, but I could almost feel his breath on the back of my head, so closely did he follow me, giving directions in a casual voice: "To the right . . . now up those stairs . . ."

We were inside the buildings all the way. It was dark; he knew the path and I did not; the only doors we passed were closed, so that I could not tell which ones led outside and which led to other rooms. I have gone over it again and again in my mind, and even now I do not see how I could have eluded him. If he had stumbled, only once—but he is as sure on his feet as a cat. I had to go where he guided me—to the tower.

It does communicate with the cells. There is a door at the end of the corridor. It had been mended, the hinges oiled, the lock repaired. (How long, I wonder, has Wolfson planned this? And I smugly admiring him, like a calf frisking off to the slaughterer's block!)

The tower is old; it must have been here for centuries, long before the monks came and built their structures around it. The stairs are narrow and steep, cut into the thickness of the walls; at each floor there is a narrow landing, stone-paved, with one door giving onto it.

Julian gave me no time to study these doors or wonder what might lie behind them; he pressed me closely, knowing that I would scramble on hands and knees rather than let him touch me.

The worst thing about the trip through the dark corridor and the dim stairs was not Julian's presence. It was my growing sense that there were not two individuals there, but three. I felt another presence behind Julian; at times I could almost hear another set of feet padding noiselessly along in his wake. When I rose to my feet on the final landing, I found that my imagination had not deceived me. Julian was at my elbow, and when I turned, I saw a head come into view around the angle of the stairs. It was a shaggy gray head, with feral green eyes and a long muzzle. I turned blindly to the door which represented the only means of escape, and with a mocking parody of courtesy Julian flung it open and stood aside for me to enter.

I saw nothing of the room at first; it was only a space into which the dog, thank heaven, did not enter. The beast stood peering in through the doorway with a terrifying suggestion of intelligence more than animal. Julian dropped to one knee and the dog turned toward him; their heads were almost on a level, and Julian spoke, the dog's ears pricking as it listened.

Julian rose to his feet.

"You will find this place comfortable, I believe," he said, and I realized that the temperature of the room was warm. There was a bright fire on the hearth and a few rough sticks of furniture—even a bottle of wine and a covered dish on the table.

"I am afraid you will have to wait for some hours," Julian went on. "There is food here, and wine—eat and keep up your strength. I don't want to take advantage of you."

"You won't," I said.

"Oh—that." Julian grinned; his resemblance to his father had never been stronger. "Harriet, I beg of you, don't judge me before you know all the facts. Oh, I am aware of what you are thinking and, on my word of honor, you are wrong about several important matters. Try to keep an open mind. No harm will come to you; your safety and happiness are the most important things in the world to me. Rest . . . have a glass of wine. . . . Before morning you will know the truth and then, I am sure, you will feel differently."

He had all his father's charm—the dangerous Wolfson charm, which could witch the fruit off the trees. Almost I believed him. Then I remembered Francis in the frigid little cell below. No facts, no truth could excuse neglect that might end in murder.

I had wit enough, though, to say nothing. Julian seemed satisfied. He started to close the door and then, as if struck by a sudden thought, opened it again.

"Since you are not a prisoner, the door will not be bolted." He waited for my reaction. But I knew him now; I betrayed no sign of hope for him to crush. "I'll leave Loki, of course," he went on. "Just outside the door. For your protection."

This time the door closed and remained closed. Just in time, too; I could not have kept my foot a moment longer. I sat down, just where I was, and shook—and cursed Julian. If he had locked the door, I might have found some way out. The dog is a more effective barrier than bolts and chains.

All this was hours ago—it feels like weeks. It is almost dusk. I have been over this room, stone by stone. It is roughly circular, with one window. The window is not barred, only blocked by wooden planks to keep out the cold. I think

I might get through that window. There is only one difficulty. The window is forty feet above the ground.

The stones of the walls and the wood of the floor are set
like iron. Those happy devices of Gothic fiction, the secret
panel and the sliding door, are missing here—or if they exist, I cannot find them. There is no way out of this room except through the door. And the dog is outside the door.

For a while I tried to comfort myself by believing Julian.
Perhaps I had leaped to conclusions; perhaps he was carrying on a plot of his own, in which his father had no part.
Perhaps he was foiling his father instead of helping him. But
I could not make myself believe it, much as I wanted to.
There may be facts I do not know, but they can only be facts
that create a greater threat. The waiting is the worst. If they
would only come! There is no way out of here for me; I can
only resign myself to what they demand. The time drags so.
I tied my hair up and brushed the dirt from my skirts and
washed my hands—yes, there is even a basin of water here.
Such concern for my comfort! It frightens me more than
threats could do.

I am weak with fatigue and hunger as well as fear. I ought
to sleep—but who could sleep? My body rebels against food.
The slab of mutton and chunk of bread provided would
hardly tempt a delicate appetite. I did pour out a glass of
wine—and then I was afraid to drink it. Suppose the food
and drink are drugged? I don't know what this would ac-
complish for them, but I can no longer fathom the twisted
depths of this plot; I can only expect the worst and act on
that assumption.

Is Ada here, in this same grim tower? There was no sound
from any of the doors below, but Julian gave me no time to
listen. I tried pounding on the floor here with the heel of my
shoe; it made a hollow echo, ghastly to hear, but no sound
came back to me. It proves nothing; the floors are thick.

The fire is dying. Shadows fill the room, shifting like dark fog. I crouch by the hearth, writing by the last glow of the red coals. The supply of fuel is almost gone. I shall not leave this room to replenish it. The door is neither locked nor barred, but the creature is still there, guarding the only way out. Sometimes it is quiet, and I delude myself into hope: Perhaps it has gone away. But I know it will never go away, not until he comes to relieve it of its charge. Whenever I approach the door, the sounds begin again—the dull, even thud of padded pacing—back and forth, back and forth. It was daylight when he left; it is dark night now. Soon he will return. And when he comes . . .

I am sick with chagrin at my own naïveté. How could I have been so blind—I, who prided myself on my superior knowledge of the world! Not a moment's doubt, not a quiver of that famed "woman's intuition" . . . Surely I must have seen some sign of the approaching terror, even if I did not recognize it for what it was. Surely, somewhere in the pages of this diary I must have recorded an event whose significance I failed to see. . . .

Later

The clues were there—when I looked for them. Easy to see now, but at the time—well, there is nothing more futile than regretting the past, unless it is railing at one's own stupidity.

What I was really searching for, I expect, was not a clue to what has happened so much as a guide as to what to do next—a magic spell or at least a casual reference to, let us say, an ancient tunnel from the tower to the moor which, by a strange coincidence, would start in this very room! A remark which I had forgotten but which now would lead to my salvation. . . . Unfortunately, life does not work that way. I am not so stupefied by fear that I wouldn't have remembered any hint of that sort immediately.

I found something totally unexpected in my investigations, but instead of being a key to freedom, it is a bigger, heavier bolt on the prison door. I have been sitting on the floor by the fire to read, partly for warmth, partly for light. As I shifted position—these stones are hard!—something crackled in my skirt pocket. I praise my self-possession, but not until I actually reached into the pocket and pulled it out did I remember the letter I found in Wolfson's drawer—the letter addressed, against all reason, to me. Well, but a few other things have happened since then. . . .

I had an impression, at the time, that the handwriting was familiar. As I studied the superscription in the dim light of the dying fire, I knew whose hand it was, and a prickle of pure superstitious terror ran down my back. I was almost afraid to read the letter. It said—

But perhaps I had better copy it entire. If he finds it missing from the drawer, he will search for it, and, without doubt, he will find it. For several reasons I would like to retain a copy.

My dear Harriet,

If my instructions are followed—which they will be—you will receive this six months after my death. That will allow time for the first part of my scheme to mature.

Take in your hands the ebony workbox I left you in my will. You will not have used it more than you can help, but now remove the topmost drawer in which the thread is kept. Underneath there is a partition of thin wood which separates the top from the bottom drawer. This partition is not fixed, as it appears to be. It opens by means of a button disguised as a nailhead, at the center back of the box. When you press down on the nailhead, you will hear a slight clicking sound. Then take hold of the strip of raised wood which runs down the partition from front to back, and lift. The partition will rise by approximately half an inch. Pull it out toward you.

In the narrow space beneath you will find my second will. It is quite in order and is dated two weeks after the first will. This, my sole valid testament, makes you the heiress to my fortune.

You may wonder, first, why I leave my money to you, and second, why I do so in such an unusual manner. I am not in the habit of explaining my actions, so I will say only that this seemed to me the best way of accomplishing my plans for my two granddaughters. Basically these plans mean they should marry, and marry well.

What do I mean by "well"? I mean that their husbands should be men of substance and position. The first requisite for a gentleman's bride is that she have money. Only in novels do handsome genteel noblemen wed young governesses or housemaids. For all her beauty Ada would find herself the wife of a struggling gentleman usher or curate if she were known to be penniless. I will not have this for my granddaughter, the descendant of a Queen of England. It will not take the men long to find Ada, and by now she should be settled, in theory if not in fact; decorum, of course, will postpone the actual marriage until after the time of mourning for me is past.

I would have waited for a year or even two, until Ada was actually married, but several considerations made me decide that you had better know the truth before that time. Ada may marry some profligate rake who will squander the money he believes to be his. Or you, with your passionate nature—which I have tried, unsuccessfully, to teach you to control—may contract yourself to some penniless fool, not knowing that you can do better. Or some other emergency may arise—I do not pretend to be omniscient.

You are not to make this will public until after Ada is married. *This is an order. The money which I have left, while quite substantial in itself, is not enough, if divided between you, to attract a husband of high social standing. Therefore you shall have the use of it in turn. I can trust you to make proper provision for Ada and to soothe her husband by a settlement which, if not what he expected, will reconcile him to the inevitable. The rest is yours, and I know you will take care of it, if not quite in the way I have done, at least in a manner which will not disgrace the family. I have observed you closely for many years. I know you well, your failings as well as your potentialities. Despite the heritage from your wretched mother, which I deplore—but which, I flatter myself, I have suppressed as much as was possible—you have a great deal of myself in you.*

I think you will not disregard my wishes even if, which is unlikely, they conflict with your own. If you should do so, rest assured that I will know. I have always been a good church member, but I do not imagine that my character will change so much between this life and the next that I will forgive a deliberate violation of my orders. I remain,

Your affectionate grandmother,
FRANCES BARTON

So she did not hate me after all.

I can be glad of that now. I can almost smile at the grim humor of that last paragraph. We went once to a séance at the home of one of Grandmother's friends. The ectoplasmic manifestations were obviously fabricated, yet I think I would be afraid to attend another such demonstration if I had deliberately foiled Grandmother's plans. One never knows. . . . If anyone could break through that "veil" they talk of, it would be she—and she would leave the veil in tatters, too.

If the inhabitants of Heaven do concern themselves, in their saintly bliss, with the troubles of those they left behind, Grandmother must be in quite a state just now. She meant well by us. Arbitrary and autocratic as her plan was, marred by what I can only regard as pride amounting to madness, it was at least designed for our good. I wonder what she would say if she knew that her well-intentioned scheme has destroyed me.

For this is the ultimate trap. Wolfson has read the letter; I found it already opened. This explains his hasty journey, to summon his confederate and explain the new development. It explains why I am now here, the object of such sinister concern. He knows that I, not Ada, am his designated prey.

I am trying very hard to be calm, but if my fingers were not clamped around this pen, I would be using them to tear at my face. It is almost diabolical, the way the whole affair has developed—almost as if some jeering Fate were taking every potential weapon and turning it against me. Even the timing of it . . .

At any other time I would have willingly changed places with Ada. I can imagine her agony of mind, loving another man, fearing convention and talk—and lacking what John Wolfson calls my "passionate nature." I could have confronted Wolfson and spat vulgarly in his face, as my mother would have done, and dared him to do his worst. He could not force me as he can force Ada. But he can force me through her.

If I refuse the marriage which will give Wolfson Grandmother's fortune ("A married woman has no property," says the law of benevolent England), he will simply destroy the second will and marry Ada to Julian. That plan will remain unaltered. The only difference is that, before, I could not save her. Now I can—by a simple Yes. It is her happiness against mine, one unspeakable marriage against another. Having the choice, I cannot condemn her to Julian's tender mercies.

Then there is Francis. Wolf does not know, yet, that his rebellious son is another weapon against me, in his hands. But he will find out. Those damnable ice-blue eyes can read my thoughts. And I think Julian knows. They will not hesitate to use Francis as they will use Ada.

I could do it. I would do it—if the money were his only goal. I am not afraid of Julian; his sort of viciousness only infuriates me, and he is not really moved by my questionable charms. If he ever tried to touch me, I would scratch his pretty pampered face to shreds. But it won't be Julian.

"It's a pity you aren't the heiress." I can hear Wolf saying it; I can see his face as he looked today, holding me. . . . The letter must have seemed to him like an answer to prayer. I wonder to whom—or what—he prays. It was bad enough then, but now . . .

I cannot, I cannot do it. Not with Francis . . . Oh, God—the door—

I can hardly read those last frantic, scribbled words. But I will leave them as they stand.

It has been half an hour since I scrawled that desperate passage. I was on the edge of a hysterical attack; the alternatives that confronted me were equally impossible. It was like being given a choice between hanging or drowning. I thought, in my frenzy, that I heard his footsteps outside. I heard the dog bound forward, growling. I staggered to my feet, stiff with crouching, and dropped the pen on the page—it has left a great black blot—and ran across the room. Consciously I have no memory of my intent, but I found myself before the window, tearing at the wooden panels with hands that felt neither cut nor bruise. If it had been open . . .

I will never know what I would have done. For as the first plank gave way before my furious attack, a strange thing happened.

Everything in the room vanished. I saw only blackness and felt nothing, not even my own body. I was outside my body, floating naked and alone in a starless void. A fainting spell? Perhaps; but all at once, like a scene that springs on the vision when a shutter is flung open, I saw my grandmother. She was sitting in her chair, as I had so often seen her—a dumpy little woman in a frilled white cap, her black eyes snapping under furled, scanty brows, a smile of contempt on her withered lips. Her lips moved. I knew she was speaking to me, but I heard not a sound.

Then, as suddenly as it had come, the vision was gone. The cold tower room again enclosed me. I was standing at the window, hands clenched upon the stone sill, and the pain in my bruised fingers made me cry aloud.

Was it the pain that brought me back from a simple fainting spell? I don't know. I only know that something had changed within me. I was still afraid—I am afraid now—but my fear is not the mindless panic that sent me running, like a trapped animal, to destroy myself. My mind is working clearly, my hands are steady. Whether that vision was sent to me from another place, or whether it came from the far recesses of my overstrained mind, it has served its purpose. I know her, as she knew me. She would not huddle, half fainting, while some villain overpowered her. She would not seek the sin of self-destruction as a means of escape— leaving others to face the consequences. She would have fought to the last breath in her body and the last cunning thought in her brain.

I am going to leave this room.

How? I don't know yet, but I must get out. The boards in the window were loose; they are now looser. My hands feel as if they had been flayed, but I can, if necessary, get through that window. It is forty feet above the ground. I cannot climb down, the stones are too even. However, I may have to try. A fall won't kill me; there are bushes—probably prickly ones—below. But it is a forlorn hope. I would probably break a limb and be unable to move. I shall try the window only if all else fails.

I have tested, again, all the stones of the wall and every plank of the floor. The only exit from this room is the door. Outside the door is the dog.

I am deathly afraid of that dog. He will not kill me; I am too valuable to be damaged. But he is big enough to hold me fast if I try to pass. I am not afraid of what the dog will do to me—I am just afraid of him.

Yet I must get him away from that door. Can I trick him? I think not. If I dropped something from the window it might lure him outside to investigate, but he would be after me before I had gotten ten feet from the tower. So I must kill him.

Brave words. But how? I have been through the contents of this room and through my scanty possessions, looking for a weapon. It was folly, of course. Only with a pistol could I damage him without endangering myself, and there is no pistol here. There is not even a knife. I looked, knowing full well that the beast could disarm me in an instant. I have not even a pair of scissors in my reticule. The contents of the bag lie scattered on the floor beside me—handkerchief, smelling salts, coins, drops—

I should have thought of it earlier. There is so little time. . . . When will Wolf return? I have no idea how powerful the laudanum is or how much is required for an animal so big. I simply poured the whole bottle over the chunk of mutton which Julian left for my dinner. The hard part was opening the door. Despite my reasoning, I felt sure the beast would leap at my throat.

He is fearfully alert—almost human. I can understand the tales the villagers tell about Wolf and those beasts—and understand as well why I keep referring to them as "he" rather then "it." He was on his feet the moment I touched the door handle, and I opened the door to find his eyes glaring straight up into mine. His teeth were bared; those fangs looked a foot long. Still he did not utter a sound. I could almost fancy that the servants' tales were true and that I was confronting Wolf himself, in his animal shape.

I stood frozen for several seconds, meeting that feral stare. Then I pushed the meat through the crack and slammed the door. I was too cowardly to wait to see if he would eat it. That was fifteen minutes ago. Has he eaten? And if he has, will the drug have its effect? How long does it take to work? I will wait fifteen more minutes. I dare not wait longer. Wolf may come at any moment. I cannot think what has kept him so long. . . .

Perhaps the drug will not affect the dog. Perhaps, instead of putting him to sleep, it will drive him mad. . . .

Ten minutes longer. I will hide this diary before I go. Some day it may be found. If the worst happens, at least someone in the world will know what became of us. I feel an urgent need for some contact, however frail, with that outer world. This is such a lonely place. There is no light, no human sound, anywhere about.

Five minutes. How quickly the time goes. First I will look for Ada, try to set her free. Then Francis . . . If he can move at all, I must get him hidden—some more sheltered place . . . Then I will start running. I should follow the road; it would be easy to lose myself on the moors in the darkness. The other dog must be with Wolf. Darkness will be no hindrance to its keen senses. If I cannot reach help before they arrive at the ruins, the dog can run me down. That dog or the other—if he wakes too soon—if he sleeps at all—

It is time now. I hear nothing outside the door. But there have been periods before when the beast was silent. . . .

Two minutes past the appointed hour. I am going now. God help me, and all other poor souls who must battle tonight against the powers of darkness.

Chapter
4

April 17, 1860

TODAY, AS I SAT IN THE MORNING ROOM PRETENDING TO SEW, one of the workmen came to the door. I heard him from where I was, asking for "the mistress," and I heard William's cold correction: "Mrs. Wolfson." William, at least, has not changed. He was reluctant to let the man in, so finally the poor fellow had to hand over his find. William brought it in to me, holding it fastidiously between two fingers. It was dirty and grimy, defaced by mold and cobwebs; but I recognized my old diary.

I have scarcely thought of it since that night—can it be only six months ago? But then I have been—shall we say unwilling?—to remember anything about that night. No, let us be honest. The sight of any object that might recall that time has sent me into a ghastly state of panic—I, who prided myself on my control. They have all been absurdly considerate of my feelings. Sometimes it makes me angry when I see them whispering and looking anxious. But not very angry; I no longer have such strong feelings about anything.

William, being totally without imagination, did not connect

the grimy little volume with my "nerves." He handed it over to me, bland as an icicle, and I took it—with, I hope, equal coolness. It was not until after he left the room that I began to tremble.

My husband would never have let me touch the diary, let alone read it. But then he never knew of its existence, or of its part in the insane events of six months ago, so he would have no reason to watch out for it—as he has watched out, successfully, for so many other "dangerous" objects. (I have seen him; he did not think I saw, but I did.)

So I sat in my comfortable chair, with my sewing—on which I do so little, day after day—fallen from my lap, holding a fat, dirty red book in shaking fingers. It had been hidden, all that time, on a ledge above the window of the tower room. Today the workmen must have been cleaning that room and so come upon it. My name—my former name—is on the cover, in gold.

The book smelled faintly of dust. It seems to have been rained upon, for there are spots of mold on the leather cover. The smell was more than a smell—it, and the very touch of the book, brought back that night so vividly that I could close my eyes and feel myself back in that dreadful room, with darkness thick outside and the fire dying. . . . Knowing that in less than sixty seconds I must open the door and discover whether I faced escape—probably only temporary—or a more immediate horror in the presence of the dog. I was there. I could feel it again, the silence, the cold, the terror. My mind seemed to hang, swaying, on the brink of a dark abyss.

And stepped back.

That is the only way I can describe it. It was as if I had faced the worst and found it endurable. I heard my own voice say aloud, "It is all over," and I knew I spoke the truth.

After a few minutes I rang for William and asked him to fetch a certain box from my room. The key to the diary was in it. I remembered, now, that I had flung the key into that box, where I kept old trinkets that were too broken to use and too cherished to throw away. For months I have forgotten the very existence of that key.

So I opened the diary and read it through, from start to finish. It has been a year since I wrote the first entry. Poor Grandmother and her sense of propriety. I did not even keep to a decent year of mourning for her. But there were other considerations which seemed more important than propriety.

I read it through to the last hysterical pages. I was certainly in a wild state then. "Poor thing," I thought, and smiled to remember that the poor thing was myself. I wonder what I would have written and thought if I had known that, up till then, I had only the faintest taste of the real terror of that night.

It came to me then that I must finish the story. I could face my memories now, but I would never be completely purged of them until I had written them down—exorcised them—cleared my mind of the clouds of darkness that still fog certain regions. For the next few days literature, not fancy work, will be the morning occupation of the mistress of Abbey Manor. I can keep the diary hidden that long, I think.

I close my eyes again, letting my fingers rest on the hard leather surface of the diary, and again the scene returns with sound and touch and feeling complete. The tower room was almost dark, the fire a bed of cooling coals. I could hardly see the last words I wrote. I remember that I wanted to go on writing—to take any cowardly pretext for postponing the opening of the door. But the final sentence was—final. There was nothing more to be said after that. I closed the book and locked it, putting the key into the pocket of my skirt. I looked about the room for a safe hiding place.

As I fumbled at the objects on the table, I found something I had scarcely noticed, having no especial need of it—a candle, in a rough iron holder. There was barely enough heat in the graying coals to catch the wick, but then I had light, and the weak glow was heartening. Equally cheering was the conclusion I drew from the presence of the candle— they had not expected to return until after dark.

Yes, but it was dark now and had been for several hours. I cast a startled look at the half-open window, and then I noticed the ledge above, higher than the head of even a tall man. I dragged the chair over to the window and climbed up. The ledge was just wide enough to hold the diary. I left it there; I could think of nothing better.

Then the door. I will not try to summon up my feelings when I put my hand on the door handle. Once was enough to experience that.

At first I saw nothing outside the door but blackness. Then I realized that I was holding the candle too high; its light dazzled my eyes and failed to illumine the floor. When I lowered it, I saw the dog. It was lying flat on the floor, but it did not look drugged. The massive head had drooped forward onto its outstretched paws, as if it were dozing. I could not see its eyes.

I knew, of course, that if the beast had been unaffected by the laudanum it would have been on its feet before this. But reason is a poor defense against fear. I had to step over the prostrate body in order to reach the stairs, and that one step took every ounce of courage I could summon up. I gathered my skirt up with one hand, lifting it high as if I were crossing a bog, and it was not until a trailing bit of petticoat brushed the dog's ears that I really believed the truth. I had won the first move. One part of my wild scheme had succeeded.

Still I was afraid to take my eyes off the monster, and I nearly fell backward down the stairs in my mindless retreat. It was no small task to descend that narrow, headlong flight with one hand holding the candle and the other trying to keep my skirts from tripping me.

The landing below, with its door, was my first objective. One glance told me that the room must be empty, for there was neither bolt nor lock fixed to the ancient slab of wood, only a rough iron handle like the one on the door of the chamber above. Yet I could not go on without making sure. I gave the door a push, and it swung inward with a screech of rusted metal that sounded like a shout of blasphemy in a temple. Silence and decay were the gods of that ancient place, and noise was a profanation.

The feeble candle flame reached only a few feet into the vast darkness of the room, but I saw enough to know that I had been correct—no one had been in this room for decades, perhaps centuries. It was a copy of the room above, except that this one was bare of furnishings. Dust lay thick upon the worn planks of the floor, and cobwebs festooned the ceiling like low-hanging clouds. I backed out, pulling the door to behind me in an instinctive rejection of the dark desolation of the room. Turning my back on the dog was bad enough; I knew I could not leave a gaping black hole behind me as well. Anything might come out of that room.

The next part of the descent was even harder because of the wind that whistled up the narrow stairwell. I needed both hands to shield the candle, and twice I came near to stumbling over my skirts. The next floor was the vital one; it was the last of the habitable rooms of the tower, the lowest floor being merely an empty space with doorways leading to the moor and the cells. If Ada were not in this room, I would have to search for her among the cells where Francis was confined. At that moment it seemed impossible that anything as healthy and alive as Ada could be present among those deadly silent stones.

She was there. I knew she must be as soon as I saw the door, for it was fastened—not with an ordinary bolt, but with a chain twisted around the doorhandle and a new heavy iron hook which had been driven into the wood of the doorframe. The splintered wood was so newly wounded that it shone white in the candle flame.

I tried to call her name, but the silence froze my tongue; I could not produce anything louder than a whisper. It was the work of a moment to unfasten the chain but it took me two moments because I did not want to put the candle down. There was rattling and banging enough as I worked, yet no sound from within. That frightened me; I knew Ada must be there, but in what state? Surely not asleep. She must be unconscious, or worse.

Forgetting caution in this new worry, I smacked the door smartly with my fist, and it swung slowly inward. Then, at last, another human voice broke the silence—a wordless, muffled cry of alarm. I raised the candle high and saw her—alive, aware, seemingly unhurt—crouched against the far wall, with both hands extended as if to ward off whoever was coming. She saw me at the same moment and knew me—with the eyes of love, presumably, since I looked like nothing so much as a wild-haired witch, and I must have been the last person on earth she expected to see. Another cry, equally inarticulate but far different in emotion, and she rushed at me. Luckily the commotion extinguished the poor little candle, for I let it fall, unheeded, as I clasped Ada's shaking form in my arms. Whatever had happened to her, she was alive and sane. That was more than I had dared hope for.

After I had controlled my own emotion, I held her away from me and gave her a gentle shake.

"My darling, there is no time for tears. We must get away from here if we can. Tell me first—quickly—are you unhurt?"

"Yes . . ."

"Julian didn't—"

Ada laughed. Her voice was still weak, but the laugh was

genuine, and a more incongruous sound never stirred that silence.

"Julian!" she said contemptuously. "Imagine, Harriet, he tried to make love to me—to kiss me! He is strong but not strong enough for that. I kicked him and I bit."

"He left you alone then?" I asked unbelievingly.

"He said—he said a night alone here might change my mind." She shuddered. "It nearly did, Harriet; I was so afraid. And he said he would send his father. When you came, I thought—"

"I know. Thank God you are unharmed. Don't be afraid, Ada."

"But you, Harriet—how did you find me?"

"No time for that story. I did find you, and now we must run. Ada, do you think you could possibly get a horse out of the stables without being seen?"

"I don't know. Why?"

"Listen," I said and shook her more vigorously. "One of us must go to Middleham and get help. If the villagers won't help, ride on to Ripon; you can hire a coach there. Here is money, put it in your pocket. To reach Middleham you must have a horse. The courtyard gates are bolted at night, but the wall is not high; you are agile, you must climb it. The only person in the stable is that poor old dotard Adam who admires you so. You can keep him quiet; bribe him if you must. Get a horse. I don't care how you do it, you must do it," I concluded wildly. "Go to Middleham, David may be there. And watch out for Julian and Wolfson—both of them are abroad tonight, God knows where. I don't fear for you once you are mounted; you can outride either of them. Do you understand?"

"Hush, Harriet, don't cry. I don't understand, but I will do what you say. But you must come with me."

"If we separate, we double our chances," I told her, trying

to calm myself. "And I can't go yet. I must try to get Francis away."

"Francis! Where is he?"

"In one of the cells here. I'm afraid he is badly hurt. If those devils find us flown and he is still here, they may—they may—"

"Francis," she repeated. "He followed, Harriet, when Julian carried me from the house. They gave me something in my soup that night. It tasted odd, so I didn't drink it all, but I was half asleep. . . . Julian dropped me when Francis struck him. I couldn't move—I could only lie there watching. Julian was no match for him; he would have won if it had not been for the dogs. I saw him fall—"

"Later," I said. "If there is a later . . . If I can move Francis, I will follow you. Perhaps you can get two horses out, but don't come back here—turn the second one loose, and I'll try to catch it. If I cannot, I will go toward Middleham on foot, hide in the trees. . . . Ada, Ada, we must go!"

We had been incredibly fortunate thus far, but I knew the desperate need for haste. I was frantic to get Ada on her way, to return to Francis. But I stopped long enough to do one thing—to replace the chain on the door. Even if I were recaptured—and I had no great hope that I would dare to leave Francis—Ada might succeed if her escape were not discovered immediately.

The wind had risen; it cut like a knife when we stepped out of the tower door. Ada still had Grandmother's sable cloak; she clutched it around her, shivering, and then suddenly whipped it off.

"Here, take it."

"No—"

"I can run faster without it, and I can't ride with it. It may keep you from freezing tonight—you or Francis."

I had just taken the cloak in my arms when from far-off,

blended with the wail of the night wind, came the distant baying of a hound.

We turned as one. In the dim starlight I saw Ada's head lift, her nostrils quivering. She was scenting the air like one of her beloved horses. Her face was so pale that it shone like a small moon against the darkness, but when she spoke, her voice was steady.

"The hound is loose and on the scent, Harriet."

"Run!" I shrieked. "Run!"

She took me at my word. I have never seen anyone run as Ada ran that night; she bounded over rocks and hummocks like a deer or a young mare. I stumbled along behind her, hampered by the cloak, to which I idiotically clung; in my mind was some vague notion of throwing myself to the dog, like a tasty bone, to distract him from Ada. But I knew it was useless. The Manor was two miles away; she could never reach it even if the dog took time out to gobble me up. The long-drawn howl came again, louder—much louder.

Midway through, the howl was drowned by another, nearer sound—the wild neigh of an excited horse.

Ada stopped and whirled to face me, her skirts billowing out. We spoke at the same moment.

"Is it . . . ?"

"It is Satan, in the far pasture. Can you . . . ?"

Without wasting time or breath on an answer, she turned and was off again. How she knew where to go, in the darkness and in her panic, I can't imagine; instinct must have led her. I always said, jokingly, that she was half equine, and after that night I can believe it. She tore her way through weeds and brambles, reached the fence and was over it, tumbling to the ground on the other side in a heap of white petticoats. I was close on her heels, whipped on by the mounting crescendo of the diabolical howling that rose now without stopping for breath.

The wind was a shrieking torrent above, beating at the bare branches of the trees and tearing the fleeing clouds to shreds. It freed the hidden moon from its covering, and in the new brilliance I saw a sight that made me catch my breath.

From far across the field the stallion was racing toward us. Its galloping hooves thudded on the half-frozen ground like drumbeats, and its mane streamed out in the wind. Ada stood like a statue where she had risen, one hand outstretched; her loosened hair hid her face, but the lines of her young body and arms were taut with eagerness. She was reaching out to the wild thing as if to a lover, and I knew that if Ada could reach the horse's back she was safe. If only the dog—

Then I realized that the baying had stopped. When I looked back, I saw why.

The hound had reached the tower. For a time its form was hidden by the masonry, but I knew better than to hope that it would stop there. When it reappeared it came straight toward us, silent now, moving in great bounds. In a matter of seconds it would be upon us.

The stallion had come to a sliding, crashing halt just under Ada's nose, as if it meant to tease her. Now it was nuzzling into her hands and skirts, seeking the tidbits of sugar she always had for it. The animal knew her, but it was puzzled and excited, aroused by the aura of human fear. It pranced around Ada with dainty little steps, avoiding almost playfully the hands with which she strove to catch its mane. She looked so small beside the animal's muscled height. It struck me with a shock of horror that even if she caught hold of it, she could not possibly mount unless she could persuade it to stand by the fence. And by that time . . .

At that moment the horse scented the dog.

Its handsome head came up, nostrils flaring redly. I forgot that I might startle it into the flight it so obviously contemplated; I ran toward Ada, screaming her name. I doubt that she even heard me. Rising on tiptoe she threw both arms about the horse's arched neck, her body brushed by the dancing hooves—and the animal responded. It stood stock-still, looking down into her upturned face; black mane and golden hair mingled in the stream of the wind.

What followed was absurd and anticlimactic—but as effective as a well-rehearsed acrobatic turn. Somehow I was on hands and knees beside the horse, feeling Ada's little slippers pressing painfully into my shoulder blades; at the same time I threw myself up, lifting her. As I staggered to my feet, swaying like a drunken scrubwoman, I saw her mounted—astride, with a gleam of grubby white stocking showing between the folds of her wide skirts. Both hands were twisted in the horse's mane and her mouth was wide open in—it sounds incredible, but it is true—a shout of laughter.

There are those who, when the danger becomes acute, rise completely out of themselves into a state beyond fear. She must be one of them; she looked like a young maenad or Valkyrie. I am not like that, I can only think of the next danger to be surmounted. I remembered that she had never ridden Satan, that she had neither bridle nor saddle, that he was believed to be unmanageable, a killer; I recalled that a hunting hound may drag down a horse. And with that last thought I saw the hound—a dark bulk clearing the pasture fence not ten feet away.

I brought my hand down, with all my strength, on Satan's flank and, without waiting to see the result, ran toward the dog. It did not leap at me. I leaped at it, arms outstretched, waving the sable cloak like a banner. At any other time I would have laughed to see how the monster checked and stumbled, astounded by my move. A cat would feel the same way if its mouse suddenly advanced on it with teeth bared.

We went down together, rolling on the ground, with my

arms clamped around the hairy neck. Only for a moment. One twist of the heavy body pinned me flat and the great jaws snapped shut—on the folds of Grandmother's cloak. As I lay on my back with the beast's hot breath in my face, I saw, with the abnormal clarity that sometimes precedes collapse, a picture I will never forget.

A length of flowing black satin soaring on the wings of the wind, the great stallion cleared the fence. Ada's black skirts blended with his blackness; she might have been part of his bone and muscle as she lay along his back, with only her white face and hands and streaming hair visible against the night. For a beautiful breathless moment the pair hung in midair, as if about to soar into the sky. Then they were gone. The hound's wet muzzle touched my cheek, and for the first and last time in that unendurable night Providence was kind enough to allow me to lose consciousness completely.

The first thing I saw when I awoke was Wolf's face.

He had arranged it deliberately, I am sure. As soon as he saw my eyes open, a smile widened the arrogant mouth that was only inches from mine. I stared dully into his eyes. He thought me paralyzed by fear; I was, instead, without feeling of any kind. It was a comparatively pleasant sensation. The worst has happened, I thought. I was wrong.

I waited for one of his mocking remarks.

"Damn you, Harriet," he said roughly, "you frightened me almost to death. Fenris is well trained, but she is a trained killer. . . . When I found you lying there under those devilish fangs, I thought—"

Astounded, I realized that he was genuinely moved. There were tears in the strange pale eyes and his face was not its normal ruddy hue.

"You canting hypocrite," I said hoarsely. "You trained

that dog to kill and set it and its mate on my scent. How dare you speak to me as if—as if you—"

In my rage I rose to a sitting position. It was an error; the air swam with little stars, and I felt myself falling back. His arm steadied me; his other hand held a glass to my lips. I smelled the scent of wine and turned my head sharply aside.

"That is why I love you," said my tormentor pleasantly—adding, with a laugh, "one of the reasons, in any case. Barely conscious after a shocking fright, and yet you have wit enough to suspect that the wine might be drugged. Here—you need the stuff, you little fool. Will this reassure you?"

He lifted the glass to his lips and drained half the contents. When he offered the remainder to me, I took it. I did need its strength. But I turned the glass and drank out of the side opposite the one his lips had touched.

"That's better. Now lie back. For God's sake," he added irritably, as he felt me stiffen, "I've no intention of making love to you—yet. I simply want you to collect your wits."

I let my head fall onto the pillow. Now I could see where I was—the tower chamber where I had spent so many nerve-racking hours. A new fire blazed high in the hearth, casting a fitful light over the man who sat beside the bed on a wooden chair. I looked about for the wheelchair and then realized my error; it could never have ascended those narrow stairs. Wolf must have climbed them on his own two legs—such as they were. A shudder ran through me and Wolf, who saw everything, saw that. His face darkened.

"You've led me a merry chase, Harriet—in more ways than one. By rights I ought to beat you soundly."

"There is no one to stop you."

The hands which rested on his knees clenched into fists. Oddly enough I had no fear of his striking me; I would rather he had.

"I don't intend to hurt you," he said with difficulty. "I hope and believe we can reach an agreement like two reasonable adults. Are you able to listen to me now?"

The shift of firelight and shadow on his strongly marked features was unnerving. At one moment the carved nose stood out like a fragment of antique statue; at the next, pits of darkness hid cheeks and eyes.

I said slowly, "I am able."

"Good." He drew a long breath and leaned back. "You have seen your grandmother's letter. That is well; it saves long explanations."

"Yes."

"I have the will. You erred there, Harriet. Why didn't you take it with you?"

"I didn't read the letter until I got here."

"I see. Well, it would have made no difference. You understand the alternatives?"

"I—think so."

"Let me make them explicit. I have no interest in that little doll of an Ada. She may marry her stable scum if she wishes."

I remembered my last wild vision of Ada and Satan soaring over the fence. Doll indeed, I thought, and almost laughed aloud. Wolf, watching me intently, leaned forward, and I hastily composed my features. I knew what was wrong with me. The wine had affected my fatigued body and empty stomach. I was as intoxicated as any roaring stablehand on holiday. I could understand now why men drank too much. I felt lighthearted, free of care, conscious of my own superior intelligence.

"Where is Ada?" I asked craftily.

"Here, in the tower." Wolf's eyes never left my face. "It makes no difference whether you know or not. You will not see her until this is settled."

I fought to keep the triumph I felt from blazing forth in

my face. He did not know of Ada's escape. Our trick with the chain had worked. If I could delay him for a few hours—till morning—I might yet be safe.

"You will release Ada?" I asked timidly. "She isn't harmed?"

"Her modesty and her maidenhead are untouched," said Wolf coldly. "My ineffectual son let himself be driven howling from her presence. But be warned, Harriet—Julian's girlish vanity is wounded. If he goes to Ada tonight, he will not be so gentle. It rests with you whether he goes or not."

"With me?"

"Don't play the fool. I want you, Harriet, you know that. I meant to have you in any case. Why, this is like a gift from the gods, can't you see that? You might have resented being my mistress; you can't object to being mistress of Abbey Manor, with a husband who admires you excessively and Ada free to pursue her own low tastes."

He leaned close, so close that I could see the fine lines under his eyes. My wine-produced calm vanished in a flutter of panic. Wine or no wine, craft or not, the man's physical nearness destroyed my will. As an enemy he was endurable; as a husband—

"No," I gasped, forgetting all my resolutions. "No, don't—"

"I could force you."

"You could not!"

"I could. You little fool, what do you know about men? Did you think, this afternoon, that I was using all my strength to hold you? I could break your bones between my thumb and forefinger. There are times when I want to, your hatred and obstinacy madden me so. If it were not that—"

He broke off, breathing heavily. I was, I confess, frozen with terror. I lay staring up at him, unable even to blink. When he spoke again, I hardly recognized his voice.

"If it were not for the fact that I love you," he said.

The words reached my ears, but not my brain.

"Love," I repeated; and then, as the sense finally penetrated, "You must be mad!"

"The poets tell us that is the true state of a lover."

"You don't care any more for the opinion of poets than I do. They are wrong."

"Oh, so you know better? This afternoon you admitted to me that you didn't know what love meant."

He was back on his favorite ground now, fencing with words. Before, his wit could disarm my inexperience. Now I did know better, with a truer knowledge.

"I didn't say that. You gave me no time to say anything. But I know that love is not what you think it."

"What is it then?" He was smiling.

"It is caring for someone else more than yourself." I stopped, seeing Francis in his futile struggle with the hounds. "It means sacrifice—giving up your life, if necessary, for the happiness of the one you love. If you really cared for me, you wouldn't force me—by any means."

"That is precisely the namby-pamby idiocy I would have expected from you," said Wolf easily. "I thought my embrace, restrained as it was, would have taught you better."

"It made me sick," I said tactlessly.

"Oh, no, it didn't. You have great capacities, Harriet. Give me a little time and I'll teach you what love means."

He bent over me and again the man's mere presence sent me scuttling for cover—in this case to the far side of the bed, where I sat up.

"You must give me time," I babbled. "I can't decide—I can't think—"

"Time is what I don't have." He spoke brusquely, but there was a self-satisfied smile on his lips as he leaned back in the chair. "You are making a mountain out of a molehill, Harriet; most people would find your attitude incomprehensible. In our civilized world marriages are normally arranged by parents or guardians, and disobedient children are punished! Suppose you had managed to get away and had told some benevolent magistrate in York the tale of Ada and her groom. I fancy he would nod his benevolent head and stroke his white beard and tell you that your wise guardian had acted quite correctly."

"Not if I told him of Ada's abduction—of your intention of forcing her—"

"Well, possibly not. But I should, of course, attribute that tale to the hysterical imaginations of two flighty young girls. Harriet, Harriet—you could find a far worse husband. I have rather advanced notions about marriage. Marriage with me can be joy and excitement, not the genteel slavery to which you would be reduced by most men. Forget the silly prejudices about love which your prudish grandmother instilled in you, and give your own impulses a chance."

It was in this mood that I feared him most. He was so reasonable and so restrained—and, though I fought it, some part of me responded to him and to his arguments. Was this the time to make my next move? He could see by my expression that I was affected. If I promised to marry him . . . There was no minister closer than Middleham. If I pretended to give in, he might let me go to Francis.

I had learned nothing from my earlier experiences with him; I was still incredibly naïve.

"If I say Yes," I muttered, "will you let Ada go, now?"

For a moment he did not answer. The firelight leaped up, and every contour of his face was redly lighted.

"Do you say Yes?" he asked.

"What else can I say?"

"You agree to marry me, whenever I say?"

"I—yes."

There was something wrong. I felt it, like a blast of wintry air. Moving very deliberately he reached inside his coat and withdrew—of all things—a small black book. Balancing it on the palm of his hand, he held it out to me.

"You will swear, on this Book?"

I did not hesitate. I stretched out one hand and placed it on the Bible. I raised my eyes and met his eyes squarely.

"I swear," I said, "to marry you whenever you say."

Some strong emotion flared in his face. It was not passion; I knew that look now. My hand fell as he withdrew the Book, and for a moment he sat looking down at the little volume with his head cocked on one side. Then his left hand moved. It went to his cravat and, in one quick movement, untied the knot. He pulled it off and dropped it to the floor.

I gave one small gasp. I saw into his mind and he saw mine; and I knew I was mad to think I could delude him.

Slowly he turned his hand and the Book fell, striking the floor with a thud, sending up a little cloud of gray dust.

"Your sworn word," he said. "I commend your lie, heart of my heart, but did you really take me for such a fool?"

There was no need for me to speak.

"I know your word isn't worth a damn," he went on contemplatively. "You would say anything. You must give me something more concrete than words."

"Why?" I gasped. "Why?"

"The obvious answer must have occurred to you. I'm not accustomed to waiting for what I want, and I've waited longer than you imagine. But there is another reason. I don't trust you, my wily darling; it makes me blush to think what you might say to a man of the cloth, tomorrow or next day. No. You will become my wife tonight—in fact if not in name. That will be sufficient confirmation of your promise."

I sat with head bowed, avoiding his eyes. He took my silence for despair, but I was, in reality, thinking furiously. How long had I been unconscious? How much time had elapsed since Ada left? If she could find help in Middleham, I might postpone my decision long enough. If she had to proceed to Ripon or York, I was lost. But I had to act on the assumption that help was coming. If the worst happened, let me delay it as long as possible!

"Let us end this," Wolf said harshly. "I have shown you the bright side of the coin; let me show you the other. If you refuse me tonight, Julian goes to Ada. My gentle Julian has some habits which you don't suspect." He caught my wrist and pulled me close. His eyes stared down into mine; they were luminous and shallow, the eyes of a wolf. "I'll show you another sight in the morning," he said. "My unfortunate son Francis seems to have disappeared, did you know that? I greatly fear that the poor fellow has met with an accident on the moor. It is a treacherous place—easy to lose one's way. I plan to send out searching parties in the morning, but if he lies out of doors for a night, in such weather . . ."

I cried out and tried to hide my face with my free hand. Wolf caught that wrist too, holding me so that he could study my tormented face.

"Julian was right, then," he said. "It may interest you to know, Harriet, that Francis will be suspected of having abducted his poor little cousin. If he is found at the foot of the tower and she is here—well, we may never get a coherent story from her. The shock of such mistreatment might well disorder a young girl's mind."

I did something then which I had thought of doing, but never seriously. I spat in his face. The gesture shocked both of us.

"Give me a few hours," I said. "Then I will decide."

"One hour." Wolf released me, so suddenly that I fell back on the bed. "One hour and no more."

He arose—and the single movement transformed him from a virile, powerful man into a hideous cripple. As he lurched toward the door, I let my eyes dwell on every deformed step. He turned, and his face mirrored the deformity of his body when he saw my avid stare.

"Stare as you will," he said. "You'll have ample opportunity hereafter to study my deformities. And while you sit scheming here, think of this."

He took an object from his breast pocket. I recognized it by the blob of red sealing wax—the letter from Grandmother. Holding it high, he tore it slowly across and then reduced the pieces to shreds. He opened his hands and a little flurry of confetti drifted to the floor.

"The only proof that a second will ever existed," he said blandly. "The will itself, of course, is in my hands. Now, Harriet—scheme away. I'll be waiting down below, if you find an hour too long."

As soon as the door closed, I went to the window. The boards were still loose; apparently they had fallen back into place and Wolf had not noticed them. I pushed the central one aside and leaned out.

The night was cold and clear; the moon rode high, unobscured by clouds. The wind which howled among the eaves of the tower had blown them all away. From the airy height I could see a great distance, even to the white curve of the road far off that turned toward the south and Middleham. Below me, outlined in shadow, lay the courtyard of the old monastery. The block of cells was dark and silent; the light from that one window would not show on this side.

I contemplated, quite in cold blood, going down to Wolf at once. Nothing moved on the distant road. Nothing would come. I was a child, still believing in fairy tales, to think it would. Francis might be dying. He filled all of my mind then. Ada was safe, and I was beyond saving. There was no way out for me that I could see; but by accepting the inevitable at once I might save Francis' life.

The only alternative that occurred to me was to do as I had planned earlier, as a desperate last resort—to try to climb down the side of the tower. I considered it with mounting approval. If I got down safely, I could at least elude Wolf for a time and, in the process, try to see Francis. Perhaps my fondness had misled me; he might not be as badly hurt as I feared. And if, as was much more likely, I fell from the wall and hurt myself, I could win a postponement of my decision. Not even Wolf would insist on sharing the bed of a woman with a broken back or limb.

I was about to lower the lifted board, preparatory to removing my long, encumbering skirts, when I finally did see something moving down below. It was a man on horseback, and as he advanced through the shadows of the gate, my heart gave a wild, stupid bound. Then the cold moonlight found the figure. It was Julian.

I let the board fall back, leaving only a slit, as he rode out into the middle of the courtyard. There was no point in letting him see this possible, if dangerous, means of escape. He came to a stop just below the tower, staring up, and I realized that physiognomy is a deceptive science. With his cap of pale hair and his long, dreaming face he might have been a young monk.

In the doorway that led to the cells a second figure appeared. It might have been that of an anthropoid, with its crooked legs and abnormally long arms. I could see why moonlight, or any other light, might be abhorrent to it; it kept in the shadows and lifted one grotesque arm in a peremptory summons.

Julian joined his father, and for a few moments the two stood conversing. The silence was so profound that I could hear the murmur of their voices, but no words were audible. Then Wolf vanished back into the doorway and Julian rode across the court. He left his mount in the mined cloister and returned, on foot, crossing the courtyard to vanish in turn through the same low doorway.

I cast one last futile glance toward the stretch of road that lay white and empty under the moon. Then something else caught my eye.

The dogs were out. They came wandering across the court, looking like savage statues that had been magically released from their stony immobility. The sight of them turned me colder than the wind could do; it would be long before I forgot the feel of the wet muzzle on my face.

It was not until I had withdrawn back into the room that the implications struck me. The dogs were out. Somehow I had assumed that they would be guarding the door, as Loki had before. With Wolf and Julian in one of the cells—why, that meant that I had the freedom of the tower. A poor freedom, under most circumstances; if I tried to enter the court, the dogs would catch me. But just now I had no intention of leaving the ruins—not with Francis helpless down below. If those two were with him—

I was halfway down the first flight of stairs before I had another sensible thought.

The darkness slowed me. I did not dare to take a light and the enclosed stairwell was as black as the bottom of a mine. I had to feel my way on hands and knees and, despite the cold, my hands were wet enough to slip dangerously on the stone. Were they with Francis now? What were they planning to do?

I found the door from the tower to the cells by groping for it. It opened, under the careful pressure of my hands, onto blackness which was less impenetrable. The light coming in from the courtyard door assured me that no one was in the corridor. They must be in one of the cells, probably the one where Francis was imprisoned. I had almost reached it before I saw the light; it came through the same narrow window which I had observed earlier, and my heart leaped at the sight of it. Thanks to the window I could both see and hear what was transpiring inside without myself being seen, and gain sufficient warning to retreat if either of them approached the door.

I stood on tiptoe to see in.

There was no fireplace in this room—part of the monkish mortification of the flesh, no doubt. The light came from candles, three of them. The yellow glow was deceptive, for it suggested warmth, of which there was none in that chamber. Wolf's breath and Julian's puffed from their mouths like clouds of smoke as they breathed. Wolf, seated on the only chair the room boasted, was enveloped in a heavy fur-collared coat. Julian paced up and down, slapping his arms against his sides.

My eyes went at once to the third occupant of the room. At first I could see nothing save a dark unmoving bulk on the low couch. Then, as if in answer to my voiceless prayer, Julian took up one of the candles and approached the bed. He bent over, holding the light low. It fell on Francis' face, on his tumbled fair hair, the livid scratches on his cheek, and on his eyes—open and aware. I caught at the bars of the window with both hands. They would have seen my hands, and my pale face pressed up against the bars, if they had looked, but neither one did. They had another victim to torment.

"He's awake," said Julian, over his shoulder. "I wonder how much he heard."

"It doesn't matter." Wolf looked like a malignant idol, gloved hands folded in his lap, eyes fixed.

"No, wait—he's off again," Julian said lightly. "Brother—Francis—wake up."

"Give him some brandy."

Julian looked up in surprise. Then with a little shrug he took a flask from his pocket and removed the top. Francis choked and coughed over the raw stuff, his struggles bringing an amused smile to Julian's lips. The brandy had its effect.

When his coughing spell was over he tried to sit up and Julian, with a mocking parody of fraternal concern, lifted him against the pillow.

"Now that he's awake, what shall we do with him?" he inquired of his father.

"Nothing."

Julian took another turn about the room. He was wearing one of the new caped coats; it became him well, giving added breadth to his slender frame.

"God Almighty, it's freezing here," he complained. "How much longer must we wait?"

"I said an hour."

"God Almighty. Standing around this icehouse, when there's a nice warm bed upstairs—"

Francis stirred at that, and Julian, seeking amusement, turned back to him.

"A nice warm bed, and something else nice and warm to go with it. Doesn't it increase your aches and pains, dear Brother, to think that only your obstinacy kept you from being in my shoes?"

The candle swooped low; Francis had to turn his head or it would have singed his hair.

"I couldn't believe it," he said, in a shockingly changed voice. "Perhaps now—I'll change my mind."

Wolf shook his head.

"Too late."

"Why?"

"Can't trust you now."

"We could sign something—an agreement."

"Why should I bother?" Wolf asked indifferently.

"She prefers me to Julian. It might be easier."

An odd smile curved Wolf's mouth. He said nothing, but Julian could not resist the opening.

"Prefers you? After that idyllic scene in the garden? That

was a clumsy move on your part, Brother. It warned me that you meant to betray us, and it convinced Harriet that you were the villain."

"Harriet?"

"Oh, I forgot," Julian said blandly. "You are unaware of the latest developments."

Wolf stirred; but Julian's back was turned to his father, and he went on gaily, "We all made a mistake, Francis. The old woman fooled us royally. She left a second will making Harriet the heiress. We found out just in time."

"Harriet," Francis repeated.

I was loath to take my eyes from his face, but for the life of me I couldn't help watching Wolf. He was upright in his chair now, and his cold gaze was fixed on Julian's back. If Julian had seen his expression, it would have cut his babbling short. But he did not turn around.

"Yes, Harriet," he said, watching Francis. "It doesn't matter, really. In fact, I would have preferred Ada. She's a pretty thing, and it would be a pleasure to tame her. Harriet rather repels me. But then she—"

He never finished the sentence, which I cannot repeat, even here. In a burst of surprising strength Francis raised himself on one elbow and broke into the vulgar description with an equally vulgar epithet, spoken in a voice which was almost his old shout. The epithet was well chosen. Julian turned red, then white. He put the candle down on the floor.

Francis was shivering violently, not so much from rage as from cold. His thin shirt was poor protection, and the fever that burned in his cheeks and unnaturally bright eyes must have intensified the chill.

"Bad enough when it was Ada you were after! But not Harriet. Keep away from her, you simpering little sadist. No judge and jury for you—I'll break every bone in your body personally if you try any of your tricks on her, you—"

I saw it coming. Francis must have too, but there was nothing either of us could have done to stop it. Julian's arm moved. I heard the sound of the blow, and Francis fell back, his head twisted at an odd angle. There was blood on his mouth—and on mine, as I sank my teeth into my lower lip to keep from crying out or moving. Surely Wolf would interfere. He could not let Francis die—not yet, not until he had served his purpose.

Julian had strength enough in those fine white hands when he was in a fury. He twisted his hand in Francis' collar and pulled him up. There was no response; Francis' head fell back.

"Leave him alone," Wolf said calmly.

"But I—"

"Leave him alone."

His voice was disinterested; he might have been speaking of a sick dog. After a moment Julian's hand relaxed. He turned to face his father.

"He'll have to die," he said sullenly.

"Not yet."

"When? After he's on his feet and able to murder me? Good God, he'll be after me as soon as he can crawl! I'll be damned if I'll take—"

"You will take whatever I tell you to take." Wolf stared off into space as if the sight of his son's face were distasteful to him. His monstrous arrogance and his contempt for Julian were unchanged, but as I studied the youthful face that Wolf ignored, the hair on the back of my neck stirred in a reversion to some primitive ancestor. I had had too much experience with danger in the last few hours to miss the feeling of it now.

"There is no need to get in such a state," Wolf went on. "He will certainly have to die—not because of his threat to you—devil take you, can't you defend yourself?—but because my plans might be spoiled by legal interference, even after they are consummated. We cannot keep Francis a prisoner indefinitely, it isn't practical. So he must be silenced permanently. But not until I am through with him."

Julian's alarming look faded as curiosity overcame rage. He took a step toward his father.

"What do you need him for? I think it's time you trusted me, Wolf. God knows I've incriminated myself deeply enough in this."

Wolf burrowed into the folds of his heavy coat and pulled out his watch. He studied it, tilting it so that its face caught a beam from one of the candles. My heart gave a sickening lurch. I had forgotten the passage of time. Now I loosened my hands—the shape of the narrow bars was printed redly across my palms—and prepared for flight. I would lie in wait for him in the tower—no, on the stairs—I would find a heavy stone, like the ones that littered the floors of cell and corridor—

Wolf put the watch back into his pocket and leaned back in the chair. So little time as that gone by, I thought dazedly. It seemed like days since I had stood outside that door.

"Not that it's any of your business," he said placidly, "but I need Francis to—er—persuade Harriet. Your surmise seems to have been correct; she fancies she is in love, as she would say, with him. She also 'loves' that silly little cousin of hers, but at the moment I think she is more concerned with Francis than with Ada. She'll acquiesce in order to save him, but she is canny enough to insist on seeing him first. So she will see him—alive and breathing, but pathetic enough to stir up all her schoolgirl emotions. After that—"

Julian nodded. "All well enough. After I have taken care of her, I shall dispose of Francis."

"You won't need to. Just leave him here. Another day, perhaps two . . . He's got the constitution of an ox. Make it three days."

"All well enough," Julian repeated. "But why bother?"

"What?"

"Why bother with threats? You have a fondness for melo-drama, Wolf. As you pointed out to me, forced marriages are made every day. I can take care of Harriet without using Francis."

Wolf turned his head almost lazily and regarded his son. His slow gaze moved from Julian's gleaming hair to the tips of his polished boots, and back.

"Go back to the manor," he said.

Julian's mouth dropped open. I had the advantage of him; I knew Wolf's real plans, and as the conversation proceeded, I had realized that Julian did not. Frightened as I was, I felt an echo of Wolf's sardonic amusement at the sight of Ju-lian's bewilderment. He was due for a shock, and if any man deserved one, he did.

"Go back?" he repeated parrotlike.

"Go back to the manor. Now."

"But—Harriet—"

"You complacent idiot." Wolf lifted his great arms and stretched enjoyably. "I don't often agree with the judgments of my elder son, but in this case I must. I would have let you take Ada—I couldn't have endured her squeals and whey-face—but Harriet is too good for the likes of you."

"But—not—for you." Julian's voice was as high as a woman's. "You mean you—"

"I will marry her, yes. Now get out."

"The money—"

"Lucky we found that second will." Wolf yawned. "An unusually felicitous combination of business and pleasure."

"Nothing for me?" said Julian in the same high voice. "Nothing for me . . . ! First abduction, then murder. I carried the girl off, I pushed Francis from the wall. I've put my neck in a noose for you and your plans. You promised me half the

money. I could live like a gentleman. I could—I won't let
you do this."

"*Let* me?" Wolf laughed.

"Give me half." Julian came toward him, swaying unsteadily. "Give me my half. I can go to the authorities—"

"With a signed confession? *You* carried the girl off, *you*
pushed him from the wall. I could not have done either of
those wicked deeds, not in my helpless state."

Wolf's features were animated. He had always enjoyed
taunting Julian, and this was the best joke of all, his son's
ineptitude and futility and his own casual command. His
eyes danced with amusement, and he looked twenty years
younger—younger than his son, whose hunched shoulders
and drawn face might have belonged to a man of sixty.

"They might not hang you," he went on, relishing every
word. "They freed one of those Edinburgh ghouls for turning King's evidence, after all—the lads who supplied
corpses for the dissecting rooms, nice, fresh corpses, manu-
factured to order. But it's a risky business. Fratricide—that
doesn't sound pretty. . . ."

Julian launched himself at his father's throat.

I had feared, even when I thought him unjustly perse-
cuted, that one day he would turn upon his tormentor. With
this final betrayal, the end was inevitable. Wolf had not been
able to predict it because he was blinded by twenty-three
years of contempt.

For a moment I thought that blindness would cost him his
life. Julian was, for an interval, mad as a Bedlamite; if he
had had a weapon, he would have struck and struck to kill.
Having no knife, he used his bare hands, but he used them
like a woman, tearing and clawing. His weight overturned
the chair, and momentarily Wolf was pinned under the
slighter man's body. Then, overcoming his initial shock with
a quickness I almost admired, he began to fight back. The

two bodies twisted and rolled, in near silence; the only sounds were the gasps of breath that came from first one man, then the other.

I watched the struggle with a cold, despicable calculation. Whatever the outcome, it would lessen the odds against me. With one man unconscious and the other weakened, I might enter the fray myself. I had long since abandoned hope of help from Ada; the crisis was now, in the next ten minutes, and she could never return in time. What I contemplated doing was bold and shocking and unwomanly; it would have been more "ladylike" to let Wolf murder Francis and seduce me. Well, I thought, clutching the bars and grinding my teeth, if that is the conduct our society demands of a lady, then I am not one.

The two men had struggled to their knees—or rather Wolf had risen so far, dragging Julian with him. I could not see precisely what was happening, for Wolf's broad back was turned squarely toward the door and his bulk obscured Julian's slimmer form. But I saw the great muscles of Wolf's shoulders bulge and tighten. I sank my teeth into my torn lip. I did not want Wolf to win. Mad or sane, Julian did not frighten me. Wolf was the greater menace of the two, and I was not sure I had the courage to face him.

For hours I had been acting under the lash of terror and had been animated by that kind of nervous energy which wreaks a fearful toll. I was beginning to feel the strain of it now. The whole scene seemed somehow unreal—the coolness with which the two discussed their fantastic crimes, the sudden, abhorrent struggle between father and son.

Then Wolf moved in a violent half turn, and I saw both their faces.

It was not Julian's features, blackened and distorted out of all recognition, that sent my hands fumbling for the door handle. It was Wolf's face—vulpine and inhuman, set in a careful frown of concentration as he choked the life out of his younger son. Whatever else he had done, I could not stand by and watch him do that. Whatever Julian had done, I could never endure myself again if I let him be murdered without lifting a finger to save him.

Before I knew my own intentions, I was inside the room and at Wolf's side, tearing at his hands. I might have been plucking at iron wires. Then he looked up and saw me. His face never changed. He simply released Julian, who fell backward with the heavy lifelessness of a sack of meal, and reached for me.

He was normally very strong. Now he was as irresistible as a windstorm. I went down under the sheer weight of him, feeling his hands on my throat and awaiting the first pressure of those hard fingers. The pressure never came. The fingers hooked themselves under the collar of my frock and jerked downward.

He was not mad. That was almost the worst moment of all, when I realized that he was not mad. He was proceeding methodically with his original plans, dismissing the black-faced thing that huddled at his feet, accepting the change of scene simply as a saving of time and effort.

Any "lady" would have fainted. I am not proud of my stamina; I tried as hard as I could to faint, and I recall my weak fury at not being able to do so. I could only struggle—quite ineffectually—and scream words I never would have admitted knowing. The struggles were as useless as the bad language.

I went on screaming and struggling even after I was beating at empty air.

It seemed an impossible effort to open my eyes. After it was done, I had no strength left for any other movement. I lay prostrate on the cold dirty floor and stared.

What I saw could not be real. Francis was lying on the cot in the corner, he could not be standing, unsteady but erect, over Wolf's supine form. He could not be holding a heavy stone. He could not—

He looked as I had seen him look before—flushed as though with too much wine, his eyes a bright, unfocused glitter. His feet were planted widely apart, and he needed that support, for his whole body swayed back and forth with the solemn gravity of a pendulum. It was not only his sickness which had reduced him to such a state; I realized that he was appalled by what he had just done. The Wolfson madness did not contaminate him. He had railed at his father, insulted him, disobeyed him—but he could not strike him down without feeling the shock.

He had, in fact, let his decent instinct ruin his aim. At the last moment, as he struck, he must have held back.

Wolf's arms moved like two quick black snakes. His hands caught Francis' ankles. One jerk was enough to topple the sick man. Francis went down with a crash that was enough in itself to knock the life out of him, but Wolf, now impatient with interruptions, was taking no further chances. He scooped up the stone that had fallen from Francis' hands, rocked to his feet, and threw it down with all his strength, straight down upon his son's upturned face.

I caught his arm with both hands—a split second after the stone fell.

That was when it happened. I have never described it to anyone—they would only smile and look uneasily at me—but something broke. I felt it, somewhere inside me, and I heard the snap of a stretched string giving way. I stood quite steadily, my hands resting lightly on Wolf's arm, and I felt nothing, neither sensation nor emotion.

At first I thought he was held in the same strange spell. He stood without moving, his face grave, his head turned slightly. He moved away from me and I stood still, watching him. He went to the window. He could see nothing, I knew that; even in daylight the window was screened by weeds. But he was not looking; he was listening. I heard the same sounds, when I bothered to concentrate. The dogs were barking. They were making a frightful din. I wondered why.

He must have heard the other sounds. I did not hear them, not then. He turned abruptly and it seemed to me that he was looking disturbed. His dark scowl moved from the window to the floor (I would not look down; I did not look down) and then to me. I returned his look, feeling no alarm, no interest; feeling nothing. And as he studied my face, his own changed.

"Harriet," he said.

I looked at him inquiringly. I knew whom he meant. I was Harriet. Harriet was I. But it was too much trouble to answer him.

"Harriet—"

He lurched toward me. Poor thing, I thought; he is so badly deformed. He took me by the shoulders and shook me, gently. His hands felt cold. I looked down and saw that my dress was torn. I took his hand away from my shoulder and pulled my dress up.

"Harriet." He sounded as if he were choking. The meaningless reiteration of my name was annoying.

"Yes?" I said. He was staring at me, rather impertinently, I thought. Then his face broke up into little fragments of expression, unconnected, inchoate. I did not like that look, so I closed my eyes. After a time he went away.

It was an odd sensation, standing with my eyes closed. It was pleasant. I could hear much better. The dogs were in a positive frenzy of excitement. They sounded like two men fighting, not like dogs at all. There were other sounds too. Horses coming, fast. Voices. Shouts and screams. Then one loud shout that rose from anger into pain into silence.

I thought I knew that voice, and briefly something inside me stirred—like hands groping for a broken thread, trying to knot it back together, I made the hands let go. Then I waited.

The other sounds continued, the voices and the howling of the dogs. There were some loud crashing noises, and the baying of the hounds stopped too. It would have been quiet then. But feet began to pound up and down, outside. Several sets of footsteps came down the stone corridor. I heard them become louder. They were just outside the door.

He left it open, I thought with a weak irritation. Now they will find me. Now they will make me open my eyes.

When I opened them, I saw two people standing on the threshold. The one in front was a boy—dark, slender, brown-skinned. He had one arm out, barring the door to the girl whose face peeped in from behind him. He looked at me and after a moment his arm dropped. The girl came in. She was pretty, despite her pallor. Her fair hair would have been lovely if it had been properly brushed and pinned.

"Harriet," she whispered. There were tears on her cheeks. They caught the candlelight like little moons. "I came as fast as I could. Oh, Harriet, darling—"

"I am Harriet," I said courteously. "Who are you?"

April 21

He came just then and I had to stop and hide my diary. It was just as well. This is not as easy as I thought it would be. I am trying to put it down, not only events, but thoughts and feelings, just as they occurred. Now I see that I had to do it that way. I had to live it again, and arrive at the climactic moment which was, then, too much for me to bear. My body stood in the cold candlelit room, awake and physically unharmed except for minor cuts and bruises. But Harriet had gone away. She was hidden deep down inside in a self-made darkness, huddled with her knees drawn up and her arms over her face. They pulled her out, partway, but she doesn't want to come, she is still clinging with one hand to the doorframe of that inner cell. If she is ever to emerge, she must let go and come freely, by herself.

He saw that I was upset and made me go to bed. The maids watched me for two days. I could not get the diary. But today the sun is shining and spring is in the air. I said I felt better and he let me get up. He is going to take me for a ride later, when he has finished the morning's business affairs. So I must end this, now.

I knew Ada, really. I was never mad, I knew who she was. After she had pestered me for a long time, kissing me and crying down the neck of my dress, I admitted it just to make her stop.

"Take me away from here," I said. "I don't want to stay in this place."

We were sitting on the bed, in the corner. It was the only possible place to sit. The room was noisier than ever, filled with people—a crowd of dark, wild-looking men who talked in a language I could not understand.

"We will go," she said. The tears kept pouring down her cheeks. She always cried like that, easily and beautifully. "We will go, dear, in just a few minutes."

"I want to go now," I said.

"Not just yet. Harriet, Harriet, what is it? You are safe now. He—he is dead, Harriet. The dogs killed him—his own dogs. They say he must have had blood on his hands or face, and the scent of it maddened them. He can't hurt you now, don't you believe me?"

"There are too many people here," I said. "I want to go away from them."

"But they are David's friends, darling. That is why I was

able to come so soon, because they were nearby. David and Francis planned it, they knew help might be needed. . . . Harriet, everything is all right now, don't look so . . ."

Someone detached himself from the crowd of men who were gathered around an object that lay on the floor. I continued to look straight ahead of me, counting the cracks on the wall, but when the man spoke, I knew David's voice.

"He's living. Bad off, but living. We'll fetch him to the manor, and Tammas will ride for the doctor."

"You told me he was dead," I said accusingly to Ada.

"He is. *He* is. But not Francis? Oh, David, I am so glad!"

I shook my head. It was a shame to destroy her shining look. But then she loved David. It did not really matter to her.

"They are all dead," I said. "I saw Julian's face. I saw Francis. . . . Ada, I want to go away from here. I will not stay in this room."

They made me go and look at him—at Francis. They were trying to help, but it was a mistake. As soon as I saw him, I knew they were lying. His eyes were closed—someone must have closed them. They had put him on a heap of straw and piled wrappings on him, and the straw, under his head, was stained and dark. They seemed to expect me to do something, so I knelt down and kissed him good-bye, although I knew it wasn't really Francis anymore. His lips were still warm. It takes the dead a long time to grow cold.

So then, finally, they took me back to the manor and Ada put me to bed. I did not faint. I never did faint, except for that one time, with the dog. I was not ill. I slept and woke up and ate and slept again. And all the while Harriet sat back in her dark place with her hands over her eyes and her ears and her mouth.

That was—how long?—six months ago. After a time I knew that Francis was still alive. I had to believe it when they took me in to see him, and he smiled and held my hand, and spoke. They had to shave off most of his hair, and his head was covered with an absurd cap of white bandages, but the scratches on his face had almost faded. The rock had only grazed his head; the bone was not even broken. But it cut a long gash, and he bled a great deal. What kept him in bed so long was the fever and lung sickness. But he has, as someone once said, the constitution of an ox. Two months later he was as fit as ever. He was Mr. Wolfson now, and the owner of the Abbey.

Three months ago he came to see me. It was still winter then; it had snowed for six days and the white drifts were piled high at every wall and tree. Snow still fell out of a cold gray sky. Ada had drawn my curtains and lighted all the lamps. She was gone that afternoon—with David; she spent with him all the time she did not devote to me. So I was alone when Francis knocked.

He sat down beside me on the sofa and took my hands.

"I want you to marry me, Harriet," he said.

"You can have the money," I told him. "Ada must have some, to buy the land and the horses David needs. You may have the rest."

"I don't want the damned money," said Francis. "I want you."

I could not comprehend his lack of understanding, so I tried to explain.

"You need not marry me out of pity, either. I am sorry about Ada and David, but he is right for her; you must see that. She never wanted to be the mistress of a fine house. She will be happy with him and you must find someone else. You don't have to marry me, Francis. I am well, truly I am. I am going to live with Ada and David."

"No, you aren't. You're going to live with me." He took me by the shoulders and stared down into my face. I thought he was going to kiss me, but instead he pulled me close to him and held me, resting his face against my hair.

"God knows whether I'm doing the right thing," I heard him say and knew he was no longer speaking to me. "Everything else I tried to do I made a mess of. Maybe this is a mistake too. But I can't stand this any longer, I've got to reach you somehow. I'll be kind to you, Harriet—as kind as one of my cursed breed can be. Let me take care of you."

It was pleasant in his arms, sheltered and safe. It was another barrier against the world.

"All right," I said.

He held me off at arm's length and studied me doubtfully.

"You will marry me? Whenever I say?"

I stiffened. The words were familiar—painfully so. But I was so tired.

"Yes."

He will want to kiss me now, I thought, and held up my face.

He did kiss me—on the cheek, like a loving brother. Then he bent his head and kissed my hands, which he still held, and I almost thought I heard him mutter, "I love you so much." But I knew that must be a mistake.

We were married a week later, in a private ceremony. No one was there but Ada and David, and a stiff old man in very correct black clothes who kept glaring disapprovingly at David throughout the ceremony. When the minister said, "Whom God hath joined together," I lifted my face and Francis brushed my lips with his. Then we all had wine and cake, and I went back to my room.

I am the mistress of Abbey Manor now, but not for much longer. Francis has sold the house and the land and all the furnishings of the house. Thanks to Wolf's love of luxury he will gain enough from the sale to pay off most of the debt to the poor young man whom Wolf defrauded. The rest he will pay from his earnings, over the years.

He has refused to touch any of Grandmother's money. With the lawyer—the stiff man in black who attended our wedding—I arranged to have half of it settled on Ada. She will be the wealthiest farmer's wife in Yorkshire. She and David have decided to wait a proper year after Grandmother's death. In the meantime he has been looking for a suitable establishment and thinks he has found one not far from York. The house is old and rambling, a cross between a cottage and a mansion, Ada says. I am not afraid for them. He loves her very much.

Francis and I are going to settle in York. He has an old friend there, a physician whom he will assist and whose practice he will eventually inherit. I will miss my handsome room here. At first I hated it, especially when I woke at night crying out with nightmares. Ada took to sleeping with me, but although she always woke me when I began to twist and moan, I never felt secure with her. After Francis and I were married, he moved into Ada's room. Then it was better. He always seemed to hear me, however softly I cried out, and then he would come in and sit on the bed and hold my hand until I woke up and knew that it was a dream.

It was only today that I understood why his presence comforted me as Ada's could not. The nightmares were always about him. Over and over, night after night, I dreamed I saw him lying dead. Part of me, the waking part, knew he was safe. The other part, the Harriet who crouched inside, could not believe it. She had retreated, closing an inner door, at the moment when the rock left Wolf's hand and she knew that nothing in Heaven or earth could stop its fall. That door was still closed and she was still caught in the nightmare like a fly in a web, imprisoned by the past and all its memories.

I little thought, when I hid my diary, that I would be the first person to read it afterward. I hoped it might serve some purpose, but I never dreamed how important that purpose might be to me. As I read it over, written down like a story—and a rather incredible story, at that—I began to realize that it is finished, done with, all in the past, like a book when the last page is turned and the covers are closed.

But there is still one thing to be written, like an envoi. I was reading over the final section when I heard his footsteps in the hall—quick, heavy, like no one else's steps. I closed the diary and left it lying open on the table. I rose to my feet. The door of my room opened, and it seemed to me that I heard another door opening elsewhere.

He stood in the doorway gazing at me, and as he looked his shoulders straightened and he let out a long breath, as if some heavy, invisible burden had been lifted from his back.

I held out my arms to him.

"My own dear love," I said.